# THE SANGREAL

## BOOK 3 OF THE MAQLÛ

## JC HOLMBERG

Library of Congress Control Number: 2022917205

This is a work of fiction and is a product of the author's imagination. Any references to historical events, real people, or real places are used fictitiously.

Learn more about the history and background of this book at:            www.JC Holmberg.com

Front cover image by Rebecacovers

Names: Holmberg, John C., 1956- author.

Title: The Sangreal / John C Holmberg.

Description: Pine Knot, KY : Tist Fiction, 2022. | Series: The Maqlû, bk. 3. | Summary: Alex Scire's search for the Holy Grail takes him from the dungeons of the Spanish Inquisition to Dracula's haunts. | Audience: Grades 6 & up.

Identifiers: ISBN 978-1-956342-11-6 (paperback) | ISBN 978-1-956342-12-3 (hardcover) | ISBN 978-1-956342-10-9 (ebook) | ISBN 978-1-956342-13-0 (audiobook)

Subjects: LCSH: Adventure stories. | CYAC: Ghosts - Fiction. | Magic - Fiction. | Fantasy. | Young adult fiction. | Historical fiction. | BISAC: YOUNG ADULT FICTION / Fantasy / Historical. | YOUNG ADULT FICTION / Fantasy / Wizards & Witches. | YOUNG ADULT FICTION / Action & Adventure / General.

Classification: LCC PZ7.1.H65 San 2022 (print) | LCC PZ7.1.H65 (ebook) | DDC [Fic]--dc23.

# To Anne,

## My voice of experience

# CONTENTS

"New beginnings are often disguised as painful endings."

**Lao Tzu**

(6th century BCE Chinese philosopher)

# CHAPTER 1
# ADRIFT AGAIN

Tears rolled down Alex Scire's face as he stared in disbelief at the dust cloud settling over the remnants of the island. He shook his head and, in a raspy voice, said, "I'm sorry, Deb, but I can't help you move on. I'm never going to search for one of the Maqlû again. All they do is bring pain and suffering."

Deborah Adler looked at her thirteen-year-old twin brother and swallowed hard to keep her emotions in check. The hardships of the last few weeks had left their mark on him. The long braids hanging down his back were dirty and unkempt. He'd lost weight that he couldn't afford to lose. And his naturally dark skin hadn't protected him from the intense Caribbean sun, resulting in sunburns on all his exposed skin. But it was the haunted look in his hazel eyes that bothered her the most. She took a deep breath and said, "I think I finally understand what you've been trying to tell me. It's hard to believe that the objects our order has been searching for all this time could be so dangerous. What I want to know, though, is how did you destroy the Pair Dadeni? I didn't see you use any spells."

Alex hesitated, thinking back to the day he'd taken the necklace their dad intended for his sister. Then he reached beneath his dirty, ragged, cut-up t-shirt and pulled the little metallic looped cross out. "I believe the ankh did it."

Deborah leaned closer. "It doesn't look like much. How's it work?"

"I wish I knew."

"Besides enabling you to see ghosts, what else does it do?" Deborah asked.

"Well, you saw what happened back in the cave. I didn't do any of that. The ankh did it all. I don't understand what it is or how it does things, but it often feels like it's got a mind of its own. For instance, sometimes, it tries to control me – telling me to go this way or that way or to do things like run, jump, duck, and whatnot. At other times, it acts like a magical object protecting me or attacking others. Still other times, it seems like it's trying to communicate with me, but I have to guess what it's saying."

"Has anyone else in the family ever used it as you have?" Deborah asked.

"I don't think so. Grandpa made it sound like the ankh has freaked out everyone who's worn it. It's one of the reasons why he told me not to tell anybody about it."

Deborah looked back at the destroyed island and said, "You know, it's strange. Our order has been searching for the Maqlû for millennia, but you've made our efforts look laughably inept with that ankh."

"At times, it does seem like it's searching for the Maqlû, but I can't tell whether it likes those objects, or not. It seems to act like a compass, pulling me towards them. Then bad guys show up, and it goes berserk."

Deborah stared at her brother as a thought, blinding in its novelty, struck her. Her voice sunk to almost a whisper as she said, "Or, perhaps, it's just following your commands."

Alex looked down at the bottom of the boat. In a barely audible voice, he said, "I don't see how, although I'll admit it doesn't destroy anything until after I'm in danger."

Seeing the distraught look on her brother's face, Deborah said, "Relax. I'm not mad at you. It's just that our order has always believed our divine mission was to find and protect those objects from misuse. But, after seeing what's happened with you, I'm beginning to wonder if we were wrong. Perhaps this is all for the best."

"Is it? The ankh destroyed half an island, killing every soul inside – just to get rid of one of the Maqlû. Can we trust it?"

Deborah winced. "Let's talk about it later. Right now, we need to focus on getting you back to civilization."

"How far from land do you think we are?" Alex asked, relieved to change subjects.

"I'm not sure, but I'm guessing we're near some of the uninhabited islands south of Bimini, which means Florida is probably 50 miles west of us, and Bimini is 20 miles north."

"Is there any place closer? I doubt the gas will last long enough to get to either place."

Deborah shook her head.

All the talking had caused Alex's throat to dry out. He tried swallowing to wet his throat, but he was so dehydrated that it didn't help. His voice cracked as he said, "I've counted on luck too much already. Florida is straight ahead. We can't miss it. So, even though Bimini is a lot closer, I don't want to turn north, miss some small island, and have the Gulf Stream sweep us out into the Atlantic."

"Then cut the engine so you don't waste gas," Deborah said. "I'll try to see where we are so we can make a better decision. Will you be all right if I leave for a few hours?"

As soon as Alex nodded, Deborah flew away. After shutting down the outboard motor, Alex sat in the bottom of the boat and leaned against the back seat. Exhausted from everything he'd been through, he closed his eyes and promptly fell asleep. A short time later, he jerked awake when something landed on his lap.

Opening his eyes, he saw the small dragon he'd seen on the island, staring at him intently with its golden eyes. But instead of grey fur, it was blue-green, the same color as the ocean.

*"Good. You're awake. I was beginning to worry about you,"* said the voice in his head.

It took a minute for Alex to shrug off the effects of his sleep-fogged mind and realize that it wasn't the little dragon talking to him but the mysterious woman he'd first heard in his head when he'd taken the ankh from his father. He started to speak, but his throat was so dry that all he could do was grunt a reply.

*"I wanted to tell you how proud I am that you've resisted the temptation of not one, but two of the Maqlû. You've done more in the last few weeks than we ever did,"* said the woman's voice in his head.

"We? Who are you talking about?" Alex managed to rasp out as he looked around for the speaker.

*"Sadie, the little Ryūjin dragon in your lap, and I. We met on Irkalla a long time ago, when I first started researching the Maqlû, and stayed with me until I died. I find it fascinating, and encouraging, that somehow, in this vast universe, she found you."*

Alex reflexively stretched out his hand and stroked the little dragon's fur. It arched its back like a cat, then curled up and fell asleep in his lap.

*"Amazing. I've never seen her take to anyone so fast,"* the disembodied voice said.

Alex looked around but still didn't see anybody. He started to call out, then changed his mind and tried telepathy. *"Where are you?"*

*"I've told you. I won't show myself to you,"* the voice in his head replied.

Surprised the telepathy worked, he asked, *"If you won't show yourself, will you at least tell me who you are?"*

*"Call me Sibyl."*

*"As in the Sibylline books?"* Alex asked.

*"The same. It's interesting that you made the connection so quickly."*

*"You've been too interested in my choices with the objects for me not to guess you were involved somehow."*

*"I foresaw the horrors of the Maqlû on my home planet and vowed to do everything I could to stop their misuse. I researched them and documented everything I learned about those objects, hoping the knowledge would allow me, or someone else, to neutralize those cursed things. But I eventually realized that if they fell*

*into the wrong hands, my books were just as dangerous as the objects themselves. So, I put unbreakable locking spells on them. Which makes me wonder how you opened the Palantir book."*

*"Could we discuss this another time?"* Alex asked. *"I'm exhausted and don't feel up to explaining my actions."*

*"I'm sorry. I was just so excited knowing you've destroyed two of those cursed ...."*

Sibyl stopped talking when Deborah suddenly appeared off the starboard side, yelling, "Quick, turn on the engine."

Sadie dug her talons into his legs and launched herself into the ocean. Alex winced and was still searching for where the dragonet had gone when Deborah arrived.

"There are a couple of islands only ten to fifteen miles away," his sister said. "I'm guessing one of them is Bimini. It's much closer than Florida, and we'll benefit by riding with the Gulf Stream. So, head north by northeast."

As soon as the small motor coughed to life, Alex swung the tiller until the sun hit his left shoulder. But the engine ran out of gas shortly after sunset. He briefly thought about using the oars in the bottom of the boat but quickly discarded that idea, knowing he didn't have the strength to row. Leaving the boat to the mercy of the wind and the waves, he curled up on the bottom and fell asleep.

He woke shortly before sunrise, with his throat afire. As the day drug on, his discomfort only worsened. His hopes of making landfall faded, and he began wondering at his cursed luck to have survived cave-ins, pirates, hurricanes, and zombies only to die of thirst surrounded by water, something Captain Every had warned him about.

His hopes jumped when a storm appeared on the horizon mid-afternoon. Even though he'd never gone to church, he started praying. Not wanting to chance it, he prayed to the Great Spirit of his father's heritage, Gaia of his mother's, and the Judeo-Christian God of his friends back home.

He got what he'd prayed for within the hour. Alex leaned back and stuck out his tongue as the rain began to fall. The water drumming inside his mouth felt heavenly, but within minutes, he stopped trying to quench his thirst and furiously bailed water out of the boat. Even though the rain lasted over half an hour, he still felt parched when it stopped. Too weak to do anything else, Alex sat back and closed his eyes.

After a short rest, he sat up and was about to scoop out more water when Deborah stopped him. "You're not going to sink, and you don't know when the next rain will come. So, leave the water and drink from the bottom of the boat as needed. It won't be the best-tasting water you've ever had, but it's better than dying of thirst."

Alex looked skeptically at the dirty water in the bottom of the boat, but as the rain had done little to quench his thirst, he hesitated for only a few seconds before cupping his hands into the water and gingerly taking a drink. The warm water tasted brackish, but it felt so good sliding down his throat that he eagerly started scooping up more.

Deborah stopped him seconds later. "That's enough for now. I don't want you getting sick, so let it sit for a while. If you don't throw up, you can have more."

Alex reluctantly let the water run through his fingers back into the boat.

He'd been grateful for the cooling rain when the sun was up, but he was still wet when the sun set an hour later. Having eaten almost nothing for three days, he found he couldn't generate enough heat to stay warm and started shivering as night came on. With the bottom of the boat full of water, he curled up sideways on the bench and propped his head against the gunwale to try to sleep. But, as Deborah had warned, the brackish water on an empty stomach didn't sit well, and soon, he had an upset stomach to go along with the rest of his aches and pains. By the time the sun rose again the next morning, he'd turned into a shivering lump of humanity.

By mid-morning, he'd again gone from one extreme to the other as the fierce Caribbean sun evaporated the remaining water in the bottom of the boat, turning it into a sauna and making his situation even more dire.

Around noon, he heard a splash. He turned to look but only caught a glimpse of something shiny and opalescent. His first thought was that Chrysophylax was coming to help him, but a school of Bonito fish surfaced just then and surrounded the boat.

Deborah tried scooping some of the fish into the boat, but her telekinetic skills were still rough, causing her to scoop only water without landing one fish. "I'm sorry," she said. "I'm afraid I'll swamp the boat if I keep helping you this way."

Alex wearily picked up one of the oars and leaned over the side. He tried hitting the fish jumping all around, but found the oar was too clumsy. Alex moved his hands up the handle and tried again. It took him several more unsuccessful attempts before he finally managed to stun one fish. He put the oar down, reached overboard, and threw the fish into the boat. With the fish still jumping around, and unsure when he would get another opportunity for food, he picked up the oar and continued batting at the fish.

He soon got the hang of it, and by the time the fish had sunk back into the ocean, he had caught five. His squeamishness warred with hunger as Alex stared at the fish, unsure whether he could eat them raw. His hunger won out. He grabbed the smallest fish, closed one eye, and brought it to his mouth.

Just as he was about to bite into it, Deborah stopped him. "You can't eat the fish like that. You'll have to take the intestines out so you won't get sick. Plus, you'll want to scrape the scales and fins off. Do you have a sharp object to do that with?"

Alex patted what was left of his pants and smiled when he felt the Swiss Army Knife their dad had given him in a pocket.

It took longer to skin the fish than he expected, as his hands were swollen, and he shook from hunger and thirst. He finally finished the first fish and raised it to his mouth, but hesitated before taking a bite of the raw seafood. Alex gagged on the first few bites but was so hungry that he ignored the taste.

He picked every bit of meat off the bones, then tossed the remains overboard. When he finished the first

Bonito, he picked up a second one and began to skin it too, marveling at what extreme hunger and thirst were driving him to do. As his body slowly turned the raw fish to fuel, he started to feel a bit more energetic. He skinned the remaining fish, then placed them in the middle seat to bake in the hot sun.

With his hunger and thirst somewhat assuaged, he asked, "When do you think we'll get to Bimini, Deb?"

"I'd guess sometime tonight," she replied. "We're drifting slower than I thought, so why don't you get some rest because when we get close, you might need to row some to get ashore."

Between the raw fish sitting heavy in his stomach, his dry throat, the uncomfortable seating in the boat, and the hot Caribbean sun, Alex spent the rest of the day trying to get comfortable. He finally overcame his discomfort and fell asleep near midnight.

A clunking sound woke him a little before dawn. He sat up and started rubbing the sleepers out of his eyes but stopped when he realized he was rubbing salt and dirt into his tender skin. It took him another minute before he was alert enough to see Deborah sitting in the front of the boat. "Are we almost there?" he asked.

His sister couldn't look him in the eyes. She dropped her head and mumbled something.

"What? I can't understand you."

Deborah looked up and, in a pained voice, said, "I'm sorry. Unfortunately, we drifted past Bimini last night. I saw the lights several miles east of us and thought about waking you, but I knew you didn't have the energy to row that far. So, I tried several magical spells to get closer, but none worked. I even tried rowing, but I can't move objects very well yet."

"So, what does that mean? Are we going to drift out to the middle of the Atlantic and die?"

"I can't say," Deborah replied. "Besides, there's a chance somebody will pick us up first. Or we could drift into the Carolina coastline. But I do have some good news for you."

"How could there possibly be good news after what you just told me?"

Deborah pulled a bulging pillowcase from behind her and held it out to Alex. "Ta-da! I spotted the *Pequod*, so I raided Diana's and Jane's room and brought you back some supplies. I'd suggest you start with the Snickers because I'm sure they're already melted in these temperatures."

Alex shouted, "Snickers!" then dove into the pillowcase. But when he saw water bottles in it, he changed his focus, grabbed one, and chugged it down. He wanted to pour some over his face to clean off some of the caked grime but decided it was too precious to waste. Instead, Alex put his head back into the opening and saw the promised snacks, some more water, and a can of nuts. He reached in, pulled out a Snickers bar, and ripped it open. It took him more time to lick the melted chocolate off the inside of the wrapper than it did to eat the bar, but it tasted heavenly. He scarfed down the second only slightly slower before looking longingly at the last one.

"I'd give it a couple of minutes," Deborah said. "Let your stomach deal with what you've inhaled. Then, if everything's still all right, go ahead and eat the last one because once the sun rises, it'll turn into mush. Besides, you need the energy."

When he'd finished the last candy bar, he leaned back against the seat, feeling full for the first time in days, and said, "How'd you get these?"

"After we drifted past Bimini, I saw some lights on the water and went to check them out, hoping I could come up with some way to get the boat to change course and come here. It wasn't until I was floating around on board that I realized it was our grandmother's ship. I tried alerting the night watch, but when that failed, I searched the ship for Diana's and Jane's room because I remembered Diana always had snacks in Stormhold. I wasn't too quiet and woke up both girls. They were initially frightened but quickly settled down when I took a pillowcase and started stuffing it with water bottles. I was surprised at how fast they guessed what was happening because they started asking me all sorts of questions about you, even though they couldn't see or hear me. It was funny because Jane even forced Diana to give up her hidden stash of Snickers. She was about to raid the ship's pantry, but I left their room because I'm still not that good at telekinesis, and this was all I could carry. You would have gotten a kick, though, from seeing their faces as they watched me carry this pillowcase down the halls without any visible support. I'm just glad for their help because I'm not sure how I'd have gotten out of the ship with this stuff without them."

"Can you go back and get some more food and water?" Alex asked.

Deborah shook her head. "Their ship was heading north at a fast clip, and it was all I could do to get back here with this bag. There's no way I could manage a longer trip."

"Well, thanks for what you did bring. This is like manna from heaven. Although, if I knew I would get a Snickers today, I'd have held out yesterday and not eaten raw fish."

"No, you did the right thing. You needed the energy then. Although it's not much, this will help you recover a little. But I'm tired and need to head to the netherworld to rest. I'll be back later today."

Alex watched his sister disappear, then looked back in the bag for something else to eat. Unsure of the future, he held off and hoped that stretching out his meager supplies would help him survive long enough to reach land.

But the supplies ran out the next day. It wasn't the end to the benefits of his sister's night-time raid on the *Pequod,* though, as he decided to use the empty pillowcase as a makeshift sunshade, making life under the intense Caribbean sun a little more bearable.

As they continued drifting along with the Gulf Stream, Deborah would occasionally scout the area, looking for some trace of nearby land, while Alex sat in the boat, trying not to think about his blistering skin, parched throat, and queasy stomach. The afternoon showers were a mixed blessing as they partially satisfied his thirst but invariably left him cold once the sun set. Every once in a while, he'd catch a glimpse of Chrys off in the distance. He figured the opalescent-colored dragon was watching over him, as fish would start jumping out of the water around the boat within minutes of each sighting. By the third day, he felt strong enough that he decided to try rowing in an attempt to hit land before the current swept out into the Atlantic. But within an hour, his hands were a mass of red blisters.

Knowing he didn't have much energy left, he pulled out his pocket knife and cut two strips of material off the bottom of the pillowcase. Then he wrapped his hands with the strips of cloth and continued rowing west.

He rowed steadily for two hours before he took his first break. By then, despite the cloth bandages, his hands were bleeding, his back and shoulders ached, and his thirst had returned with a vengeance. He slumped to the bottom of the boat, exhausted from the effort.

"That was rather foolish," Deborah scolded. "You're barely surviving as it is."

"I don't have much choice," Alex said. "If I'm to live, I must make landfall soon. Otherwise, the current will sweep me out to sea, and it won't matter how much energy I save now." He rested a few minutes, then resumed rowing.

The breaks became more frequent as his thirst, hunger, and soreness grew steadily worse. Just before sunset, something bumped against the boat and turned it, so it faced more westerly. A second later, it picked up speed. Alex leaned over the side and spotted a flash of opalescence. *"Chrys, is that you?"* he called out.

*"Yes, little one,"* the dragon's voice sounded in his head. *"A storm is coming up, and I fear it will sweep you out to sea if I don't intervene. And no matter how upset my uncle and the High Council will be if they*

*learn of this additional intervention, I couldn't let you perish out here."*

"What's going on?" Deb asked.

Alex briefly thought about trying to hide the dragon's presence but decided there was no harm in telling his sister. In a hoarse voice, he said, "There's something else you should know. I didn't believe magic existed a year ago, and you're probably thinking dragons don't exist either."

"What! You've got to be joking," Deb said. "Either that, or you're delirious from all you've been through."

Alex tilted his head towards Chrysophylax and said, "If you look closely, you'll see flashes of opalescence in the water. That'll be Chrysophylax. I met him in Lamanai. He just told me that a storm's heading our way and is pushing us towards land to take us out of harm's way."

"I didn't hear anything," Deborah said.

"That's because he communicates via telepathy."

"And when did you get the ability to speak telepathically?" Deborah asked.

"I think the ankh gave me the ability. But don't worry, I can't hear anybody else's thoughts."

"Why's he helping you?"

"It's a long story," Alex replied. "I'll tell you about it when I feel better. But I trust him."

Alex looked to the east, where he saw dark clouds starting to crowd the skyline. The storm Chrysophylax had predicted hit a couple of hours later. At first, it was just high winds. But then the seas grew choppy. Soon after that, the rain came pelting down.

The storm threw the little boat around for the rest of the day and long into the night. If it wasn't for Chrysophylax continually righting the boat, Alex was sure he'd have ended up in the water. The only benefit from the storm was that Alex was able to fill up his water bottles and drink enough water to satisfy his thirst for the first time in over a week.

To keep up his spirits, Alex kept reminding himself of how much worse being adrift on the ocean before he reached the Fountain of Youth had been because, this time, he had Chrys and Deborah to help him.

The boat ground to a halt in the middle of the night. Alex stuck his arm into the raging waters, hoping he'd touch either Chrysophylax or the sea floor, but as he leaned over the gunwale, a wave crashed into the boat, nearly toppling him. Unsure how far they were from the coastline and not wanting to die, he quickly pulled himself back in and said, "I guess I'll have to wait till morning to find out what we've run aground on. I just hope we survive the night."

# CHAPTER 2
# **BLACKBEARD**

The storm grew fiercer as the hours went by. Occasionally, the clouds would part and let in enough moonlight for Alex to see they were in the middle of a forest of dead, skeleton-like trees. Looking at the eerie forms rising around him, Alex shouted, "Where in the heck are we? It looks like we've landed in some sort of nightmare dimension."

"I don't know," Deborah replied. "I'll fly around and check it out. I'll be right back, so please, stay out of trouble while I'm gone."

"Hey, I don't go looking for trouble. It finds me."

Deborah shook her head and flew off.

The sea grew ever stronger, smashing into the boat again and again, forcing Alex to cling to the sides. During a lull in the storm, he stuffed all the filled water bottles he could into his shirt, then leaned over the side, looking for a way down. He instantly regretted the motion as the boat tipped and spilled him into the surf below.

The next moment, a wave lifted him and slammed him into the nearest trunk, knocking the air out of him, along with half his water bottles. The water retreated, unceremoniously dumping him into the churning surf. It took him a few seconds to gather his wits and stand, but as soon as he got to his feet, the next wave crashed into him and knocked him back down. Before he could get to his feet, another wave slammed him into a dead tree, ripping his sunburned skin to pieces.

Ignoring the pain, Alex focused on making it to land. But it took him two more waves before he finally managed to reach the shore. He fell to his knees, too weak to go further but grateful he was on land again.

The waves hitting him from behind finally forced him back to his feet, whereupon he scrambled over a nearby dune to get out of the waves and the worst of the wind. But as soon as he crested the dune, he saw a group of men standing around a strange yellowish-green fire a hundred yards up the beach, singing and talking loudly. Alex half-stumbled, half-ran towards the fire, not noticing that the ankh was beating a steady warning against his chest. It wasn't until he got close that he realized it was a group of pirate ghosts. Unsure whether they were friendly or not, he backed up a few paces, hoping the sound of the rain and waves, and the darkness would mask his presence.

When he thought he was far enough away that they couldn't see him, he turned and ran. He'd only gone a few steps, though, when an icy-cold hand clamped onto his shoulder. Two more cold hands gripped his wrists and drug him across the sand before throwing him in front of the fire. Despite the flames dancing several feet into the night air, Alex felt no heat.

A large man with a tri-corn hat and braided black beard covering half his face stepped out of the shadows and looked down at Alex. He was a fearsome-looking man with dark eyes that seemed possessed by some demonic light. The man looked ready to head into battle with two cutlasses strapped around his waist and a pair of pistols stuffed into the sashes he wore over his blue coat. "What do we have here?" growled the pirate.

"A bit of sport," yelled one man from the circle surrounding Alex.

"Shark bait," called another.

The pirate standing over Alex said, "Nah. What we have here is a spy. And not just any old spy, but a living one who came all the way to the afterworld to see us. What do we do with spies, men?"

"Hang 'em," the band of ghosts shouted in unison.

Alex scrambled up and held out his hands. "I'm not a spy," he said. "I've been adrift at sea for days, saw this fire, and came here hoping someone could help me get home."

The assembled pirates roared in laughter. Their leader leaned in and asked, "Do you know who I am, lad?"

"No…no, sir. Please, you must believe me. I mean you no harm."

"I'm Blackbeard. And I don't take prisoners unless they'd make a good fighting man aboard my ship. But by the looks of you, you're so scrawny you wouldn't last a day." He turned to the surrounding pirates and yelled, "What shall it be, mates? Shall I make it quick and kill him with a blow to the head? Or shall it be a cutlass up his soft, tender gut?" Blackbeard's eyes lit up as he said, "Or, how bout' a noose around the neck so we can see him dance?"

A roar went up on the third suggestion. "So be it," Blackbeard said. He leaned in so close that their noses almost touched and added, "It's the yardarm for you, matey."

Alex felt the ankh's power suddenly surge through him the instant Blackbeard grabbed his arm. A bolt of blue energy shot out of him and hit the burly pirate in the chest, knocking him back several feet. Stunned, Blackbeard lay on his back for a few seconds before he recovered his wits and jumped to his feet. With a growl, he lunged at Alex.

Without thinking, Alex leapt through the ghostly green flames and started running. He felt hands grabbing at him, followed by cries of pain. He heard what he thought was his sister's voice chanting some incantation, but he didn't look back. Soon, his sides were heaving, his breath came in ragged gasps, and his legs grew wobbly. He descended a steep embankment, slipped on a stone, and tumbled into a marshy area.

Hoping he'd escaped, Alex listened for the pirates, but he couldn't see or hear anything – except for the storm. He got to his feet, climbed the embankment, then turned away from the beach, heading in the direction the ankh pulled him. The rain stopped, and with the dunes and trees blocking the wind blowing off the ocean, Alex felt more comfortable than he had in days.

He stumbled through the dark with branches lashing at him, tripping on unseen obstacles. Despite his exhaustion, he kept pushing on until the ankh finally quieted down. As soon as it did, Alex pushed aside some palm fronds and collapsed onto a small mound to catch his breath. He stretched out, placing his hands behind his head while staring at the moon as it played hide and seek in the clouds.

His breathing had just returned to normal when he heard a loud grunting sound. Startled, he sat up and, to his horror, saw a monstrous boar running toward him.

## CHAPTER 3
# THE CONQUISTADORS

Alex jumped to his feet, looking for an escape route. In the dim moonlight filtering through the tree canopy, he spotted an animal path and ran towards it. But he tripped on a root in the darkness and fell. Alex heard the grunts of the giant hog scurrying towards him and instinctively kicked. He was surprised when he felt his foot crunch against the beast's mouth. As he got up, the hog swung its head. One tusk grazed his calf, knocking him off his feet and sending him rolling down into a muddy area.

He tried getting up, but he was stuck in the black muck. Alex looked back to see how close the beast was and was surprised when Chrysophylax suddenly appeared and slammed into the boar, disappearing with it into the nearby marsh. There was a brief rustle of grasses, a loud terrified squeal; then all was quiet as if neither creature had ever been there.

Alex stared at the spot for only a moment before he scrambled up the bank and plunged headlong down the animal path. He kept running away from the beach until he collapsed onto the ground, his breath coming in ragged gasps. He looked for another way out of the dense forest, but it was still too dark to see much. Deciding to wait until it was light, he found a nearby tree with some low-hanging branches and climbed up to get away from other predators.

Finding a large nook, he curled up and fell asleep. A blast of cold air woke him up a short time later. He opened one bleary eye and was surprised to see Deborah hovering a few feet away. Reluctantly, he sat up and rubbed his eyes to wake up. "What'd you find?" he asked.

"Well, there's good news and bad news," she replied. "It looks like we've run aground on one of the outer bank islands on the eastern coast, so we're not too far from the mainland."

"I'm assuming that's the good news," Alex said. "And the bad?"

Deborah couldn't look Alex in the eyes when she said, "Although I spotted some buildings on the far side of the island, I didn't see anyone."

"What about food?"

She grimaced and said, "I'm not a survivalist, but I didn't see much that's edible on the island unless you go hunting. However, I did spot a lot of places where wild boars have rooted up the plants, so you'll have to watch out for them."

"You're a little late on that warning," Alex said. "One's already come after me. Luckily, Chrys took care of it."

"I can't believe I missed him," Deborah said. "I so want to see what your dragon looks like."

"He's kind of a recluse, so you'll just have to wait for another opportunity, although, given my experiences of when he shows up, I prefer you never see him. But let's get back to what's important. Are you sure there's no food around? I lost most of my water bottles but still have a few left, so what I really need is food."

"There are all sorts of birds around – herons, egrets, pelicans, and a bunch of smaller birds. Maybe you can get lucky and find some eggs."

"Not at this time of year," Alex said.

"Well, I've seen some loggerhead turtles nesting. Maybe you can watch where they bury their eggs, then dig them up and eat them."

"I can't do that," Alex said. "They're an endangered species. Maybe if I'm starving, I'll consider it, but I hope to be back in civilization long before that happens."

"There are two other food sources I've spotted, but I hate to mention them." Without waiting for a response, Deborah said, "I know you've had your fill of raw seafood, but I did see some horseshoe crabs and clams on the beach. The waves are still pretty strong, but they've died down enough that if you're starving, you can hunt for them now. Or we can head for those buildings I saw and wait for someone to come. I'm sure it won't be long because I saw some lights off to the west this morning."

"Is there any way of getting to the mainland?" Alex asked.

Deborah shook her head. "Nope. There's a big salt marsh and a lot of open water between here and there. There are other islands, but they won't help you."

"It doesn't sound like there are a lot of good options. The best one appears to be waiting at those buildings you mentioned. Do you know the way?"

When she nodded, Alex climbed down and followed her to the left on the path he'd found the night before.

They'd only gone a short distance, though, when several of Blackbeard's men swooped down on them.

He ducked instinctively when two of the pirates shot their pistols at him. But the lead balls harmlessly sailed through him, as did a third pirate's cutlass. Alex whirled around when he heard a scream from behind him and was just in time to see one of the pirates grab his sister and yank her into the air. He completely forgot about the other attackers and ran after her. A second later, one of the pirates clobbered him with a fallen branch, giving him a painful reminder that even though weapons of the spirit world might not hurt him, those in the land of the living could. Dazed, he didn't react when two of the pirates grabbed him. The ankh reacted, though, and blasted them into the nearby treetops.

Silence descended over the forest as Alex waited for his head to clear. When he could finally stand, he got up and looked around for his sister, but there was no sign of her or Blackbeard's men.

Figuring his best bet was to look for the buildings Deborah had told him about, he set off down the path despite having no idea where it would lead. He kept slogging through the dense forest of live oak trees, palms of all sizes, and a few scattered magnolias and pine trees until he came to an open area with dead trees scattered about. Alex was so glad to see an opening that he didn't notice the vegetation was covering a swamp until he fell into the dark, gooey mess.

He came up sputtering, gagging from the stench. Alex wiped the muck off his eyelids, cautiously opened his eyes, then waded over to a patch of grass and tree roots. He pulled himself out and dipped his fingers into the cleanest water he could find to start cleaning the gunk off his face. After a few minutes, he gave up and, with a heavy sigh, resumed his search for a way out.

Alex spotted where the path had veered away from the swamp and headed down it, but after an hour of fruitless wandering, he decided he'd gone the wrong way and started retracing his steps. Several times, he heard motorboats and voices in the distance, but each time he headed for them, he ran into a swamp he couldn't cross.

As the sun dipped lower in the sky, Alex looked around for a tree to sleep in. Spotting an ancient live oak, he pulled himself onto the lowest limb and started climbing. From time to time, he had to knock off some of the Spanish Moss so he could see his way, but he finally found a resting spot thirty feet above the ground where the limb spread out to form a lumpy bowl.

Alex tested the spot and decided it could hold his weight, but the bark was so stiff and scratchy that it was impossible to get comfortable. Knowing he only had a little more time before it got too dark to move, he climbed through the tree, gathering moss to pad a makeshift bed for the night. Then he took out the only remaining water bottle he had left and took a sip, hoping it wouldn't have to last him much longer.

Though exhausted, he couldn't fall asleep as his growling stomach and the swamp sounds grew louder as the night got darker. The worst part of the night, though, was when the swamp slime hardened, causing his skin to chafe every time he moved. Despite all the discomforts, he eventually fell asleep.

Shortly after midnight, a light rain began falling. At first, Alex thought the tree's leaves would keep him dry, but he soon found otherwise, as every time the wind blew, the rain that had collected on the leaves above would dump on him. He gave up trying to stay dry and instead focused on catching rainwater to drink. But he collected very little, leaving him even more aware of his growing thirst. The rain did have the benefit of washing off some of the slime, but it left him soaked to the skin and shivering. When he finally drifted off to sleep again, he couldn't help but think that a year earlier, he would have considered it the most miserable night he'd ever experienced. But now, it wasn't even in the bottom ten.

Alex woke with a start, feeling like something was off, but unsure what had disturbed his sleep. He sat up to look around, but it was still dark inside the forest, as the sun had yet to rise. Alex pulled out the ankh to check it for warning signs, but it lay quiet against the palm of his hand. After several minutes of watchful waiting, he decided it was just his nerves were on edge, and he closed his eyes to get more sleep. But no sooner had he closed them than he heard a faint metallic noise in the distance.

His hopes for rescue soared as the noise became more distinct, eventually turning into the clanking of metal. He was about to shout for help, but froze when the lead person came into view. Below him was a column of marching ghost soldiers, swords at their sides and muskets on their shoulders, all wearing the metal chest armor and distinctive morion helmets of the conquistadors.

Hoping they would lead him out, Alex waited until the last ghost was out of sight, then descended and headed after them. He followed them on the grassy path he'd been wandering along the day before until they turned onto a much larger sandy path. Half a mile later, Alex's hopes soared when they passed over an earthen causeway separating the marsh he'd kept running into the day before and open waters.

A short time later, the soldiers disappeared into the side of a grassy shrub-covered hill. At first, Alex thought it was a dune, but he quickly ruled that idea out when he realized that even those on the beach hadn't been as big or as steep.

When he thought it was safe, he came out of hiding and scrambled up the mound's slopes, hoping to use the added elevation to figure out where he was. Halfway up, the ground gave way. He tried leaping to the side but was too late and fell into a shimmering blue opening, like the one in the temple in Lamanai. Alex hit a big metal object that caused him to flip over and hit his back on a wooden structure, sending him tumbling further into the darkness. The last thing he remembered before blacking out was his head hitting a metal object near the bottom of the pit.

A sliver of sunlight was streaming in when he finally came to, in what felt like a freezer room. Shivering, he tried sitting up but instantly regretted the motion, as a searing pain shot through his head. He closed his eyes and waited until the pain had subsided.

But when he reopened his eyes, he saw a half dozen lances pointing at his chest. Hoping he was dreaming,

Alex tried sitting up, but a sharp jab from one of the spear points told him he wasn't.

Wondering what new type of trouble he'd landed in, he tried surreptitiously looking around and was surprised to find he was on a ship's gun deck turned on its side. Before he could learn more, another conquistador appeared, apparently of higher rank, as his breastplate had a gold lion standing on its hind legs clawing at an unseen enemy, unlike everyone else's plain metal ones.

"Get up, señor, and come with me."

"Who are you?" Alex asked.

One of the soldiers jabbed their lance into his side as an answer. Alex winced as the metal tip dug into him, sending a small trickle of blood oozing down his side. He struggled to get to his feet and limped after the soldier through a small doorway to the left.

Alex had difficulty following the soldiers as he had to climb over cannons and other debris littering the ship. The business edge of a lance kept prodding him every time he stopped or was slow to get over an obstacle.

Despite his fears, Alex felt somewhat relieved when he entered a cabin where all the furniture had been set upright and stood on what used to be the left side of the room. The soldier standing behind the desk was different from the other ghosts. He was about the same height as Alex but had penetrating brown eyes and close-cropped grey hair. He wore black armor with gold inlay and had a jewel-encrusted saber hanging by his side.

The soldiers behind Alex snapped to attention. Their leader came forward and bowed his head. "Here's the prisoner, Capitan. I'm sorry for the delay, but it took quite a while before he awoke. Do you want me to dispose of him now, as he's only a child and can't be of any use to us?"

The Spanish captain snapped, "Silencia, Lieutenant! It's not your job to decide what to do with him." He turned to Alex and tried to stare him down, but Alex returned the stare without blinking.

The Spanish captain walked over and put his face inches away from Alex's. "I'll ask you only one time. What are you doing here? How did you find this place?"

Alex tried speaking, but his throat felt like it was on fire. He swallowed, hoping to wet it a bit, but he was so dehydrated that it didn't help. A lance prod drove him to say in a raspy voice, "When I landed on this island a couple of days ago, I ran from some ghost pirates. I was in a tree this morning when your soldiers passed underneath, so I followed them here, hoping they would lead me back to civilization. When your men disappeared, I climbed up the mound to get a better view, and that's when I fell into this ship."

The captain peered at Alex. "How is it that you can see and speak to us? Are you using black magic?"

Alex shook his head. "It's a long story, but no, I can't do any magic. So, if you'd point me in the right direction, I'll leave and promise I'll never return.

The captain glared at Alex. "You want me to believe that you just happened to stumble onto my ship when nary a soul has come near this place for over three centuries. And you want me to believe that you just happened to find your way into our afterworld. No. It's not possible. You're lying."

In an icy-cold voice, the Spanish captain ordered, "Take this boy outside and execute him. But make sure you dispose of his body some distance from here. I don't want his corpse to lead someone else to us."

The soldier bowed his head. "Si, Capitan." Then, he motioned for the soldiers to escort Alex out.

A sharp poke in his ribs caused Alex to lurch forward. He stumbled back through the gun deck in a trance, unwilling to believe that he'd come through so much only to die alone – where no one would ever find him. Alex felt for the ankh and was surprised it was thrumming excitedly against his chest.

The blast of hot, humid air when he exited the ship, was a relief after the cold below, but another poke brought his thoughts back to his predicament. Half a dozen conquistadors surrounded him and prodded him to walk away from the ship towards a nearby saltwater marsh.

As he trudged along, Alex wondered if all condemned prisoners felt as numb as he did. It was like he was marching in slow motion to his death. He made a silent promise that if he got out of this predicament alive, he'd go back to Colorado, curb his curiosity, and never leave home again, no matter how much others begged him to help them.

When they got near the edge, the troop leader shouted, "Stand him next to the water. I want to make it an easy meal for the alligators and hogs."

A glint of metal in the tree line off to the side caught Alex's attention. He looked into the woods, hoping some miracle rescue was about to happen. Instead, the ankh changed from thrumming on his chest to thumping him – warning him that danger was near.

Time slowed as he watched three soldiers with muskets line up in front of him. He heard the command to ready arms, then the clinking of metal as the soldiers raised their muskets to their shoulders.

Alex weighed his chances of running through the spirits versus jumping into the water and taking his chances on avoiding becoming some hungry animal's meal – the memory of his encounter with the giant hog made up his mind. Alex looked into the heartless eyes of the soldiers and saw one lancer who seemed to pity Alex's situation. Without waiting, he charged the unsuspecting soldier and grabbed his lance. He heard a roar from the tree line and looked to see what was causing it. His heart skipped a beat when he saw Blackbeard and his fellow pirates charging across the field.

# CHAPTER 4
# SIEGE PERILOUS

The next thing Alex knew, he was lying flat on his back as the soldier had taken advantage of his concentration lapse and flipped him over, using the lance as leverage. Alex rolled to his left to avoid the soldier's lunge but didn't quite make it, as the edge of the lance sliced open his side before plunging into the ground where he'd been an instant before. Alex twisted around and lunged for the weapon, managing to grab it before the spirit could pull it out of the sand.

The soldier let go of the lance and had just started pulling his sword out when one of the pirates shot him through the heart, causing him to dissolve into dust. Alex jumped to his feet, but instead of attacking the conquistadors, he turned on the pirates. He thrust the lance into the nearest ghost's chest, sending the pirate to the next stage of the afterlife. Knowing he didn't have much energy left, Alex knew the battle needed to end quickly if he were to survive. He saw Blackbeard, with several burning sticks stuck in his beard, fighting towards the Spanish captain's blind side. Alex ran towards Blackbeard and arrived just as the pirate raised his sword to strike the Spanish captain. Alex thrust his lance into the pirate's right side and shouted, "Don't do it, or you'll end up being a pile of dust before you can turn your head."

Blackbeard froze. "Now, don't be hasty, lad. I'm lowering my arms real slow."

Alex pulled the lance out and pointed it at Blackbeard's heart, saying, "Just in case you don't think I'm serious." Without taking his eyes off Blackbeard, he said, "Captain, take his weapons away."

The captain raised his sword, but before he could swing it, Alex raised his hand and said, "No more bloodshed. If you kill Blackbeard, I'll put this lance through your heart. Now, both of you, call off your men and stop the battle."

The Spanish captain lowered his sword and shouted to his men to stop fighting, while Blackbeard did the same.

When silence had descended on the battleground, Alex said, "Captain Blackbeard, tell your men to leave and never come back."

Blackbeard grumbled something, then shouted, "To the ship, men. There's no booty here for us." Within seconds, the pirates had vanished into the forest.

Alex shifted his lance towards the Spanish captain. "Now it's your turn. Tell your men to leave." Thinking of the ankh's powers, he added, "And I should warn you. I have a secret weapon that will protect me against you and your men."

The captain sheathed his sword and called out, "Follow them and make sure they leave this island."

"But, Capitan," the lieutenant protested. "We can't leave you here with that boy. He's a practitioner of the dark arts and is dangerous."

"That's an order," the captain shouted. "Now go and leave us alone. I'll be fine."

"Si." The lieutenant saluted and called his men together. Within a minute, they too had disappeared."

Alex lowered his lance slightly.

"What do you want?" the captain asked. "If you were going to kill me, you'd have done it by now. Are you here for my treasure?"

Alex frowned and shook his head. "I have no idea what you're talking about. I told you. I found this place accidentally. All I want to do is go home. Besides, I just gave away one treasure and have even less desire for yours."

The Spanish captain studied Alex for some time before he suddenly bowed and said, "Captain General Don Juan Esteban de Ubilla at your service. Please, come with me. I have something I think you've earned."

Alex followed the captain towards the opening he'd fallen through earlier but hesitated when he saw the blue lights of the afterworld again.

The captain, who was already on the gun deck, looked up and asked, "Aren't you coming? I assure you; no harm will come to you."

"Just give me a sec," Alex said. "I'm a little nervous because I don't have the best luck when I enter the afterworld." He took a couple of deep breaths, then climbed in.

The captain led Alex to a small desk in the middle of his cabin and pointed to the drawer. "Please, open it."

Alex looked askance at Captain Ubilla but slipped his fingers into the pull and tugged at the drawer. It didn't budge.

"Try again. It's hard to open at this time of year because of the high humidity and its age."

Alex wiped his hands on his ragged camouflage pants, then tugged harder. The drawer burst open and sent him tumbling backwards. A large leather book popped out, flew through the air, and landed on his groin, causing Alex to ball up in agony. After the pain subsided, Alex slowly uncurled, then sat up and gingerly straightened the book on his lap. Grimacing, he asked, "Why did you dismiss everyone to show me this moldy old thing?"

The captain pointed at the book. "Look at the cover," he replied.

Alex squinted at the leather binding in the dim light coming into the cabin. "It's hard to make out because of all the mold on it, but the first word looks like it starts with S."

The captain looked expectantly at Alex as if it explained everything. When Alex didn't say anything, Captain Ubilla said, "It's my family's diary of our search for the Sangreal."

One of the soldiers appeared in the doorway and said, "Pardon, Capitan, but a motorboat is coming. They're still a couple of miles away, but they don't appear to be the usual fishermen or tourists. I thought you should know because they seem to be looking for something." The soldier glanced at Alex and added, "Or someone."

The captain nodded. "Gracias. Now, please, give us a few minutes alone."

Figuring the motorboat might be his only chance to escape wherever he was, Alex headed for the exit. He was halfway there when the captain called out, "Please, señor, take this book with you."

Alex glanced at the old leather journal and took another step towards the exit.

"At least listen to what I have to say while you wait for your rescue," the captain said. "Many lives could be at stake."

Alex inwardly groaned and turned back towards where the captain stood. "What's so special about that book?"

"Have you ever heard of the 1715 Spanish Plate Fleet?"

Alex screwed up his face. "No. Should I have?"

"You must hear my story so you know how important this book is, and why you should take it with you." He paused to gather his thoughts, then, with a faraway look in his eyes, said, "This has been in my family for centuries, with each eldest son swearing to protect it with his life while simultaneously trying to solve the riddle of the book. I didn't take my vow seriously, though. Instead, I chose to seek my fortune here in the New World. I was so successful that I became the Captain General of the 1715 treasure fleet. Because of the wars in Europe, King Phillip had postponed the treasure fleet's voyage to Spain two years in a row. So, the fleet I commanded had the largest treasure ever, and this ship was my flagship. My part of the convoy started in Vera Cruz, where we took on the Mexican portion of the treasure. My counterpart, Captain General Zubiza, loaded his cargo in Cartagena. We delayed our departure several more weeks, waiting for treasures from the Orient."

"We sailed for Havana, but once again, we had to delay our voyage because of a request from King Phillip for us to bring certain jewels back to Spain for his soon-to-be bride. We finally left Cuba on the 24th of July, almost two months later than originally planned and, more importantly, in the middle of the Atlantic hurricane season. Since there hadn't been a treasure fleet for three years, we assumed pirates and our enemies would be lurking for us near the usual convoy routes, so we took a more northerly route, choosing to stay close to the Florida coastline to avoid detection. In the end, our delays, the cumbersome nature of our ships, the course change, and the heavy treasure caused our doom."

"I was at the head of the column when the wind suddenly died. The next morning, a hurricane struck. Most of the ships in the flotilla quickly sunk. However, we managed to stay afloat long enough for the storm to drive us here. Unfortunately, most of my men perished during the storm. And those of us who survived, died soon after we ran aground here and are the men you saw today."

"Why haven't you moved on?" Alex asked.

"Most of my men think we're stuck here because we must continue guarding the King's treasure."

"But that's stupid," Alex said. "This treasure of yours is probably just a bunch of metal and stones. It can't help you much in the afterlife. Besides, why do you care if anybody finds your dead king's treasure? You can't stop anybody from taking it."

"Perhaps you're right, but at least the time I've spent here has allowed me to study the book I hold in my hands – the one I promised my father to guard with my life."

"So, what does it say?" Alex asked.

"I could only read part of it because it's written in old English, Arabic, and other languages I don't recognize. But I believe the book holds information on a treasure infinitely more valuable than the immense fortune I have on board here."

Despite his concerns, Alex was intrigued. He stepped forward and asked, "What is the treasure the book talks about?"

"I don't know. It might be the Templar's lost treasure or maybe some holy relic. I know my ancestors devoted their lives to protecting this book and its secrets. We've escaped detection for centuries – until today. I never thought there could come a time when I would pass on my family obligation, but I believe you should look after this book. You can see the dead, showed compassion for the pirates, and forgiveness towards us. It wasn't chance that you walked into our life."

"What am I supposed to do with this?" Alex asked.

"The same thing my father told me – guard it with your life. If possible, find and protect whatever this book is about." He thrust it into Alex's hands and said, "Please, take it."

Alex was about to reject the captain's request when he thought about the ankh and everything that had happened to him.

Before Alex could say anything else, the sound of engines reverberated through the cabin. "Come," Captain Ubilla said. "God moves in mysterious ways. He has brought you to me and sent someone to rescue you." The Spanish Capitan motioned to Alex. "I have one other thing to give you before you go. I have found this sort of thing can help in various ways."

He went to one of the chests and took out a gleaming gold ingot.

Alex's mouth dropped open.

"This is for you to use as you see fit. I'll wrap it up so robbers won't attack you and carry it out since you'll need to use at least one hand to climb out."

Seconds later, Alex was back on the trail. Captain General Ubilla stuffed the ingot into the crook of Alex's arm. Then he pointed to his left and said, "The docks are that way. Good luck, and may God bless your path."

Shocked at how his luck had changed so quickly, Alex stumbled off in the direction the captain had pointed. He'd only gone a short distance when he heard cries of joy. Turning around, he saw the mound he'd just exited collapse. Amid the choking dust cloud, Alex saw the captain shimmering for just an instant before disappearing.

Even though he'd seen spirits move on before, the disappearance of the conquistadors, after centuries of waiting, moved him. He swiped at the tears running down his cheek, then continued on his way.

# CHAPTER 5
# HIM WE CAN RESCUE

Thinking his ordeal was almost over, Alex felt what little energy he had left suddenly drain from him. He shuffled along the sandy path without noticing his surroundings until he came upon an open grassy area with a handful of buildings scattered around. It was only then that he realized the engine sound had disappeared. Fearing he'd lost his opportunity for rescue, Alex broke into a trot.

He halted when he rounded the island's ranger station and saw a dilapidated-looking boat at the dock. Alex's emotions quickly shifted from the euphoria of rescue, to wondering if he would be safe on board with the golden ingot in his possession, to questioning whether the ship was even seaworthy.

Seeking reassurance on whether it was safe to approach, Alex put his hand over the ankh and was relieved to feel it lying quietly on his chest. He shifted the ingot onto the book and waved while calling out.

As he wound his way down the ramp to the dock, a short, stocky man with long dreadlocks was finishing tying the stern line to the dock cleat. Another Black man, much taller than the first, with short hair and a bright floral shirt, jumped out of the boat and strode to where Alex stood.

He swallowed and managed to croak, "You don't know how glad I am to see you guys. My name's Alex Scire and I'm marooned here. Can I get a ride back to civilization with you?"

In a thick French accent, the tall man said, "Of course. I'm Jean Paul, and this is my friend Francis. But how did you get here? You're stranded on an uninhabited island, miles from the mainland."

Alex avoided the question, saying, "It's a long story. Do you mind if I go aboard now? I'm exhausted and don't know how long I can stand up." The remainder of Alex's adrenaline stopped pumping, letting him suddenly feel all his aches and pains and causing his knees to buckle.

Jean Paul helped Alex to his feet and asked, "Of course. Where are you going?"

Alex hesitated. "I want to go home, but all you need to do is get me to a place with an airport. I can get the rest of the way from there." Seeing the two men skeptically eye each other, Alex quickly added, "Or Salem, Massachusetts. My grandmother lives there, and since I don't know where I am, either will do."

Jean Paul raised his eyebrows, looked at Francis, and said, "We just happened to be taking a detour to see this island before we headed to Maine, so we'd be happy to drop you off in Salem if you want."

Alex looked at the boat and frowned.

Seeing Alex's skepticism, Jean Paul said, "Don't let our ship's looks fool you. She might be old and worn, but *La Amistad* is seaworthy, and has never let us down."

"I appreciate the offer, but you can drop me off at the next city, and I can fly home."

Jean Paul looked Alex up and down. "No offense, but you don't look like you can even afford a phone call."

Alex started to reach for his pack but realized it was probably at the bottom of the ocean, along with his wallet. "I'm sorry. I've been through so much lately that I'd forgotten I'd lost all my stuff."

"Don't worry about it," Jean Paul said. "How can we say no to you in your situation. We can give you a clean, dry bunk, three meals a day, and it'll cost you nothing."

"I don't want to impose on your hospitality…" Alex never finished the sentence as he fainted.

***

Jean Paul knelt beside Alex and felt his pulse. Then he lifted one of Alex's eyelids. Speaking in French, he said, "This has to be the boy they're looking for – the same one we saw in Port Royal."

Francis knelt on the other side of Alex and picked him up as if he was as light as a feather. "Does it matter who he is? Look at him. He looks like death warmed over, and he needs our help. Grab his stuff and bring it to the main cabin."

"But where will we sleep?"

"It's not important," Francis said. "I won't sleep until he's better. Now get out of my way."

Within minutes, they were underway, but Francis didn't come topside again until long after they'd made their turn north in the Atlantic. Standing beside Jean Paul, who was at the wheel, he said, "Make for Salem at full speed. I have no idea how he's still alive. I'll do what I can, but if he's to recover, he'll need the help of the witches."

Jean Paul smiled. "Always the soft spot for those less fortunate, eh, my friend? But shouldn't we take him to one of the hospitals in Savannah?"

"They can only help him so much, and I can do almost everything they can here. He's dehydrated, has blisters on every exposed part of his body, probably has sunstroke, and looks like he's starving to death. Plus, he's got wounds all over his body, including a fresh one. Taking him to a hospital will only delay his recovery in the long run. Besides, his sudden appearance will beg too many uncomfortable questions. I prefer the fewer who know about his situation, the better."

"What about Enkidu?" Jean Paul asked. "Do we tell him that we've found the boy?"

"We've worked with him for many years, but he has his own agenda – which I don't trust," Francis replied. " I'd prefer we ensure the boy is safely in the witches' hands before telling him."

"This is so strange. What do you think is going on?" Jean Paul asked.

"I've no idea. What I wonder about, though, is why Sharur guided us to him again. It feels like Enlil is using Sharur to guide us to the boy. It doesn't make any sense."

"Maybe when he wakes up, he'll tell us what's going on," Jean Paul said. He paused, then asked, "By the way, did you see what he brought aboard?" Without waiting for a reply, he said, "He had no food, water, or money - nothing but a gold ingot and an ancient journal. Who goes wandering around in the middle of nowhere with those things?"

"Nobody," Francis replied. "I've wrapped up those items, but they're not ours to worry about. They're his, and we are but his guardians."

## CHAPTER 6
# BECAUSE WE DO NOT DARE

Chrysophylax bellowed his greeting as he landed outside his Uncle Nabu's laboratory.

*"Thank Marduk, you're back,"* Nabu said telepathically. *"I've been worried about you. Some of the High Council members have been asking why they haven't seen you in such a long time. I think they suspect you've snuck off world."*

*"They've definitely tightened security at the portals,"* Chrysophylax replied. *"I came back through the most remote wormhole at night and barely evaded detection. Why are the Elders so riled up?"*

*"They've always been suspicious of me, and now with you disappearing, I believe they've leapt to the conclusion that we're plotting an insurrection. I think it's also because the Ryūjin are excited about something."* Nabu looked around his lab and sighed. *"I hate to admit it, but I miss the pest that used to stay here. It disappeared about the time you left for Earth."*

Chrysophylax said, *"She followed me to Earth and, I believe, has gone off with that boy."*

*"What! Why would it do that?"* Nabu asked.

*"I don't know. I'd have asked it if I could understand it, but you know their type. They get so excitable that the images they send are just gibberish."* Chrysophylax paused, then added, *"Although, at times, it seemed like the boy could understand it."*

*"Interesting,"* Nabu replied. *"Remember when I told you about Sibyl, the Irkallan girl I met a long time ago. She believed the Maqlû were dangerous and created the Sibylline books in an attempt to understand and stop the misuse of those objects. She's also the one who found and gave me the ankh and always had one of those pesty Ryūjin dragonets hanging around her. Its behaviors would suggest it's the same one as hers, but I can't tell because you know how they all look alike. Enough about them. Tell me, what happened on your mission? What did you learn?"*

Chrysophylax took a deep breath before saying, *"I believe he's destroyed another one of the Maqlû."*

*"Interesting."*

Chrysophylax was surprised his uncle took the news so calmly. *"I thought you'd be furious, or at least shocked. What's happened to have changed your mind so much?"*

*"I've given a lot of thought to what you said the last time you were here and have decided that maybe the High Council is right. Maybe we should stay out of human affairs. That goes for both of us, which is why I've already stopped trying to control the destiny of the ankh and the Maqlû."*

*"But...."*

*"No buts,"* Nabu said. *"You need to let go of your fascination with that boy and stay here on Berellus. The Elders are nervous and will punish anyone going against their wishes. And I know you – you're itching to return. But I'm telling you, you need to stay here. Make your presence visible, so they don't suspect you've left the planet against their orders. I don't want to see*

*anything bad happen to you. Now go. See Mireu. She's been asking about you."*

*"I understand what you're saying, but I'll stay only until things calm down. I can't explain why I need to return, because I don't understand it myself, but I have to go back to Earth and see this out."* Chrysophylax walked out to the ledge outside his uncle's laboratory and launched himself into the air.

# CHAPTER 7
# SOME OTHER BEGINNINGS END

Jean Paul stepped up to the gate's video camera security system and pressed a button on the keypad. A few seconds later, Brother Robert Stafford answered. "Finally. What news do you have about the boy?"

"Either come out to the street to talk to us or let us in," Jean Paul said. "I'm not talking to you through this." A buzzer sounded, and the gate silently opened.

As Francis drove their rented car up the winding driveway through a grove of trees, he asked, "Why are we here? You know I don't trust him."

"He broke with Gilgamesh and Pythia ages ago and has done a lot of good since then with his Magos Order," Jean Paul replied. "Plus, I'm curious what his interest in the boy is, which is why I am adopting Machiavelli's suggestion to keep our enemies closer."

Francis growled in reply.

They exited the forest and entered a grassy meadow with a large pond. On the far side lay a stone cottage overlooking Salem Sound. A short, powerfully built man in dark brown robes and a tonsure haircut stood in the doorway, waiting for them.

There were no handshakes nor polite greetings when the three met. Instead, Stafford led Jean Paul and Francis around to the back patio, but before they even sat down, he asked, "Well, did you find him? What was he doing?"

"Aren't you going to offer us drinks? Or at least say hello?" Jean Paul asked.

"Yes, yes, of course. Pardon my manners. It's just that the boy has unnerved me. I don't know what to think of him." Stafford entered the cottage and came out with the drinks a few minutes later. He was so anxious for news that he asked, "Well?" before he sat down.

"He was near death when we found him, so we took him to the witch's house to heal," Jean Paul said. "I don't know what he went through, but it must have been horrible, as it looks like it'll be some time before he physically recovers. And who knows how long it'll take to heal the mental scars of what he's been through."

Stafford ignored Jean Paul's concerns. "So, how did you find him? The witches had the Coast Guard out looking for him for days. I heard he went overboard during a freak storm near Tortuga, but they never got a single lead on his whereabouts."

"We first spotted him with two young witches in a remote spot in Port Royal. How he got from Belize to there, though, only Gaia knows. But we saw him and his friends for only a moment. One second, they were there, and the next, they were gone. They just disappeared into thin air."

"What sort of magical spell did he use?" Stafford asked.

"That's just it. We don't think the boy used any magic, as he appeared unconscious when he disappeared. And we've never known any witch who could perform the type of spell required for such an act."

"But you two are the greatest trackers in the world. Why did it take you so long before you found him again?"

"We don't know how he evaded us," Jean Paul replied. "All we know is that he disappeared in Port Royal, went overboard near Tortuga several days later, then somehow made it to Blackbeard's Island a week later. What I don't understand, is if he went overboard near the Windward Passage, how did he get to Georgia? The currents wouldn't have taken him that way. And I doubt someone picked him up, because he was in one of the most desolate places on the eastern seaboard. The only reason we were able to find him was because we followed one of Francis' hunches." He shuddered. "I can't imagine what the journey was like for him."

"Did he have anything with him?" Stafford asked.

Jean Paul glanced covertly at Francis and shook his head. "All he had were tattered clothes, sunburns, bruises, and scrapes. He must have a tenacious hold on life because it's a miracle he survived."

"Are you sure he didn't have anything else?"

"Do you have so little compassion that all you can ask about are his possessions?" Jean Paul asked. "Shouldn't you care more that he was on death's door? He must have been willing himself to live because he collapsed before we even got him on board our boat. And he was so out of it that he didn't wake up during the entire trip here. Besides, why are you so interested in what he had with him?"

Stafford pounded his chair arm. "Dammit, there's more at stake than the boy's life. I need to know if he found one of the Maqlû."

"If he found one of them, he didn't have it on him," Jean Paul replied coolly.

Stafford stood and began pacing across the veranda. After several minutes, he sat down and said, "I appreciate your efforts at bringing him back safely. I don't know what he was doing down there, but I'm sure it has something to do with the Maqlû. Whether he's a help or a threat is the question."

"What will you do now?" asked Jean Paul.

"I'll use my contacts within Elizabeth's household to get information on what the boy did. If that doesn't work, I'll go right to the top."

Francis leaned forward and placed his fists on the table. "I'm warning you. No harm is to come of that boy, or you'll answer to me. Understand, he's under our protection from now on." Before Stafford could reply, Francis kicked his chair over and said to Jean Paul, "Come. We have better things to do than talk to the likes of him." He took a few steps, then turned. "One more thing. Until you change your ways, don't ask us for help again. Our priorities are too different. We're done with you and your friends."

## CHAPTER 8
# BY THE TRACKS WE LEAVE

Even though he ached all over, Alex felt too comfortable to open his eyes when he finally woke. His throat felt less parched than he remembered it being, but a grumbling stomach reminded him not everything had changed, although it wasn't as bad as he'd remembered on those endless days on the ocean. Something didn't feel right, though, when he shifted and felt his sunburned skin rub uncomfortably against the sheets. It took him a few seconds before he remembered that he hadn't slept in sheets for weeks. Panicked at not knowing where he was, Alex tried sitting up. But an unseen hand gently pushed him back down in the bed. A soft voice with a light Scottish accent said, "Ye need to take it easy."

Alex tried opening his eyes, but they didn't want to open. He waited for a few seconds, then tried again. At first, everything was blurry. After a few more seconds, a pair of blue-grey eyes, peering out of a mass of ginger-colored hair, came into focus. "Jane? Is that really you? Where am I?"

"Ye're back in Salem," she replied.

Alex felt something else was off and lifted the sheet to peek underneath. When he realized he wasn't wearing anything, he looked up, his face beet red. "Where are my clothes?"

Jane laughed. "Really. That's what ye're worried about? I've spent a lot of time nursing people, and there's nothing I haven't seen before. Besides, yer clothes were falling apart by the time ye got here."

He felt his chest and realized the ankh was missing. In a panic, he started pounding the bed, trying to find it. Jane laid her hand on Alex's. "Relax. I've got it safely hidden. I know ye don't want anyone else seeing it, so as soon as ye came in, I took it off ye."

Alex fell back against his pillow and asked, "How did I get here?"

"I have no idea what happened once ye went overboard," Jane said. "All I know, is that two gentlemen found ye down on an island off the Georgia coast and brought ye here. I don't know how ye survived because ye had more than yer fair share of injuries. The men who rescued ye took care of ye pretty well, but they didn't clean that nasty wound on your side well enough, so I had to cut it open and get all the puss out before I sewed ye back up when ye got here."

Alex reached down to his side and felt a thick bandage. Seeing some dry clothes at the foot of his bed, he said, "Turn around so I can get dressed."

Jane shook her head. "Ye're not going anywhere for a while."

"I'm getting up. I can't just lay around here."

"Yer staying right where ye are until ye get better. Doctor's orders. Ye need more food and rest before ye can start moving around again."

"Who's the doctor? Let me talk to him," Alex said.

One of Jane's eyebrows arched, and a grin spread across her face.

Alex moaned. "Don't tell me you're the doc."

"Guilty as charged. Ye should thank me by the way. If it were up to yer grandmother, ye'd be in a hospital right now, and we wouldn't have been able to use any of our magic or herbal remedies to help ye heal. Ye also wouldn't have gotten as good of care as Diana, and I have been watching over ye twenty-four-seven."

Alex saw that someone had moved a recliner chair into his room, along with a pillow and blankets. He looked at Jane and said, "Thank you for everything both of you have done for me."

Jane smiled and said, "Jest hearing ye talking again is payment enough."

Alex's stomach growled just then. "Can I at least have some food?"

"Now that's music to my ears," Jane said. I'm going to keep you on a rather bland diet for a while, but ye can have as much as ye want. Hold on. I'll be right back."

A few minutes later, he heard a knock on the door. Diana entered, her wavy brown hair, clean white t-shirt, and jeans a stark contrast to the last time he'd seen her.

Diana rushed over and clasped his hand as tears ran down her cheeks. "Thank Gaia you've come about. I thought we'd lost you."

Alex didn't know how to respond. Trying to lighten the mood, he said, "You shouldn't have worried. I had some guardian angels looking out for me."

Diana sniffed and wiped the tears off her cheeks. "I don't see how you can make jokes after what you've been through, but I'm glad to see you again. How are you?" she asked.

"You mean what we've been through," Alex corrected. "But to answer your question, I'm fine."

"How can you say that? Just look at you," Diana exclaimed.

Alex was glad Jane walked in with a food tray just then, so he didn't have to figure out what to say next. He sat up and shifted his attention to the food but grimaced when he saw what was on the tray. "Is this all I get – chicken noodle soup, some type of yogurt, and apple juice?"

"Ye need to build up the bacteria in yer intestinal system," Jane said. "You might think you want a steak or some spicy Mexican food, but believe me, ye'd quickly regret it."

Alex didn't hear the last words as he was already greedily slurping the soup. He was surprised, though, at how quickly he got full. When he thought his belly would burst, he put his spoon down."

Jane immediately picked it up and dipped it into the yogurt. "Na, lad, ye have to have some of this. It'll help yer gut repopulate with good bacteria."

Seeing Alex eyeing the yogurt skeptically, Jane said, "It's just Greek yogurt and a few other spices I've added, sweetened with a little bit of honey to help ye recover faster."

Diana rolled her eyes and said, "I'm sorry for you, Alex. That yogurt is one of Jane's infamous concoctions with about a dozen ingredients – supposedly all healthy. But I've never been able to stomach it. Besides, this is payback for having your sister steal all my Snickers. At least, we thought it was your sister. Was it?"

Alex nodded. "We managed to find a boat on some deserted island and were heading towards Bimini, but she discovered we were too far from shore and would never make it. So, she started scouting around for help and saw your ship. When she couldn't figure out how to get anyone's attention, she did the next best thing and raided your room to get some supplies for me."

"Why didn't she come back and get more?" Jane asked.

"She said she's not very good at telekinesis yet, and that's all she could handle. Plus, you were moving so fast away from us that she didn't think she could return with more supplies." Alex swallowed the spoonful waiting at his lips, grimaced, and lay back. "Are you happy now?"

"It's a start," Jane replied.

"I want to thank you both for all you did for me." There was a long, uncomfortable silence before Alex added, "By the way, how long was I out for?"

"Counting the trip up here, about a week," Jane replied.

Alex gasped, lay back on his pillow, and moaned, "A week! How could I lose so much time?"

The food soon started taking effect, and his eyes grew drowsy. Hoping he wasn't being rude, he said, "I'm sorry, but I'm already tired and ready for a nap."

Diana picked up the tray and left, leaving Jane alone with Alex. As he drifted to sleep, his last thought was of someone lightly brushing hair off his forehead.

It was several days before he was eating normally and able to get around the house. But, even then, his movements were slow and pained.

Jean Paul and Francis came by to see him as soon as they heard he was moving about and were talking with Jane and Diana in the drawing room when Alex shuffled in. He immediately went over to Jean Paul, hugged him, then turned to Francis, who hung back. Alex stood with his arms wide open until Francis came forward and engulfed him in a bear hug.

Alex accidentally bumped into a small baton-like object hanging at Francis' side. An image of himself, Diana, and Jane in the open lot in Port Royal flashed in his head, followed by an image of him standing in the meadow on Blackbeard's Island. They were so realistic, that, for a moment, he thought he was relieving parts of his journey through the Caribbean. Then he realized he wasn't having a flashback. Instead, he was seeing those places from someone else's perspective. Shocked, he staggered back and stared at Francis. "How did you do that?" he asked.

Seeing he'd made his Haitian rescuers uncomfortable, he pointed at the metallic object with flying buttresses joined on each end and quickly added, "It's just that thing shocked me."

Jean Paul seemed to relax. "It's just an old artifact Francis found ages ago and has become sentimental about. He carries it with him everywhere he goes. He's even given it a name – Sharur."

The ankh beating excitedly against his chest told Alex they weren't telling the whole truth. He stared at the object, wondering if it was something he should be concerned with or whether it was like the ankh he wore. Alex sat down on the sofa and closed his eyes.

Jane quickly sat down beside him and felt his forehead. "Are ye all right?" she asked.

"Yeah. I'm fine. Just a little tired from being up and about so much." He turned to their guests and said, "I can't ever thank you two enough for saving my life."

"It was nothing. I'm sure you'd have done the same for us." Jean Paul fiddled with his baseball hat for a minute, then abruptly said, "We should go and let you rest. We just wanted to check on you."

Alex suddenly jumped up and asked, "Did anyone reimburse you for your costs? I don't remember where you said you were heading, but this had to be out of your way. I'm sure it would have been a lot easier for you guys to drop me off at the first hospital rather than bring me all the way up here."

"Your thanks are all we need," Jean Paul replied.

The two men were walking out the door when Alex called out, "Wait. Wasn't I carrying something when you found me?"

Seeing the anxious look on his face, Diana quickly said, "Your stuff is in a bag in your closet. And don't worry. We didn't look inside because we know how secretive you like to be. But I've got to ask, what's in it? It weighs a ton."

Alex held up a finger. "Wait a minute," he said. "I'll be right back." He returned a few minutes later, holding the gold ingot wrapped in one of his old t-shirts. Holding it out, he said, "This is for saving my life."

Jean Paul's eyebrows shot up. "Do you know what you're doing? This isn't necessary."

Alex grinned and said, "I don't want it. Besides, I don't remember your boat too well, but I got the impression you need to do some work on it."

Jean Paul took the ingot and bowed. "If we can ever be of any service, please feel free to call on us."

Diana showed them out of the house. Returning to the drawing room, she closed the doors and asked, "You just shocked the heck out of them. So, out with it. What did you just give them?"

"It was nothing," Alex replied. "It's just something I found right before they rescued me. I thought they could use it more than I could."

Seeing the looks on both girls' faces, he said, "Not here. Let's go upstairs."

After settling into his bedroom, he said, "Don't worry. It wasn't any magical object. It was just a gold ingot someone gave to me."

Diana jumped out of her chair. "You gave them what! That's…," she did a quick mental calculation and said, "worth over half a million dollars!"

Jane had a totally different reaction. She chuckled and said, "Only ye could be lost at sea and show up with a small treasure to show for it."

"I had no idea how much it was worth," Alex said. "Besides, how would I explain it? Despite all the trouble they went through, they never asked for anything. It was the least I could do for them. By the way, what have you told my grandma about what happened on our little adventure?"

Jane glanced at Diana, who flung up her hands. Seeing she was on her own, Jane said, "We're quite proud of how we avoided telling her yer biggest secret – that ye can see ghosts."

Diana interjected, "But Jane wimped out and forced me to make up lies about how we got around the Caribbean."

"You still haven't told me what you told her," Alex said.

"I told her you were very persuasive and kept talking people into giving us rides. I also told her that we felt compelled to follow you because we wanted to make sure you didn't cause us any trouble," Diana replied. "At least it was part of the truth."

"We kept saying we were seasick whenever her questions hit too close to home," Jane added.

"I'm just glad your grandmother hasn't been around Jane much because Jane never gets sick – not even colds," Diana said. "She's the envy of everyone at Stormhold.

Jane snorted. "Don't kid yourself. Elizabeth knows there's more to the story than what we've told her. She's kept her doubts to herself, for now, although I don't know why. I can't help but wonder if Lady Yvaine has told her not to snoop around too much." Turning to Alex, she said, "Ye should know, though, that we also told her we think ye found and lost the Palantir in the cave-in in Lamanai. Neither of us felt right to have everyone keep working on a fool's errand."

"How'd she take it?" Alex asked.

"Elizabeth wasn't happy, but she did better than I expected," Diana replied. "The Elders debated whether to search through the cave-in rubble but decided against it because, in the end, they didn't believe our story. My mom, however, went ballistic. But you have to expect that when we're talking about you."

"What did you tell her about how you got on board her ship during a hurricane?"

Diana winced. "Please don't be mad, but we weren't sure what to tell her. She jumped to the conclusion that you used some form of magic to transport us through the storm, and we didn't disabuse her of the idea."

"Great. Now your order is really going to be afraid of me." He sighed, then said, "I guess it's not the worst thing you could've said. But I have to say, this is kind of funny." Seeing the confused looks on their faces, he said, "I never thought I'd see the day when you'd be backing up each other's lies, covering for me."

"I think you're rubbing off on us," Diana said. "We, or at least I, am beginning to feel a little bit of rebelliousness seeping into my blood."

"What happened to Deborah?" Jane asked.

"She saved my life when I washed ashore on the first island, then stayed with me until we ended up on Blackbeard Island. I haven't seen her since." Alex looked out the window and murmured, "I just hope she's okay."

"So, did you find the Fountain of Youth?" Jane asked.

"What people think of as the Fountain of Youth is an abomination," Alex replied. "It's why I'm going home as soon as you say I'm fit to travel. I'll figure out some other way of helping my sister move on that doesn't have anything to do with those nasty Maqlû objects."

"What are ye talking about?" Jane asked.

"They're nasty things that corrupt everyone. Your order should leave those objects alone. Put it this way – Deb agrees with me."

"What caused the change of heart?" Jane asked.

"I'd rather not talk about it."

"Well, will you at least explain how you found a gold ingot and that old journal?" Diana asked. "We're both dying to know."

"There's not much to tell," Alex said.

A buzzing sound stopped the conversation. Diana pulled her phone out, looked at the message, then put it back in her pocket.

Alex smiled and said, "I see you've got another phone."

"No thanks to you," Diana retorted. "Luckily, my mom was so happy to see me that she didn't scold me too much about ruining another phone."

"I think you should call it Kenny," Alex said.

Diana scrunched up her face. "That's a stupid name. Why would I call it that?"

Jane chuckled and asked, "Haven't you ever watched South Park? Kenny's a character who keeps dying and coming back to life in the next episode – just like your phone."

"Ha, ha. Very funny," Diana replied. "By the way, I don't know if you saw it, but one of the ghosts from the *Fancy* brought your pack over from the ship and dropped it off. It's in the closet with the journal."

"Yeah, I saw it. Thanks," Alex replied.

He started to lie down on his bed but stopped when Jane said, "We're not done with ye yet, bub. I can understand why ye brought back the ingot, but I don't understand why ye brought back that old journal. What's in it?"

"I don't know, but I'm surprised you haven't looked inside. Some Spanish ghost captain gave it to me and asked me to solve the riddle in it. He said it's the key to a secret treasure worth protecting. You guys can have it because I'm done with my adventuring days."

"What riddle?" Jane asked.

Alex yawned. "I don't know, and I don't care."

Jane stood up, motioning for Diana to do the same. "I'm sorry," she said. "We've overtaxed ye. Get some rest, and I'll check on ye later."

Diana picked up the ancient journal and walked out of the room. Neither she nor Alex noticed how long Jane gazed at him before closing the door and going downstairs.

# CHAPTER 9
# IF HISTORY REPEATS ITSELF

Diana was halfway to her room when she realized Jane wasn't behind her. She retraced her steps and saw Jane closing the door to Alex's room. "What are you doing? Don't you want to see what he found?"

"Of course I do," Jane replied. "I was just making sure he was resting." She motioned for Diana to lead the way and followed her upstairs.

Diana dropped the book on her desk and waited until Jane had closed the door behind them before blurting out, "You're good at reading people. What do you think he's hiding?"

"Who knows? At least he shared more information than he's done in the past. Did ye notice how little he said about what happened after he went overboard? It's like someone magically transported him 1000 miles, even though I know that's not what happened. But if he did make landfall early on, why did he leave the first island? The odds of living would have been much better if he'd stayed on land. And how could he have survived being adrift on the ocean for so long?" Jane paused for a moment, a faraway look on her face, then snapped her fingers. "Remember that rogue wave that hit our ship a few days after the storm?"

"Yeah, so?"

"Where's yer computer? I've got to check something."

Diana handed her laptop to Jane, who eagerly took it and sat on Diana's bed. She remained silent for several minutes until she jumped up and shouted, "That's it!" Jane ran to where Diana was sitting and plopped the computer on her desk. "That's got to be him."

Diana read the article, then looked up. "I don't get it. So what?"

"Ye read where they detected an earthquake near Bimini and discovered that one of the smaller islands had sunk into the sea. Well, the Caribbean Tectonic Plate meets the North American Plate far south of Bimini, so that quake shouldn't have happened. I can't help but wonder if Alex somehow found the Fountain of Youth and destroyed one of the Maqlû objects."

Diana looked skeptically at Jane. "That's a huge reach. How could he cause an earthquake?"

"I don't know, but we know the Maqlû are incredibly powerful. And ye saw what happened in Lamanai. I bet he destroyed whatever was there, just like he did the Palantir. Besides, didn't ye hear the bitterness in his voice when he was talking about the objects? Something must have happened there that shook him so badly that he's decided he won't keep searching for the Maqlû to help his sister."

The two sat in silence until Diana motioned for Jane to pull up a chair. "Speculating on what he did or didn't do is fruitless. The only way we'll ever know what really happened is if he opens up and tells us. So, while we're waiting for that miracle to occur, let's look at the book he brought back. Maybe that will give us some clues. Plus, I'm dying to know what's in it because he valued it more than half a million dollars."

"I wouldn't be so sure of that comparison," Jane said. "It sounded like he didn't know what was in it either and was jest bringing it back because someone asked him to."

"Good point," Diana said. She turned to the book and opened it, but after flipping through a few pages, she flung her hands in the air and groaned. "Of all the books he could have brought back, I can't believe he found one written in multiple languages. This is going to be much harder than I thought. We're both fluent in Spanish, and I know French, Italian, and a little Arabic, but I don't know any of the Slavic languages. Do you?"

"No, but we have several linguistic experts in our order that could translate this," Jane said.

"I can't believe I'm saying this, but it has to be someone we can trust. Do you know anyone like that?" Diana asked. "They'd have to be supportive of Alex, or at least open-minded, because you know whoever helps us will want to know where we got it, and we won't be able to hide Alex's involvement forever."

"No offense, but that would rule out yer mom."

"None taken. She's had it in for him since day one. What about his grandmother? She's the head of the Salem Grove and would have contacts throughout the order."

Jane shook her head. "Even though she's given mixed signals about Alex, she's still pretty traditional. The only person I know who might help is Nadia."

"I know she can speak Arabic, Russian, Turkish, and a half dozen other languages fluently, but I've never gotten a good read on her," Diana said. "At times, I think she's a rebel, but at other times, she seems as traditional as I used to be. I'm just not sure whether she'd go along with us on this or spill the beans to the High Council."

"I guess I could ask Lady Yvaine for help," Jane said. "She'd know who could translate it and keep it a secret. Of course, I'd have to figure out what to tell her because she's still unsure how to deal with Alex."

Diana looked up from the book. "I know this is way off subject, but how old do you think Lady Yvaine is? She never seems to age, and she's been around forever."

"I don't know. What's your point?"

"Think about it. How often have you seen Lady Yvaine stand up to the other High Priestesses and challenge their way of thinking? Whatever the issue, she's always proven right in the long run. And right now, even though she's unsure about Alex, she's his only defender on the High Council. Why? What does she know that nobody else does?"

"Maybe it's simply that she's smarter than the rest of us," Jane said. "I still don't understand what ye're driving at, though?"

"Every adult in the order I've talked to has berated us for going off with Alex – except for Lady Yvaine. I know she wants you to stick to him like glue, but what about me? Does she want me to go with you guys on his escapades, too? If so, why? Is she secretly hoping we help him? If so, does she want us to study the book or give it to someone like Elizabeth? Does she want us to jump into action and follow him blindly into the unknown?"

"We shouldn't go into anything blind," Jane replied.

"But we have – both in Lamanai and in the Caribbean. And this book is already starting to feel like more of the same."

"Good point. Well, then, let's not be blind about it. Let's get cracking. Even though we might not know all the languages in it, I'm sure we can figure out the gist of it."

They spent the rest of the day and night poring over the old book, stopping only to check on Alex and get snacks to stay awake. The sun was just starting to rise when the door banged open, and Elizabeth Adler, Alex's grandmother and high priestess of the Salem Grove, came barging in.

Diana was still rubbing her sleep-encrusted eyes when Elizabeth asked, "What's going on? I haven't seen nor heard from either of you in a day. Are you plotting some new shenanigans with my grandson?"

Jane, who'd taken a nap on Diana's bed, got up and walked over to where Elizabeth stood. Towering over the older woman, she ignored the icy-grey eyes boring into her. "We're doing research, per Lady Yvaine's request," she said.

"She never mentioned anything of the sort to me," Elizabeth replied.

"That's because I haven't updated her on the most recent developments. But, as ye well know, she asked me to investigate yer grandson. And that's what I'm doing. Diana is assisting me."

Elizabeth glanced down at the book. "What are you two studying so intently?"

"We're trying to figure out what this is about," Diana said, tapping the opened book. "Your grandson found it but wasn't interested in it, so he gave it to us. Since he has a knack for finding interesting things, we decided to study it to see if there's something we should delve into."

Elizabeth winced. "And?"

"We're not sure because we can't read all the languages in it. But from what we can tell, this book is about a religious relic, probably the Sangreal," Diana said.

"Don't you mean the Holy Grail? That's just a fairy tale in the King Arthur legends."

"And most people look at magic the same way," Diana argued. "Yet we know differently."

Elizabeth rolled her eyes. "Okay. So, what have you learned?"

"Not much, as we can only read part of this. One of the things we've learned is the term Sangreal came first, eventually evolving into the Holy Grail over time. The rest is either boring journal-like entries or a riddle. But I think there's something to it."

"Well, it doesn't matter. I've talked with Lady Yvaine. She told me that you two have been gone long enough, and I'm to send you both to Stormhold immediately."

"What about Alex?" Jane asked.

"Since he can hobble around the house, I'm sending him back to his grandfather. He's been a distraction long enough." Elizabeth slammed the book closed, scooped it up, and swept out of the room.

# CHAPTER 10
# THE BEAR DANCE

By the end of the school year, everything that had happened the previous summer had faded into a dim, unpleasant memory for Alex. His life seemed perfectly normal. Even the ankh hanging around his neck had been inactive since he'd returned to his grandfather's house. The only proof of what he'd been through were the physical scars all over his body.

After getting off the bus on the last day of school, his cousin Chipeta said, "You know, the Bear Dance is this weekend. And just because I haven't mentioned it for a while doesn't mean I've forgotten."

Alex looked sheepish as he replied, "You're good. I was hoping you'd forgotten, and that's why you'd stopped pestering me about it."

"Are you kidding? There's no way I'm letting you get out of it. It's one of the biggest events of the year. People come from all over to see it. Besides, it's fun, and I think you'll like it."

"I don't understand why it's such a big deal," Alex grumped.

"It's a shame your dad didn't tell you anything about our tribal history," Chipeta said. "In the old days, they held the Bear Dance at the sound of the first thunder of the year, which was usually in March. It signaled it was time for the different bands of our tribe to come together after the long winter – just like the bear emerges from his hibernation. It was a chance for our people to sing new songs they'd dreamed of around the winter campfires, show off their new clothes, swap tales, and, importantly, a chance for the young men and women to meet."

"What am I supposed to wear?" Alex asked.

"You've got it easy. You can't wear your baggy camo pants or shorts, but you can wear the shirt and jeans you've got on. But I won't let you wear that dorky Tilley hat you're always wearing. It might have been handy on your trips, but it'd look stupid in the corral. Instead, I've got a bowler hat and a nice beaded vest for you."

Alex grimaced, trying to imagine what Chipeta had gotten him. "What about you?"

"All women have to wear shawls and dresses that go below the knees. But we need to eat and clean up before we leave, so don't dilly-dally."

Two hours later, they pulled into the parking lot outside the dance corral. Their grandfather, Ignacio, switched off the engine and said, "The dancing's already started, so you two go on in. I'll be in later."

Alex saw a large sign at the entrance and stopped to read it, but he was so nervous about the dance that the only thing he took away from it was no cameras. In an attempt to delay the inevitable, he swerved towards the food truck, but Chipeta caught his arm and pulled him away. As they wound their way through the picnic area outside the entrance to the corral, Alex stopped when he saw the brush blocking his view of the dancing inside. "I thought I'd be able to see what's going on before I had to dance. What am I supposed to do?"

"You've got the easy part, as the girls do all the work, like usual. When we go in, I'll sit with the other women and girls on the left side of the enclosure while you sit with the men and boys on the right side."

"Why can't we sit together?"

"Because it's not allowed." Seeing he was about to protest, Chipeta cut him short, saying, "That's just the way it is. You should also know that this is a woman's choice dance, so someone will signal the women to line up before each dance. Then, when the announcer tells them to, the women walk over to the men's side. We pick out our dance partners by flicking our shawls at them. If someone picks you, you're expected to join the dance to show respect towards women. And don't think you can avoid it because the Cat Man will be there."

"Who's that?" Alex asked.

"The Cat Man enforces the rules. He usually wears a black shirt, carries a stick with a red flag, and stands near the center of the corral."

"Will you dance with me first?"

Chipeta shook her head. "Relatives can't dance with each other."

"So, what do I do if I get selected?"

"That's the easy part. For tonight, and most of the next two days, it's line dancing. The Cat Man will draw lines in the dirt where the women and men are supposed to stand. You take your position across from the woman or girl who selected you, then grab the hand of the person on either side of you. It's a pretty simple dance. All you have to remember is to step back and forth with your left foot while your right foot steps in place. Just mirror the women's movement. We step with our right feet and keep our left feet in place. Just feel the music and try to keep in step with the rest of your line. C'mon now. No more stalling."

Chipeta pulled him through the entrance, then pushed him to the men's side. He sidestepped one of the two small cedar trees inside the corral, found a chair, and sat down without acknowledging the man and boy on either side of him. Alex watched intently at what was happening in the current dance, hoping it would last long enough that he could figure out what to do, but it ended almost immediately.

He'd felt self-conscious when Chipeta had given him the hat and vest, but he sighed in relief when he saw several other boys and men wearing similar clothes. A couple of minutes later, one of the men at the back of the dance corral, where all the musicians were sitting, called for the women dancers. Over a dozen women, ranging from young girls to grandmothers, stood up and began collecting at the center of the corral. One of the musicians started singing, signaling the women to choose. Alex's heart raced, torn between the fear of no one selecting him and the hope of sitting out the dance so he could see what went on.

A woman, who looked about the same age as his grandmother, approached and flicked her shawl at Alex. Half-panicked, he followed her to the middle of the corral and stood across from his dance partner on a line the Cat Man had drawn. There was a pause in the singing as all the dancers settled in. But instead of calming his nerves, the quiet caused Alex to forget his cousin's instructions. In a half daze, he felt the men on either side of him grasp his hands.

The Cat Man walked up and down the line, making a few adjustments to the dancers, then stepped to the end of the lines. A few seconds later, the chanting and raspy music started, and the lines began to move. As he feared, Alex was woefully out of step.

The women's line was in much better unison as all the female dancers seemed to move as one while the men swayed back and forth in an undulating line. Alex tried watching everyone's feet, but it didn't help him. He was so focused on getting in step that he lost track of time and was surprised when the song ended.

Thankful he'd survived the first dance, he thanked the woman and returned to his seat. But all too soon, there was another dance call. This time, a younger girl selected him.

The second dance went a lot smoother, and he returned to his chair, thinking the whole event wouldn't be as bad as he'd feared. No one selected him for the third dance, but a fringed blue shawl snaked out on the call for the fourth dance and snapped a few inches in front of his face. He looked up and saw Jane standing in front of him.

# CHAPTER 11
# CHIMNEY ROCK

Alex spent the next three days of the Bear Dance festival and the nearby Pow Wow, trying to figure out why Jane had shown up out of the blue. He sensed it had something to do with the journal he'd found and knew that whatever she wanted meant trouble lay ahead. But as the weekend went along, he was surprised she never mentioned it.

On the last night of the festival, Chipeta drew him aside and said, "Grandpa had a long talk with Jane last night and suggested I take you up to Chimney Rock to talk things out tomorrow."

"What did they talk about?" Alex asked warily. "And why you? If Jane has something to say, shouldn't she be talking to me about it?"

"It was actually Jane who suggested we talk. Grandpa just recommended the location."

"I still don't understand," Alex said.

"Jane didn't give me any details, but she said you'd gone through hell and back last summer and that you probably had some fears that are holding you back from, what she thinks is, your destiny. She thought you'd be more comfortable sharing your worries with me. If we're going to do this, I think we should get it over with, so we'll head out early tomorrow."

"Don't I get a say in this?"

"No, so get some rest. Oh, and dress warmly tomorrow. It'll be cold up top."

It seemed like he'd barely fallen asleep when Alex heard someone knocking on his door. Having forgotten his cousin's plan, he snuggled up to the warm spot on his bed where Sadie had taken to curling up with him every night and pulled the blankets closer. A renewed pounding followed by, "C'mon, sleepy head, wake up. We need to get going," finally got him to open his eyes and grumble a reply.

It wasn't until he stumbled into the kitchen a short time later that he realized it was pitch black outside. "What time is it?"

"Four thirty," Chipeta responded. "Now let's get going. Grandpa is waiting outside in the truck with our food and drinks."

With one eye shut against the lights in the room, Alex put a finger to his lips. "Can you be a little quieter? I'm still waking up."

Chipeta pushed him out the door, and half an hour later, they pulled into a small gravel parking lot. She hopped out and thanked their grandpa for the ride.

Alex climbed out, shouldered his dad's old army backpack, and followed Chipeta under the gate. A quarter mile further, they ducked under a chain stretched across the road next to the park's visitor center.

They climbed in silence up the three-mile-long gravel road, with the moon and stars lighting their way. The higher they climbed, the more Alex fell into a reverie as he listened to the soft breeze whispering through the piñon pines.

When they finally reached a paved parking lot marking the end of the road, Alex said, "Remind me what they used this place for. Grandpa brought me up here last year, right before he suggested I go off on that blasted vision quest, but I forgot what he told me."

"The Chaco Canyon people had a religious and astronomical observation area up on top of Chimney Rock," Chipeta replied.

"But I thought Chaco Canyon was all the way down in New Mexico."

"It is, but a few decades ago, a teenage girl proved they could communicate with people in Chaco Canyon eighty miles away, although she used mirrors instead of massive bonfires. We can talk more when we reach the top, but we should get going because I don't want to miss the sunrise."

Chipeta led him to a rocky trail at the end of the pavement that was much steeper, narrower, and rougher than the road they'd come up on, so both lapsed into silence to focus on climbing until they paused at some rock walls on their left.

"These are some of the ruins of the Pueblo Indians that lived here over a thousand years ago," Chipeta said. "We'll get a better look at them on the way back when there's some light. But right now, you need to pay close attention to where you're walking. There are a few places where this trail comes close to the edge, where it's almost 1,000 feet to the bottom. So, don't be ashamed to bend over and use your hands on the climb."

A little while later, they passed another, much higher wall, but Chipeta kept on going, leading Alex to the same rock he'd sat on a year earlier.

"This is as far as we're going," she said. "It's dangerous enough to climb down and get over to

Chimney and Companion Rock in full daylight, but there's no way I'd try it in the dark."

The eastern sky was turning a light blue when Alex sat down on the rock table and let his legs dangle over the side. A light breeze from the east caused him to bundle back up before finally settling down to watch the sunrise.

There was enough light to see the two rock formations Chipeta had mentioned, so he asked, "Which one is which?"

"The far one is Chimney Rock because, well, it looks like a chimney. Both sets of rocks are over three hundred feet high from their base. I've hiked to them several times, but I usually stop here because it's a tough and scary climb. On clear days, you get great panoramic views. I like sitting up here and staring into the distance."

Alex sighed when a thin yellowish-white strip of light appeared on the horizon, highlighting the shades of blue above it. "This reminds me of sailing around the Caribbean last summer. The captain and I would watch the sunrise and listen to the wind slapping at the sails while the waves lapped against the sides. Thanks for bringing me up here."

"I'd like to see the ocean sometime," Chipeta said. "But we're not here to talk about me. You've been so quiet about what happened last summer that both Grandpa and I are worried about you. Who is this captain you mentioned?"

Hoping Chipeta wouldn't delve too deeply, Alex replied, "Oh, someone I knew. But he's gone now."

"Why won't you talk about what happened? Jane told me that you opened up a little after Lamanai, but then clammed up again when you returned to Salem. She and Grandpa hoped you'd talk to me."

There was a long silence before Chipeta said, "Does whatever going on with you have to do with the ankh?"

Alex's eyebrows shot up. "He told you about it?"

"Grandpa said that if I were to help you, I'd need to understand some of what you're going through. He told me his grandmother and mother wore it, as did he and your dad. Grandpa feels guilty about what's happening to you because seeing the spirit world freaked him out so badly that he gave the ankh to your dad when he was a teenager and thinks it screwed with his mind."

"I didn't know all that history, but at least now I understand why my dad acted the way he did."

"Doesn't the spirit world bother you?" Chipeta asked.

Alex shook his head. "Not all the time. I've met some really cool ghosts, including the captain, a spy, a Viking, and my sister."

"You've talked to your sister?" Chipeta asked in a stunned voice. "What about your parents?"

"Nope. That's part of the problem," Alex replied. "You see, Deb's upset because our parents moved on immediately after their death, as most spirits do. But my sister is stuck in the afterlife. At first, she thought she'd move on if I helped her find some magical objects her order had been searching for, but it hasn't worked out."

Another silence descended until Chipeta touched Alex on the shoulder and pointed to the east. "Look, the sun's about to rise."

Alex looked past Chimney Rock to the snow-capped San Juan Mountains, where the horizon had changed to orange, driving the yellows, whites, and blues higher into the sky. The continuing transformation of the sky temporarily pushed his worries out of his mind, allowing him to enjoy the sunrise.

He didn't move again until the sun lost its orange tint. With the sunrise having finally released him from its spell, Alex sighed, reached into his pack, and grabbed one of the breakfast sandwiches Chipeta had made. He'd only taken a couple of bites when he pointed to the base of Companion Rock and asked, "Did you see that?"

"What?"

Alex didn't respond as he stared intently at the steep rocky slope below him. A puff of smoke rose above a large boulder and drifted towards them.

"Damn! I know we've had another dry year, but I can't believe a wildfire is springing up here now," Chipeta said. "I'll call this in, but pack up. We've got to get going. The breeze is blowing straight towards us, and who knows how long we have before it's a raging inferno."

Alex didn't move as he scanned the mountainside below him. "It's not a wildfire," he said. "There's at least one guy down there, and I'd bet there are more."

"What is he doing. Why would someone want to start a fire up here, especially at this time of day?"

"You wanted to know what's bothering me?" Alex asked. He pointed at the smoke and said, "It's this type of stuff. I'd bet almost anything that those men are after me."

"Why would anybody be after you?" Chipeta asked.

Alex didn't answer as he kept watching the smoke. Seeing two men jump out of their hiding spot and run across the mountain face below them, he shouted, "Run!"

"Slow down," Chipeta called out as Alex ran back towards the Great Kiva. "If you hurry down that slope, you could fall and die."

"I'm not worried about the fire," Alex replied. "I bet those guys are trying to drive us into a trap. We've got to find a way out of here before it's too late."

A blast of cold air washed over Alex, causing him to look around for ghosts. He spotted a dozen Indian spirit warriors flying towards him and pushed his cousin back against the Kiva wall just before they flew past. Then he watched in fascinated horror as the ghosts swooped down on the two unsuspecting men, unleashing a dozen arrows. He heard howls of pain, then silence. It wasn't until both men fell to the ground, arrows poking out of their torsos, that Alex realized the ghosts hadn't been carrying weapons from the spirit world.

Two spirits broke off from the pack to put out the smoldering fire while the rest flew into the forest below, searching for the remaining assailants. Alex cringed several minutes later when he heard more cries of pain in the distance.

An old Indian with a careworn leathery face came up the path, passed through Chipeta, then hovered a few feet in front of Alex. He wore a buckskin shirt, vest, and pants, had twin braids draped over his shoulders, oversized hoop earrings, and a leather pouch hanging on his chest. "Those men will no longer bother you while you're on our lands," the spirit said. "We will continue to ensure your safety, but please finish whatever business you have here and leave. We find it unpleasant to continue resorting to violence to protect you."

"Wait, are you saying there've been others?" Alex asked, afraid of the answer.

The old spirit warrior nodded. "Both the living and the dead."

Alex was so ashamed of the carnage that surrounded him that he couldn't look the ghost in the face when he said, "I'm sorry for all the trouble I've caused you, but I want to thank you for your protection."

Chipeta gasped, causing Alex to break off the conversation and turn to see what his cousin was upset about. He was just in time to see the two men's bodies fly past her. "Are they dead?" she asked, a horrified look on her face.

Alex grimaced. "Probably. Let's go home; I don't want to stay here anymore."

"Wait. Two men, maybe more, just died, and you're just going to walk away as if nothing happened," Chipeta said.

"This is the type of stuff I ran away from, and why I don't want to talk about last year." Alex turned back to look for the warrior he'd been talking to, but the ghost had disappeared.

Chipeta spun him around, grabbed his arms, and shook him. "I won't pretend to understand what you've been through, but not talking about it is the worst thing you could do. You need to meet your problems head-on. If you don't, they'll fester. So, tell me, what's going on?"

Alex sat down, leaned against the kiva's wall, and stared out, unseeing, over the valley. It was a long time before he said, "I don't understand what's happening, but I thought this stuff would end when I stopped searching for the Maqlû."

"Are those the magical objects you said you were trying to find to help your sister?"

"Yep."

"Is that all you're going to say? At least two men just died, and all you say is, yep."

"What do you want me to say?" Alex retorted. "Ever since I took my dad's ankh, strange things have been happening, including a lot of deaths. Although, up to today, at least as far as I knew, it was only spirits dying in the afterworld."

There was another long silence until Chipeta said, "I'm sorry. I'm freaked out by what just happened. If I hadn't seen it for myself, I could never have imagined what Jane was talking about. And by the way, when did you learn to speak something that sounded like Shoshonean?"

"I didn't," Alex said. "The ankh acts like a universal translator with ghosts, so I can communicate with spirits in their native language, even though it sounds like English to me. I don't know how it works, but it does."

"So, what were you talking about with thin air?"

Alex shifted uneasily from foot to foot and said, "One of the warriors was politely asking me to leave because he's tired of killing people, both the living and the dead, to protect me."

Chipeta gasped.

"I didn't know that type of stuff was happening around here," Alex said. "I was hoping I'd put it all behind me when I stopped searching for the Maqlû. But I'm kicking myself because it shouldn't have surprised me."

"How can you say that? You couldn't have expected what just happened," Chipeta said.

"See, that's where you're wrong. For instance, when I was in the Caribbean, dozens of ghost pirate ships, with hundreds of men, were chasing after me. It was only slightly better in Lamanai."

"Who could you have ticked off so badly that they'd send so many men and ghosts to kill you?"

"A couple of ghosts mentioned some woman named Pythia, but the only person I know by that name died a couple of thousand years ago. They've also mentioned some guy named Gilgamesh, but he died almost five thousand years ago. And you know where I used to live. There's nobody around even to tick off. So, I can only conclude that it's the ankh causing my problems."

"Then why don't you get rid of it?" Chipeta asked.

"Because I can't. I tried throwing it away once, but my resolve lasted only a couple of seconds," Alex replied. "It's like I'm addicted to it.

"You know what? Ignore what I just said, because I'm not being honest with myself. The reality is that I'm unwittingly creating my enemies. People are greedy, and by going after those magical objects, no matter how good my intentions, I'm threatening them."

"So, do something about it. Don't sit here and let them take the initiative. Besides, you should know you're not alone." Chipeta paused, then said, "I have to tell you that I haven't been totally honest either. I suggested we take this trip today, because Jane told me she's worried about you and thinks you'll be safer at Stormhold than here. She asked me to try talking you into going back with her, because she assumed you'd turn her down if she asked."

When Alex didn't say anything, Chipeta grabbed his hands. "Can I say something?" Without waiting for him to answer, she said, "I don't know what others might advise you, but here's what I think. You might be a little safer if you stay here or go hide in that Stormhold place Jane wants you to go to, but not much. I can see that trouble seeks you out, cousin. But don't run from it. Run towards it. Go find your destiny. The Great Spirit challenged you when he had you take the ankh. So, embrace it."

"But the ankh was meant for my sister. And now she's dead, and I'm alive and stuck in this never-ending nightmare. The only reason I left here last year was to understand why my mom and sister lived apart from us. I stayed away because I thought I could help my sister. But now, I don't believe finding any magical object will help her move on. And besides, I don't fancy joining her in the afterlife anytime soon."

Chipeta glared at Alex. "You sound like your father – running away from your problems."

Stung by Chipeta's words, Alex stood up and hiked down in silence. But by the time they got back into their grandpa's truck, Alex had changed his mind. They had barely pulled out of the gravel parking lot at the entrance when Alex said, "Grandpa, I appreciate everything you've done for me this past year, but today reminded me that no matter how far I run, I can't escape my fate. So, I've decided to embrace it and go with Jane to Scotland."

"I understand," Ignacio said. "Your father and I made a different decision – one where we tried to hide from our fate. Go and know you're always welcome here, son of my son."

Chipeta turned around and smiled. "I'm proud of you. I also think you're doing the right thing."

Early the next morning, Alex hopped out of his grandpa's truck and placed his bag beside Jane's at the bus stop.

# CHAPTER 12
# IF YOU KNOW THE ENEMY

The nighttime breeze was a pleasant contrast to the hot, sunny day, causing Pythia to linger as she stared at the stars. Knowing she couldn't keep postponing the inevitable, she sighed, then took the steps to her home's hidden opening above Delphi on Mount Parnassus. She silently chanted the opening spell and slipped in as soon as the rock door slid open. A few scattered candles came to light, illuminating the narrow stone hallway while casting eerie shadows against the walls. She headed down the short corridor and passed between the two limestone columns that framed the opening into a small grotto where a tall tri-legged stool and table stood in the center.

Pythia climbed onto the stool, pulled back the purple veil covering her jet-black hair and emerald green eyes, and gazed into the octagonal-shaped bronze cup with the elaborate script on its sides sitting in front of her. She was about to stick one of her fingers into the silvery liquid and chant the spell that she hoped would bring it to life when she abruptly changed her mind and headed to her study, where she turned on her computer and called her former associate.

***

Eight hundred miles away, Brother Robert Stafford flung open the doors to his study and stormed in. "What's so important that you wake me up at this hour? I haven't been sleeping well because of that blasted boy and now this."

His older brother, Sydney Carton, got up from his chair and pointed at the large monitor at the end of the room, where Pythia's face appeared. "I'm sorry, but this call won't help with your insomnia."

Stafford sat down and slammed his fist onto the table beside him. "Damn him. What's he done this time?" He looked up at his brother, who was over half a foot taller, slimmer, with short-cropped grey hair and glasses.

"That's what we'll find out if you calm down and listen to what Pythia has to say," Carton replied.

Stafford rubbed one hand over the shaved area on his head and took a deep breath. "I thought we'd agreed to talk tomorrow. Why the urgency to talk tonight? Were your attacks successful?"

"What do you think?" Pythia paused, letting her rhetorical question sink in. "Of course not. I've dispatched dozens of spirits to go after him, promising them just about anything their greedy little hearts desired. And I have nothing to show for it. I don't understand how he's survived so far. At least I knew he had Captain Every as his protector in the Caribbean. But I know of no one guarding him now that he's at home. Even the witches have deserted him."

A buzzing sound drove Stafford to pull out his cell phone and check a text message. After reading it, he threw his phone on the table and shouted, "Damn!"

"What's wrong?" Pythia asked.

Stafford twisted a large signet ring around on his finger, then reached over, picked a cigar from the box on the table, and lit it. He pushed the lighter and box towards his brother, who shook his head. Stafford lit it, then puffed on it for a minute before saying, "I apologize for my outburst, but I'm unsettled by that boy. Not only have all my attempts to eliminate him failed, but I just learned that he left home with one of the witches. I've already alerted all our agents to be on the watch for him, but based on his history, I don't put much stock on them sticking with him."

"You're not telling me something. What's really bothering you?" Pythia asked.

"Well, last fall, I learned the Salem grove was all in a twitter about something the boy had found. Then, they went silent. I didn't think anything of it at first because the boy headed home at about the same time. But that text I just got alerted me to the fact that several witches just flew to Europe to consult with their Spanish counterparts."

"So?" Pythia asked.

"The witches tend to meet in groups only at their headquarters in Scotland. So, to meet now means something's afoot. And we need to find out what."

"I've told you many times that I disagree with your goals," Carton said. "But, as an outsider, let me suggest that for you to succeed, you first need to figure out why your efforts to get rid of him keep failing. For instance, if Utnapishtim and Urshanabi have intervened, you have a totally different problem than if the boy has hooked up with some warlock."

"Why would you mention The Guardians?" Pythia asked. "How are they involved?"

"My brother asked our old friends, who now go by the names Jean Paul and Francis, to track the boy down last summer," Carton replied. "And despite having Sharur, they had an extremely difficult job trying to track him. They eventually found him on an uninhabited island off the coast of Georgia, brought him back to the witches and, in no uncertain terms, told us the boy was under their protection. And you know them. They don't tend to meddle in human affairs, unless they think it's for the greater good.

"All of which leads me to believe it's unwise for you to pursue the boy," Carton said. "I mean, just look at what your efforts have achieved so far. They've been nothing short of disastrous. Not only have you lost a lot of good agents, brother, including several members of our order, but you've also caused the Guardians to get involved in this mess. And you, Pythia, you said you've lost countless agents and at least one of your magical objects. Clearly, your approaches aren't working. Which is why I think you should look at the situation more broadly."

Stafford glared at his brother and raised one eyebrow. "You've chosen not to get involved in this until now. Why the sudden interest?"

"I'm not interested in helping you get rid of the boy, but I'm struck by all the unusual events that have happened in the last year. I haven't identified any pattern yet, but it feels like there's some sort of great unraveling of our past going on. And I want to understand that."

"You're not making any sense," Pythia said. "What's your point?"

"That's just it. I don't know what the point is. But, for instance, did you read about the earthquake where half of a small deserted island in the Caribbean sank into the ocean last summer?" He paused. When Pythia and Stafford shook their heads, Carton said, "If you draw a line from where the two witch girls suddenly reappeared near Tortuga, to where the Guardians found the boy, guess where the island was located?" Without waiting for a response, he said, "Smack dab in the middle. I also studied the geology of the area. There's no way it was a natural phenomenon. Someone, or something, caused it, but I don't think the boy is powerful enough to do it alone. Which probably means he's in league with some powerful warlock or witch we're unaware of. The boy has made no aggressive move towards us, which tells me we should leave him alone for now and learn more about him. Otherwise, I fear it won't end well for us if we keep intervening."

"Let's say you're right. Who could he be working with? It can't be the Bandruí," Pythia said. "And if it's not The Guardians, then who? And why?"

"Exactly," Carton said. "Those are the questions we must answer before trying to stop the boy."

Pythia shook her head. "I disagree with your conclusion because I believe what Sun Tzu said, that in the midst of chaos, there is also opportunity. We must strike before he realizes we're after him."

"How can you be so casual about another person's life?" Carton yelled. "We should not be the judge and jury. Leave him be. I beg of you. Let us study him and figure out what's going on."

Stafford slammed his fist on the table again. "You don't understand, brother. I haven't had a good night's sleep since he tricked me into giving him *The Sibylline Book*. I fear he's after the Maqlû, and I worry that he'll find one of them and be able to master whatever he finds. If he does that, he could defeat all of us. The stakes are too high, which is why I believe we need to ensure he doesn't interfere anymore."

Carton threw his hands up in the air. "I give up. There's no talking sense to either of you. You're on your own." With that, he left the room.

"I know your brother has always been cautious, but when did he become like this?" Pythia asked.

"It's been happening gradually over the last century," Stafford replied. "He's grown weary and has no fight left in him anymore. Ignore him. We need to proceed as we've discussed and stop the boy before he can do any more harm." He drummed his fingers on the table for some time before saying, "I have to say something that I'm reluctant to mention. My greatest fear is not that he finds the Maqlû – it's that he'd destroy them. And you know what that could mean for us."

"Who would want to destroy them?" Pythia asked. "Anyone who masters them would be like gods."

Stafford sighed. "I hope I'm wrong. Enough of that pessimism, though. Let's get down to business and figure out how to stop the boy once and for all."

## CHAPTER 13
# NOTHING IS PREDESTINED

Ignacio wrapped an arm around Alex's shoulders and said, "I know you must go on this quest, but be careful, as there is much danger ahead of you."

"There's danger everywhere I go," Alex replied. "Besides, didn't you tell me to embrace my destiny?"

"Yes, but I never imagined you'd undergo all these trials," Ignacio replied.

"Me neither, Grandpa, but I've realized I only have two choices. Do nothing, and let danger come to me. Or attack it head-on and figure out what's happening. Jane said that the head of her order, Lady Yvaine, will help me figure out what's going on, and I've got to take advantage of her offer." He hugged his grandfather and said, "And don't worry; Jane's already promised to remind me to call you often." Then he hugged Chipeta and ran after Jane onto the bus.

He'd barely settled down when Jane asked, "All right, what's going on? I'm not complaining, but what made ye change yer mind and decide to come with me to Stormhold? I asked yer cousin, but she got a haunted look on her face and clammed up."

"Let's just say I realized I can run, but I can't hide."

Jane sighed. "Fine. I know ye well enough that ye won't tell me what happened yesterday. I jest wish I knew what goes on in that head of yers."

"I'm afraid ye'd be disappointed," Alex replied. "What's Lady Yvaine like?"

"She's nae like the other women in the order. She's an independent thinker who wants ye to come to Stormhold so she can get to know ye better."

"If she wanted to get to know me better, she could've used the phone, come here, or invited me to Stormhold during Christmas vacation. My guess is there's something else going on, and you either need my help or want to make sure I stay out of the way."

"Wow, that's a pretty cynical attitude," Jane said.

"But am I right?"

Jane dropped her head and mumbled, "Yes."

"Does this have something to do with that book I gave you last summer?" Alex asked.

Jane nodded. "Yer grandmother took the book from Diana and me and has spent almost all her time since then studying it. Translating it was straightforward. The hard part has been making sense of it, as most entries are either speculation or boring diary-type information."

"That doesn't explain why you've traveled halfway around the world to come get me," Alex said. "What's happened for you to come now?"

"Well, part of that is simple – ye're on vacation for the next couple of months." Jane yawned and said, "Now, if you don't mind, I'm going to get some sleep. We got up way too early."

Alex stared out the window for the next few hours until they'd put Pueblo behind. He felt movement beside him, turned, and saw Jane brushing her long ginger-colored hair.

Seeing Alex staring at her, Jane blushed and said, "I'm sorry. I didn't have time to brush my hair this morning, and I've got so many tangles that I couldn't take it any longer. Is this bothering you?"

All he could do was shake his head as he was too entranced to say anything. After she'd finished brushing and tying her hair into a braid, he turned back to look out the window at the prairie rolling by. It wasn't until after they'd passed Colorado Springs that he finally worked up the courage to get the whole story out of Jane. He turned towards her and said, "I've been thinking and believe you know more than you're saying. So, why don't you tell me what this is really about?"

"I can see ye won't stop pestering me until I tell ye," Jane said. "Ye're right. Lady Yvaine wants you in Stormhold because of what's in that book ye found last summer. What I'm about to tell ye is based on the brief time Diana and I spent with that book of yours, information I've pieced together, and rumors."

"What about it? Is it valuable?"

"Ye could say that. If it's what it seems, ye could say it's priceless."

"Are you ever going to tell me what you're talking about?" Alex asked.

"It's about the Sangreal."

"What's that?"

Jane rolled her eyes. "This is when I wish Diana were here. She'd get all excited and give ye a detailed history about it. The short version is that the Sangreal, or Sangrail, or San Graal, are the early names for an object that people eventually called the Holy Grail."

"No way. So, it really exists, and that journal the ghost gave me is its history?"

"It's not that simple," Jane said. "Most people would assume it was a hoax or myth, but yer grandmother has concluded that it exists. And even though it's not one of the objects our order has ever sought, yer grandmother wants to search for it. She doesn't want yer help, but Lady Yvaine asked me to convince ye to come to our headquarters outside of Stirling, Scotland, and advise us as yer grandmother searches for the Grail. I've been reluctant to talk to ye because I don't think we should involve ye."

"So, you're saying that the situation is exactly what I thought. Your boss wants to keep me under wraps in Stormhold while my grandmother searches for the Sangreal. That way, I can't interfere and cause something to go wrong. I know I swore off searching for magical objects, but I'm hurt that no one thinks I can help."

Jane flushed a beet red and looked away.

"You look like you're guilty of something," Alex said. "What else aren't you telling me?"

Jane took a deep breath and said, "They never considered asking for yer help, as they believe yer a warlock, which is why I was the one who talked Lady Yvaine into inviting ye to Stormhold. Because, if the Sangreal is real, I'm pretty confident ye can help. And I don't want ye to go with yer grandmother because I'm worried about what might happen if ye search for it. I don't want ye to go through what ye did with the Palantir and the Fountain of Youth."

"So, even if I could find it, my grandmother wouldn't accept my help if I offered it."

Jane shook her head. "She's still pretty upset with ye. Diana told her that ye found and accidentally destroyed the Palantir, and, surprisingly, she believed ye'd done that and pulled everyone out of Lamanai. It just added to our order's concerns about ye. Our members have never been nice to ye, and nothing has changed for me to believe things will be different now. Just look at Diana. Even though you've saved her life and shown her a world she never dreamed of, she's still as confused as everybody else about what makes you tick. And, if you don't like any of my other reasons for trying to keep ye out of this search, I believe there's a high probability that this is a wild goose chase. People have been looking for the Grail for over two thousand years without any success. I doubt it ever existed."

"I don't see why you're so skeptical. I mean, people thought the Fountain of Youth was only a myth too."

Jane whirled around in her seat and grabbed Alex's shoulders. "Wait. Are ye saying that ye found the Fountain of Youth?"

Alex held a finger to his lip. "Shhh."

"So, what happened?" Jane whispered.

"I still don't want to talk about it."

"I figured whatever happened to ye last summer was a bad experience. So, why would ye want to chase after another one of these myths? All it means is more danger for ye."

Alex turned to stare out the window. "You're right. It makes no sense, but I want to help. No – make that I need to help find it."

"What is so important that ye'd want to risk yer life trying to find it? Do ye have a death wish or something?"

"No. I'd like to believe I'd search for it to help my sister move on in the afterlife. After all, the Grail isn't a magical object – it's a holy relic, so it can't corrupt people. Right? But I fear that since people in the order are talking about this search, outsiders will have heard about it too. And whoever keeps attacking me will think I'm going after it too. So, I'd rather be proactive rather than let trouble come to me." He turned back to Jane. "You said something about my grandma searching for it. Where is she now?"

"Na, na, na. Ye're not going to rope me into one of yer hair-brained adventures that easily," Jane said. "I'm supposed to bring ye back to Lady Yvaine, and that's what I intend on doing."

"Oh, come on. Come with me and help me find it. You're the only one who seems to be okay with me. Besides, since you're sixteen and I'm still fourteen, the airlines and customs won't ask as many questions if I'm traveling with you."

"Are ye daft? I told ye. I'm supposed to bring ye back to Scotland. I can't imagine what Lady Yvaine would say if I went off with ye on another one of your madcap adventures."

When Alex didn't say anything, Jane waved her hand in front of his face. "Hello. Is anyone in there?"

Alex sighed. "I guess you're right. I should consider this a summer vacation in Europe and not risk my life going after some myth."

Jane studied him for some time, trying to get a read on his intentions before she finally sat back in her seat. Two days later, they arrived in Edinburgh.

# CHAPTER 14
# **MISPLACED**

"What!" Lady Yvaine yelled as she slammed her hands down on her desk and jumped up. "How could you lose him? I sent you after him because you have a sixth sense about these things. You always know what's happening with other people – at least you do with the women in the order. You found him in Belize when everyone else thought he was dead. You stuck with him when he disappeared in the Caribbean. You even managed to bring him all the way across the Atlantic. So, how could you lose him at the airport?"

"I'm sorry," Jane said. "Somehow, I lost him at customs. I looked everywhere. I even tried going back in, but they wouldn't let me. I asked airport security to help, but they couldn't find him either. He seems to have jest disappeared."

Her hands trembling, Yvaine plopped down into her chair and shook her head. "Where could he have gone? You said you believe someone's after him. Did someone kidnap him, or did he just get lost?"

"If I had to guess," Jane said, "I'd say he's headed to Spain to help his grandmother find the Sangreal."

"But why? He has to know how the members of our order will treat him."

"I warned him that things might actually be worse now that everyone believes he destroyed the Palantir."

Lady Yvaine stared down at the crystal letter opener in front of her while drumming her long, slender fingers on her desk. She abruptly stopped and looked up. "You don't seem surprised. Why?"

"Don't assume I know what he's doing. I don't. I'm only guessing. He told me there were two reasons he might go after the Sangreal – one personal, the other from a sense of duty."

"I hear a but."

"But I fear it's something else driving him this time." Jane walked to the window and stared at the lake below Stormhold. "Looking back at everything we talked about since I met up with him, I probably should've had him on a leash before we got off the plane because he tried to convince me to go to Spain with him. I thought I'd convinced him otherwise."

Lady Yvaine studied Jane's face, trying to understand what her assistant was thinking. She finally gave up and sighed. "You know, in some ways, you two are a lot alike."

Jane blushed and put a hand to her face. "What! No, that can't be." After a slight hesitation, she asked, "How so?"

"Well, for one thing, you're both inscrutable, which is probably why you two get along so well. But, back to the problem at hand. Do you have any suggestions on what we should do?"

Jane smiled. "Aye."

"You have that smile on your face that I find so disturbing," Lady Yvaine said. "What are you thinking?"

"Well, ye know he's quite resourceful, extremely determined, singularly focused, and a bit odd. So, I'm guessing that he'll be in Seville shortly."

"Did you tell him where they're convening?" Yvaine asked.

"Of course not."

"Then how will he know to go to Seville? Most people in his situation would index to Barcelona or Madrid."

"In some things, Alex is completely clueless. He's a shy, bumbling boy who's eager to please others. But jest like ye think I have a sixth sense about people, well I think he's got a sixth sense for trouble. And if I'm right, we'll find out soon enough where he's gone. If I'm wrong, who knows when or where he'll show up."

Yvaine started drumming her fingers on her desk and staring at the bookshelves across the room. It was some time before she looked up and said, "Well, what are you waiting for?"

Jane shook her head. "I'm sorry. I don't understand what ye're asking."

"If you're going to find him, you better get going. If you hurry, you might beat him there. I'll call ahead and have them ready my jet. And as for earlier, I'm sorry for blowing up at you."

Jane smiled and said, "I understand yer emotions better than ye think."

Yvaine waved her out, saying, "That'll be all for now, but thank you for trying." As she watched Jane run out of the office, she wondered what her assistant wasn't telling her.

## CHAPTER 15
# THE HOPE OF TODAY

Elizabeth greeted Diana and Sophie outside of customs in Seville's airport. After exchanging hugs, she said, "I'm so glad you agreed to help me search for the Sangreal over your summer break."

In her thick accent, Diana replied, "I appreciate the invite, but I don't understand how I can help. My mother is the Grail lore expert, and I know other members of the Bandruí are far more qualified for this than me."

"I did want your mother for her particular knowledge," Elizabeth said. "But I wanted you for your knowledge of my grandson. Since he found the journal, I thought your insight into him might help us occasionally."

A snort of disgust from Sophie caused Elizabeth to cast a quelling glance at her fellow Druid.

"I appreciate your faith in me and hope to live up to your expectations," Diana said, "but why don't you ask Alex for help? He's the one with the super-finder powers. And, although I don't understand him most of the time, he tries to do the right thing."

Elizabeth winced. "Excluding him was one of your mother's requirements to get the two of you for the summer. Besides, my grandson's not reliable. He's a loose cannon."

Hoping not to antagonize either woman so early in the trip, Diana said, "I don't want to disappoint you, but

I still think you'd have a better chance of finding the Grail if you brought him along."

"Well, that's not going to happen," Sophie snapped, driving Diana to drop the subject.

Their conversation drifted to other topics until they arrived at a large two-story building with plastered white walls and a striking golden-colored front entrance surrounding double bronze doors. Once inside the Spanish Grove's villa, a young girl guided them into a paved brick courtyard lined by dozens of arches on two levels of covered porches. Diana was so entranced by the villa's quiet splendor that she wanted to linger, but she fell into step with her mother as they entered a room halfway down the left side of the courtyard.

The rich, burgundy-colored walls, gilded decorations, and classical paintings that graced the parlor made it seem to Diana that she'd stepped into a sultan's palace. It took her a minute before she noticed an elderly lady lying on a divan on the far side of the room. The woman wore a long black formal dress with a red and gold embroidered pattern.

"It's so good to see you again, Lucrecia," Elizabeth said. "Señora de Leon, may I present Sophie and Diana Bennet, the young women I've told you about."

The lady raised a delicate white hand in greeting. Sophie nodded casually at the elderly lady, but Diana, embarrassed by her mother's rudeness, took her hand, and curtsied. "It's so nice to meet you, Señora. Lady Yvaine asked me to send you her regards."

"How kind of her. How is she?"

"Lady Yvaine is fine and wants to thank you in advance for your help with this search," Diana said.

"She is most anxious to learn if the journal will lead us to the Sangreal."

The conversation shifted to small talk while a middle-aged woman set out the contents of the tea tray. As soon as the doors closed behind her, Señora de Leon sat up, dropping all pretense of her earlier indolence. She looked at Elizabeth and said, "I'm glad Lady Yvaine didn't force your grandson on us for this search, as she did the Palantir. No disrespect, but I can't bring myself to trust him. I still don't understand why Lady Yvaine continues to flaunt our rules about him. There's never been a good warlock yet."

"Rest easy," Elizabeth said. "He's headed to Stormhold as we speak so Lady Yvaine can keep an eye on him this summer."

Diana was surprised at her boldness when she cleared her throat and said, "But he's done nothing to harm us. He's saved my life, and my mother's and has found and willingly given the *Palantir Sibylline Book* to our order. And now, he's given us the journal. I'll be the first to admit that his actions are often strange, but I have seen no indication that he's a danger to us."

"That's enough, Diana!" Sophie snapped.

"But it's true, Mom."

Señora de Leon looked at Elizabeth. "Is this the type of help you were expecting? I'd never countenance that type of back talk. She's an apprentice, not a priestess."

Before Elizabeth could reply, Diana cut in. "I know you don't want to hear it, but I can't stand by and see you talk about him this way. I once thought as you do, but I've learned he's much more than meets the eye. I only came here at Elizabeth's request. I think he would help us much more than any ancient books or maps you might have. I can't explain why, but I believe it to be true."

"It's easy for you to say that, but you haven't been around long enough to see all the bad things men have done, and continue to do, against members of our order. I realize what a huge break his finding of the Grail journal has been for our order," Señora de Leon said. "Maybe he's not dangerous to us now, but he will be, and that's why I cannot allow the boy to help us. If you're unwilling to live with that decision, then you should return to where you came from. But, if you're done arguing, we should get down to business."

Knowing she was fighting a losing cause, Diana nodded and sat down.

There was a long, uncomfortable silence until Elizabeth broke it by asking, "Why aren't more members of your grove attending this meeting, Lucrecia? I thought Lady Yvaine said I'd have your support."

"You have, but you've spent nine months studying the journal. You know it inside out, but I've only heard snippets of information. So, before I bring anyone else in on this project, I want to hear more about what you've found because I don't want to waste anyone's time if I believe this is a wild goose chase."

Sophie leaned forward and added, "I've known you my entire life, Elizabeth. You know I've supported you on every decision in the past except with regard to your grandson. I believe we should focus on dealing with him instead of chasing after yet another magical object

– especially since we haven't found any in over a century."

Diana opened her mouth to argue, but Sophie cut her off. "I know what you're about to say – that he found the Palantir, then accidentally destroyed it. I don't buy that story. I think it was all a plan to weasel into our order so he could destroy us from within. I'm a student of our order's history. We can't trust boys who are born to members of our order. They have always been a threat and always will be."

"I hear what you're saying, Sophie," Elizabeth said. "I've spent many a sleepless night worrying about the threat my grandson poses to this order. But as I've told you, Lady Yvaine has been very explicit in her instructions. We are not to harm him, so she's watching over him in Stormhold. Now, can we get on with the matter of the journal – the purpose of this meeting?"

Diana held up her hand. "Jane and I only looked at the book for a few hours and have been at Stormhold ever since you took it from us. We've only heard bits and pieces of what you've discovered, but I understand that we could be looking for just about anything from a cup, to a dish, to a treasure, or even a stone. The tales of what caused it to be holy are just as varied, ranging from the cup that Jesus drank from at the Last Supper to the vessel that collected his blood on the cross. Some even think the Holy Grail could be the Templars' treasure. So, have you figured out what we're looking for?"

"No. It could be any of the things you mentioned. But if we can find it, it will be precious beyond imagining – maybe even more powerful than the

Maqlû." She smiled as she added, "And if it's only the fabled Templar treasure, well, I'm sure we can figure out what to do with it."

She picked up the leather journal lying on the table in front of her. "This is the book in question. The earliest entries date from the mid-sixth century. The last entries were from the fifteenth century. I've carbon-dated the paper and tested the ink, and it appears authentic. I know there's a low probability of finding the Sangreal, but I believe we'd be breaking our oath if we didn't try to find it."

"I get it," Señora de Leon said. "But countless people have searched for the Grail through the centuries. And nobody has found it."

"True, but what makes this journal different is that there was a letter in the back of the book written by Vlad Tepes III, addressed to the Holy Roman Emperor Frederick III, asking for his help in protecting the Grail from the invading Ottomans. Vlad knew the Turks outnumbered him and that they would hold the Grail as a constant threat over Christian Europe if he lost. But he didn't, and the rumors about the Grail subsided. So, my conclusion, and quite frankly my hope, is that it's still wherever Vlad hid it."

"How do you expect to find it with so little to go on?" Sophie asked.

"I was thinking the Spanish grove could trace the response to the letter since the family who kept this journal for centuries was Spanish. I also believe this is the right place to start searching because Seville is home to the Archivo General de Indias."

"We'd be up against astronomical odds trying to find what happened to that letter after all these centuries," Señora de Leon said.

"True, but we should try." When there were no further objections, Elizabeth said, "Fine. Now let's get to it."

# CHAPTER 16
# BE THE CHANGE

Alex was standing in front of an ATM in the Seville airport when he heard a familiar voice from behind him say, "Ye're a sneaky little devil."

He whirled around to see Jane standing behind him in one of her ankle-length, brightly colored floral dresses. Feeling guilty at having run away, he tried apologizing, but all that came out were unintelligible sounds. At last, he managed to stammer, "I'm sorry about ditching you. But, since you were so insistent on going to Stormhold, and I couldn't persuade you to come with me, I decided to go alone. That way, no one would yell at you." Seeing a smirk on her face, he said, "What'd I say that's so funny?"

"Your plan didn't work. Lady Yvaine's already yelled at me for losing ye. But I'm curious about why ye chose to come to Seville. I'd have thought ye'd have tried Madrid first."

"I don't know much about the different cities in Spain, so I just booked the first flight out, which was to here. I didn't realize it had two layovers. So, why are you here? I thought you were supposed to go to Stormhold."

"My job is to try to keep ye out of trouble." Jane shook her head and said, "I don't know how ye did it, but whatever method ye used for selecting your destination, ye chose well. Yer grandmother's here in Seville."

"How'd you find me, since I'm here by chance?"

Jane smiled. "I jest assumed that ye'd make a lucky guess and come here since yer grandmother's here."

"Interesting. Now, if only I could figure out how to use this ATM."

It took some time for him to pull out money, as he'd never set up a pin for his bank card, but with Jane helping him download his bank app to her phone and set it up, he managed to get money out. When they'd finished, Alex asked, "I know this is a little late to think about it, but where should I stay tonight?"

"I wondered how long it would be before you asked that question. I've already booked a two-bedroom Airbnb for the night. Now, all we have to do is call an Uber."

As they left the terminal, Alex looked at the dark grey-green clouds overhead and said, "I thought it was always sunny here."

"It normally is. Ye must have brought yer luck because those clouds don't look good. Let's hurry before it starts pouring."

Luckily, it didn't take long to reach the appointed pick-up spot because the rain started falling as they got into their ride. By the time their driver let them out, though, it was pouring. Jane led Alex down a narrow cobblestone alley, where they had to weave around several large potted plants before reaching a shallow arched opening where they ducked in to get out of the rain.

Alex had to speak up because of the loud, rumbling thunder when he asked, "Where are we staying?"

"Here, but I'm waiting for the contact person to give us the key."

Half an hour later, when no one had shown, Alex looked down the alley and said, "There's been a person standing under that other awning almost this whole time. Do you think it might be who we're looking for?"

Jane grunted, then ran down the alley. Alex watched as the two women talked and was grateful when Jane motioned for him a minute later. When he arrived, she said, "Apparently, there was a mix-up. This is where we're staying for the night."

"Thank god," Alex said. "I was beginning to worry we'd have to sleep on the streets. It wouldn't be the worst night in my life, but it's not something I wanted to experience. I can't imagine what it's like for those who live that life every day." He looked up to the still dark clouds and said, "I've never seen anything so ominous looking in my life, nor have I heard thunder continue non-stop for almost an hour. This isn't a good sign for the start of this trip."

"It's nothing to worry about. Ye're jest being superstitious," Jane said. "It'll be okay."

He was surprised at the temperature difference when he stepped outside the next morning. Sweat was soon pouring off him as he followed Jane to a café on a large boulevard, where they sat at one of the tables outside underneath a large umbrella.

With his stomach grumbling, he was looking forward to a big breakfast but was disappointed when he found that the only food he could get at the street café was a toasted baguette with a thin slice of ham. Promising himself a better meal later, he closed his eyes to rest when Jane excused herself to go to the bathroom. However, it seemed like only a minute later, he heard someone calling his name. Still suffering from jet lag, he reluctantly opened his eyes and nearly fell out of his seat when he saw Diana running across the plaza, wearing a simple white blouse, knee-length jean dress, and a white floppy-brimmed straw hat. Unsure how to explain his presence, he pulled his Tilley down and hoped she hadn't seen him.

A few seconds later, he heard her breathlessly ask, "What are you doing here? I thought you were in Scotland."

Knowing he couldn't avoid her, he reluctantly raised his hat and looked up. It'd been almost a year since he'd last seen her, and he couldn't help but think she was even prettier than he remembered. He was still thinking about how to reply when Jane arrived and spared him from having to respond.

Diana sat down beside Alex and asked, "When did Lady Yvaine change her mind about you guys coming here?"

"She didn't," Jane replied. "Alex pulled a fast one, ditched me in Edinburgh, and came here to help his grandmother find the Sangreal. When I realized I'd lost him, I followed him."

"I'm confused. Everyone here thinks Lady Yvaine is keeping Alex locked up in Stormhold, and I'm pretty sure they don't want his help. In fact, they'll be furious when they find out he's here."

Alex threw his hands into the air and said, "I don't know what I was thinking."

"That's not true," Jane said. "Ye know exactly why ye came. The only issue is whether ye're going to work with yer grandmother or not."

"But how did you know to come to Seville?" Diana asked. "Did Jane tell you where we were?"

"Of course not," Alex replied. "I realized I couldn't sit still doing nothing, so I took the first flight to Spain."

Diana turned to Jane and asked. "How did you know he would come here?"

"Easy, when I realized there's a corollary to Murphy's Law, called Alex's Law," Jane replied. "It says that he'll be wherever you least expect or want him to be at the worst possible time. Even then, I wouldn't have found him, except he took a flight with layovers, and I managed to catch up with him in the Seville airport."

He turned to Diana and asked, "So, you don't think my grandma will want my help?"

"Nope."

"Don't worry," Jane said. "We'll help ye."

"I'm not agreeing to help," Diana said. "There's no way I'm going to stroll into the Spanish Grove and announce that I'm going to help Alex instead of them."

"That's not the type of help I was thinking about," Jane said. "Yer mom would probably call the authorities and say we're runaways or worse, that he kidnapped me."

"So, what type of help are you thinking of?" Diana asked.

"I haven't given the issue much thought."

Diana grunted, then leaned over and punched Alex lightly.

"Ow. What was that for?"

"Because you keep doing things that throw my life into chaos." She leaned over and punched him in the arm again."

"Ow! What's that one for?"

"That's for scaring the heck out of me last summer. I thought you were dead. Then, when you showed up out of the blue, you were too sick for me to express my frustrations with you adequately. I wish you'd think about others before you do your crazy stunts – like today. I can't believe you came here."

Alex looked over at Jane and saw she was lost in thought. He leaned over and, in a quiet voice, asked Diana, "What have they learned from the journal so far?"

"There's a ton of information in it, but the big aha is that it does something that no other Grail myth or story has done – link it to Romania and Vlad Tepes."

"Who's Vlad Tepes?" Alex asked.

"Really? You don't know who he is? You probably know his nickname, though – Vlad the Impaler."

"He sounds creepy, but the name still doesn't ring a bell."

"Bram Stoker is said to have used Vlad Tepes as the inspiration for his fictional character Dracula," Diana said.

Alex's eyes practically popped out of his head.

Pleased at the impact she'd had, Diana smiled. "I thought you might be interested in that."

Alex's smile faded. "I am, but for the opposite reason of what you're thinking. It would mean that finding the Grail will be even more dangerous than I thought."

"Relax. Vlad's been dead for centuries," Diana said.

"But what if he turned into a vampire and is still alive? Maybe you should call this whole thing off."

"Are you kidding?" Diana replied. "The more we study your journal, the more everyone in our order gets excited about it."

"What if you do find it? What then?" Alex asked.

"What we always do – we'll safeguard it," Diana replied. "We already have a couple of magical objects we guard round the clock. The Grail will be no different."

"I'm confused about one thing, though," Alex said.

"Only one thing?" Diana replied.

"That's brutal. My question is, what are we supposed to call it? I've heard you use both Grail and Sangreal."

"It's had several name changes," Diana replied. "The Sangreal was one of its earliest names, but since the Medieval Ages, pretty much everyone calls it the Holy Grail. But why the change in interest? Last fall, you swore off searching for any magical object. Yet you've gone through a lot of trouble to get here."

"I know, but something came up back home that caused me to change my mind," Alex replied. "But, now that you mentioned the linkage between the object and Dracula, the opposite of holy, I'm wondering if I should give up before it gets too dangerous."

"You think differently than everyone else, but the more I get to know you, the more I trust your instincts. Maybe you should come to the villa and tell your grandmother about your fears," Diana said.

Jane rejoined the conversation and said, "Ye were jest saying that they don't want anything to do with him. I doubt if they'll ever accept him."

"What if I find the Grail?" Alex asked. "Do you think they'd change their mind about me then?"

"My gut says that no matter what you do, they won't accept you," Diana replied. "But I wouldn't worry about it. Right now, the biggest danger is that it'll bore you to death. All we've been doing so far is reading and debating what to do with that journal you found."

All of a sudden, Diana reached out, causing Alex to recoil. "Relax," she said. "I'm not going to hit you. All I want is your credit card."

"What for? Jane already set up my ATM card."

"I'm going to put your data into my phone so I can pay our expenses for whatever comes up."

"What do you mean?" Alex asked.

"No matter what your grandmother and the others say, I know you well enough that I'm pretty sure you're not going to sit around and twiddle your thumbs. And, as we've been talking, I've decided I'm coming with you. Since we'll need money to go on this search, and I haven't found many ATMs around here, we'll need credit cards. Thus, my request."

"I never said I was going anywhere," Alex replied.

"Ye've already come 5,000 miles and said you want to help find the Grail. How can we not interpret that as ye're going in search of it?" Jane asked. "And, if I didn't make myself clear, I'm coming too."

"But…."

"But nothing," Diana said. "Now, give me your cards."

"What if you ruin Kenny again? You know fancy technology has limitations," Alex said.

"Well, they say the third time's a charm. Besides, there's no way I'll let you ruin another phone."

Alex pulled his wallet out of his backpack and handed over his credit cards, saying, "I didn't ruin the first two."

"Yeah, but I got into those situations because of you." After Diana handed them back, she asked, "Do you want to see a little bit of the city?"

"Wait, you were just talking about finding the Grail, and now you're talking about sightseeing. Which one are we doing?" Alex asked.

"It sounds like ye don't have a plan, but I trust your instincts. So, until ye decide which way we go, I'm with Diana. Let's look around the city a bit. Where would ye suggest we go, Diana?"

"I'd like to see the Alcazar, but we'll need tickets. But I can go online tonight and order tickets for tomorrow."

"What's the Alcazar?" Alex asked.

"It's the oldest royal palace still in use in Europe and part of the UNESCO World Heritage site here in Seville. I hear it's fabulous. But, with what's left of this morning, I'd suggest we see the Plaza de España and walk around the outer gardens of the Alcazar. Then this afternoon, we can see the cathedral, when the lines will be shorter. It'd take us hours to get in if we went now."

It was soon so hot under the blazing Castilian sun that Alex was glad he'd brought his Tilley hat. They walked past the central plaza, where the Cathedral of Seville and the National Archive buildings stood across from each other, and past the outer walls of the Alcazar to get to the public gardens beyond. A group of Flamenco dancers caught their attention, so they stopped to watch. Diana tossed some coins into the performers' basket when the dance was over and said, "Come on. We're not far from the entrance."

As they walked towards the outer gardens, Alex was surprised at how many languages he heard from the other tourists. He could identify the French and German speakers, was surprised at the disparate number of British vs. American accents, and thought he heard at least two, if not three, Asian languages. It was like nothing he'd ever experienced before, and was so fascinated that Diana had to keep prompting him to keep up.

Alex was amazed at how beautiful the Alcazar's public gardens were. He kept stopping to watch the parrots flying about in the trees or bending over to smell the flowers and was surprised when he felt a tinge of disappointment when Diana led them out of the gardens.

It was a long walk to the Plaza de España, but they missed the park entrance and walked past the Regional Military Museum entrance twice before realizing the plaza was inside. Diana's attempt to describe the place didn't do it justice. Alex thought they'd entered some fairy tale palace as the inside of the stunning building curved gracefully around a giant open plaza with a canal cutting through the middle.

After an hour of wandering around the plaza, Alex felt another twinge of disappointment when Diana drove them out, preventing him from spending more time looking at the different tiled provincial alcoves. She led them towards the cathedral plaza, but before long, Alex had grown so parched from the heat and walking that all he could think about was getting something to drink. They found a small café to have an early lunch, but he was so thirsty that Jane had to tell him to slow down on gulping his Fanta. He was glad he followed her advice because lunch was much more satisfying than the breakfast sandwich he'd had. When he'd finally finished eating, he leaned back in his chair and asked, "What bizarre things have happened in the city?"

"I don't know if it was the most bizarre thing in this town ever, but it's certainly the most ignominious," Diana replied. "The Spanish held the first auto-da-fé of the Inquisition right here in Seville. They symbolize everything horrible about the Inquisition, which the Catholic Church and the King and Queen of Spain sponsored."

Alex held up his hand and asked, "What is that auto da whatever you said?"

"They were religious ceremonies where government officials brought out accused heretics and subjected them to church proceedings in public," Diana said. "They executed the first people in Seville who went through the process by burning them at the stake."

"That's horrible. Where did this happen?" Alex asked.

"I'm not sure, but I'd imagine it would be near the cathedral in an open area where the masses could watch the spectacle."

Alex pushed back his chair. "I'd never thought I'd say this, but I'm interested in seeing this cathedral you're talking about."

As they crossed the crowded pedestrian and carriage-horse-only plaza a few minutes later, Alex felt the ankh tugging him forward. Surprised, he froze, staring at the cathedral towering over him while Diana and Jane kept walking.

Once Jane noticed he wasn't with them anymore, she ran back and asked, "What's wrong?"

"Something doesn't feel right," Alex replied. His voice trailed off when he saw a male and female ghost passing through the cathedral's stone walls. He did a double take and took off at a jog, yelling back, "C'mon. I just saw something I need to check out."

# CHAPTER 17
# IS THERE A WAY

Friar Tomás de Torquemada apparated and looked around the damp, dark dungeon. The medieval torture chamber was larger and better equipped than the ones he'd labored in centuries earlier, but it still felt like home.

As he waited for the allies the witch Pythia had promised him, his thoughts drifted towards her promise of eternal life. He didn't doubt she could resurrect him, for after all, she was a living person who could talk to the dead. That, plus the fact that he'd just received the promised Hand of Glory she'd told him she would send, had made him confident he would soon return to the world of the living to resume his cleansing of undesirables from Spain.

He didn't have long to wait but was surprised when he recognized the middle-aged couple who appeared. Torquemada bowed to the newcomers. "Your Catholic Majesties."

The woman dipped her head slightly in greeting and said, "Friar Tomás."

"Why did Pythia send you?" Torquemada asked. "You have no skills I know that would help in this mission." He raised the grey shriveled hand he was holding. "Unless she gave you a magical object as she did me."

"That thing is a blasphemy," Queen Isabella said. "Imbuing a part of a human body with magic is unholy and is the devil's work."

"Your majesties should not be so hasty to condemn the use of magic in the pursuit of a higher goal," Torquemada replied. "Remember why we started the Inquisition. We did it to find and punish those who didn't adhere to the true faith. Now that we're getting a second chance to finish what we started, don't you think we should use whatever means are necessary to rid our world of heretics? Surely there's no harm if we do it in God's name."

"Maybe, but we have no wish to dirty our hands with the type of work that the witch asked us to do," King Ferdinand said.

Torquemada sneered. "Of course not, Your Majesty. You always left the dirty work for me and others to handle. I guess it was too much for me to think that Pythia would send someone who would be willing to do whatever was necessary to find the Holy Grail."

"Why shouldn't our subjects be doing the work?" Ferdinand asked. "Bella and I are focused on the future of our country, and you are competent enough to handle the heretics just fine."

Torquemada leaned to one side to see what the former king was holding behind his back. "What's that you're hiding?"

Ferdinand blushed and shook his head. "Nothing."

"That witch gave you a magical object, too. Didn't she? Come now. Show it to me. You needn't be ashamed of accepting such a gift from her. I'm sure you did it for our worthy cause."

After hemming and hawing, Ferdinand held out a short metal scepter with a flaming star set inside a circle on top. "She said it's the Scepter of Shamash.

Supposedly, it can focus the sun's rays and set fire to whatever I aim at. I haven't...."

Torquemada cut off what the dead king was saying and held up a hand for silence as he looked around the darkened dungeon.

"Is there anything wrong, Tomás?" Isabella asked.

"I thought I heard something." The friar looked around again, then turned to the queen and asked, "Do you sense anything strange?"

Isabella and Ferdinand both shook their heads. "What is it?" the ghost queen asked.

"Pythia told me we should be wary of a boy with a strong aura, and I sense one that worries me. But I don't see how he could have known of our meeting. Besides, he can't see us, so we shouldn't worry about him." After scanning the dungeon one more time, he shrugged and said, "I guess it's just my nerves."

"I've never seen you so spooked before," Isabella said. "Is this task that dangerous?"

Seeing the worried look on her face, he tried to put her mind at ease. "How could it be dangerous? We're already dead."

"But the Grail is different," Isabella said. "Just look at you, Tomás. We haven't even begun looking for it, and you're already nervous. Maybe we shouldn't be searching for such a holy object. Who knows what it could do if it's real, and not like all the fake holy objects the Church has created over the centuries to make money. Maybe it's better if it stays lost, for I'm beginning to fear this quest will lead us from the righteous path we took all those years ago of protecting the one true faith."

"You'd probably be right, dear if it weren't for the object in question," Ferdinand countered. "Finding the Grail is a holy mission that will give us purpose again. You talk about maybes, but what if God is punishing us for not completing our work of rooting out the heretics in our country? I fear that until we accomplish that task, we will remain here in the afterworld and never go to Heaven. It's like the witch told us – our only chance to alter our fate is to find the Grail."

"Are you really willing to do what it takes to find it?" Torquemada asked. "It will be messier work than what you're accustomed to. Your hands will be dirty and bloodied before we finish this."

"What's your plan?" Isabella asked.

"The witch suggested I follow a boy who, she believed, would lead us to the Grail. She warned me that he's more dangerous than he looks, but I have learned that a group of witches he's associated with are also looking for it, using information he found. They fear he's a warlock and will get rid of him if he crosses them. So, I plan for him to lead the witches to the Grail, let them dispose of him, then we swoop in and take it from the witches."

Seeing Isabella and Ferdinand hesitate, Torquemada added, "Remember, if what Pythia says comes true, when we return to life, we can rid this country of heretics, and you can mount the throne again."

Isabella looked at her husband, looking for confirmation. When he nodded, she turned to Torquemada and said, "You're right. We cannot forsake our country in its time of need."

# CHAPTER 18
# **TRAPPED**

Both girls set off after Alex, wondering what new scrape he was leading them into.

The three ran across the Plaza del Triunfo to the cathedral's St. Christopher's gate. Alex stopped, put his hands on his head, and groaned when he saw there was a line curling around the inside courtyard. "I can't believe this. I'll never find them now."

"What's so important to run around in this heat for?" Diana asked when she finally caught up.

Ignoring her question, Alex looked around for another entrance and asked, "Is there any faster way of getting in?"

"No, you'll have to wait in line like everyone else," Diana said. "But at least it's a short line. What's got you so riled up?"

Alex pointed off to his right. "I just saw some ghosts enter the cathedral over there."

"What's so special about that?" Diana asked. "You see them all the time."

"True, but I have a bad feeling about them. They looked like they're up to something."

"Relax," Jane said. "With your spidey-senses, I'm sure you'll find them again. But now that we're here, we might as well get in line."

Alex found the next half hour nearly unbearable as the line seemed to move at a snail's pace. When he finally reached the security checkpoint, he hesitated, wondering if the scanners would catch the knives in his pants and backpack, even though none of the airport scanners had.

Diana nudged him forward, then yelped and jumped back.

Alex was almost as surprised as Diana when he belatedly realized the ankh had activated its forcefield. He turned and saw her dancing around, a pained look on her face, clasping the hand she'd touched him with close to her chest.

"What did you do?" she wailed.

Seeing everyone staring at them, he said, "I'm sorry. I tend to build up big static charges at times." Then, with a red face, he hurried through security.

When Diana got through, she glared at Alex, then stomped away. Jane came beside him and whispered, "I'm assuming that was yer necklace. Can't ye control it?"

"Not when it's trying to protect me," he whispered back. I'm guessing it was helping me get through security because I have a couple of knives on me."

After walking through the museum portion of the cathedral, Diana led them off to the right. Alex's embarrassment vanished as soon as he entered the cathedral and looked in awe at the vast interior. In a daze, he followed Diana into the central nave, wondering aloud, "This is monstrous."

"It's the third largest cathedral in the world in floor size and largest by volume," Diana said. "What amazes me most is that it has eighty magnificent side chapels. When I came here before, I grew numb seeing all the marble altars, statues, gold and silver reliquaries, and crosses."

Alex nodded and moved on. He'd only taken a couple of steps when Jane nudged him and said, "I don't get it. A little while ago, ye were anxious to get inside and pursue yer ghosts. Now, ye're acting as if ye're just a tourist. Which, by the way, I find refreshing."

"Don't let my looks fool you. I'm scared, so I'm trying to distract myself. But I still have a bad feeling about those ghosts," he replied.

"I hate it when ye get those types of feelings," Jane said. "It gets frustrating chasing after ye when we can't see what's happening. What are you expecting? Should we get out of here?"

"I don't know," Alex replied. "But since we're here, we should at least wander around and see if something looks out of place."

They hadn't gone far when they came to a chapel with a large sculpture in the front center of the alcove where four men wearing crowns carried a large bronzed coffin above them. "Do you know what this is?" Diana asked.

"Of course not," Alex replied. "You're the history buff."

"This is the tomb of Christopher Columbus."

"I don't get what the big deal about him is," Alex said. "The Indians were in the Americas thousands of years before him and the Vikings centuries."

"Recognition and glory don't always go to the pioneers. The ones who get the glory are the ones who document their achievements, then brag about them first."

Something bumped into Alex's leg, causing him to look down and exclaim, "Sadie! What are you doing here?"

"How could you know this cat?" Diana asked. "You just got here yesterday."

Confused by the little dragon's presence, Alex stammered, "Well, uh, I don't know. I, uh, I call all cats Sadie." An image of a darkened doorway flashed into his mind. Without thinking about his company, he looked down at Sadie. "What are you trying to say?" he asked.

"You need to take a chill pill," Diana replied. "I didn't mean anything by the question. I was just curious why such an odd-looking cat would come up to you in a cathedral in a foreign country and start rubbing on you."

Alex waved away her comments, saying, "I'm sorry. I was thinking of something else." He looked around, trying to figure out what Sadie was telling him, and was surprised to see the plainest wall he'd seen in the cathedral – simple dark wood paneling. He followed Sadie around the memorial and saw a beat-up, dark, multi-paneled door tucked into the bottom corner of an enormous picture in the back left corner of the chapel – the same doorway image Sadie had shared. He approached the door, bent over, and looked into the keyhole.

"What are you doing?" Diana asked.

Without looking up, he replied, "I'm getting goosebumps from whatever's behind this door, but all I see is a small stone passage leading towards the outside of the building."

"I know what you're thinking, but don't do it," Diana said. "Something bad is bound to happen. At the very least, some guard will see us on the security cameras and arrest us. By the way, where did your cat go?"

Alex could see Sadie in the corner, but she'd changed her colors and blended so well that the little dragon was nearly invisible. Turning his attention back to the door, he reached out to lift the latch, but the door didn't budge. "It's locked," he said.

"Of course it is," Diana said.

"Please?" Alex begged.

Diana rolled her eyes and huffed. "Fine. Step aside."

"I'm shocked at ye, Diana," Jane said with a grin. "I do believe he's totally corrupted ye,"

"You're one to talk. I bet you think this is fun, but if they catch us, I'm blaming you two." She looked around to see if there were any security personnel, then pulled out her talisman. In a voice barely above a whisper, she chanted,

> *"I summon now the mists*
> *To hide us from the light.*
> *Let us walk enshrouded*
> *Hidden from their sight."*

Pausing only briefly, she added,

> *"Listen to me and abide*
> *Open this door and push it aside."*

Alex heard two clicks and felt his heart pounding as Diana lifted the latch and slipped in. He motioned Jane forward, looked around to see if anyone was watching, then followed them in and shut the door.

Jane and Diana had crammed themselves into a small space to the right that ended on the outer wall. To his left was a narrow stone hallway with well-worn stone steps, barely wide enough for one person to walk through. He hesitated for a second, then headed down. The stairs soon turned and led to a small, dimly lit dead-end room.

A rat scurried across the floor, causing Diana to scream, "I hate rats. Why did you bring us to a place where the first thing we see is the thing I hate the most?"

Alex shushed her, then turned back to study the stone wall where the steps had ended. He spotted a small bump in the upper right corner of the wall, reached up, and pushed in on it. Stones ground against each other as a hidden door slid open.

They crept down two more flights of stairs, ending on a long stone-flagged balcony overlooking a large room with flickering lights. Alex could hear voices as they crept along the hall, so he turned and put a finger to his lips to warn Jane and Diana to be quiet.

The three ducked behind stone balusters and peeked at the scene below them. A dozen flaming torches sat in wall sconces, providing enough light to show it was a medieval torture chamber. A pair of metal coffin cages hung from the ceiling in one corner, with partial skeletons inside and bones on the floor below, while a Judas Cradle occupied another corner. The wall opposite where they were hiding had a pair of racks with two more skeletons and a Catherine's Wheel. Along all four walls were dozens of sets of manacles, with about a quarter of them still holding the bones of some long-forgotten soul who had died in the chamber. Below Alex were two long tables with various torture devices ranging from head crushers to knee splitters, a variety of whips, several pairs of copper boots, and a large bronze bull with a lid. The grisly sights caused Alex to shudder at the cruelty the inquisitors had inflicted on people in the room.

After getting over his initial shock at seeing all the torture devices, Alex spotted the two ghosts he'd seen outside. They were a rather plain-looking couple. The man wore an orange waist-length tunic over a white linen shirt, black hose, and a black brimless cap that covered a thick bush of salt and pepper colored hair. The woman wore a floor-length brown dress with a subtle red floral pattern and a simple white bun cap.

They were standing opposite another ghost that reminded him of Brother Stafford. He was a short, rotund man with a tonsure haircut, long, sagging jowls, and dark beady eyes. Instead of Stafford's brown robes, though, the spirit wore a white, ankle-length tunic with a matching scapular and capuce, covered by a black cappa with the hood falling back over his shoulders.

Alex whispered, "Those ghosts I saw outside are down there, along with some monk."

"I'll take your word for it, but this place is creepy," Diana whispered. "I say we get the heck out of here."

Alex shook his head. "I need to find out what's happening." He peeked over the balcony and was listening to the conversation when he suddenly felt two arms link through his. Surprised, he let out a faint squeal, then quickly slid back down and held his breath, hoping the ghosts hadn't noticed. He didn't move for several minutes before he finally worked up the courage to look over the balcony again.

"What was that about?" Jane asked.

"You startled me when both of you grabbed my arms," Alex replied.

"We did that because we learned in the Caribbean we could see and hear ghosts if we were touching ye," Jane said.

"Oh, yeah. I forgot. Sorry about that."

"Well, did ye learn anything?" Jane asked.

Alex shook his head. "They were too far away to hear them. But now that they're gone, we can go."

"You're going to have to speak up," Diana said. "I can't hear what you're saying, and I can't read your lips in this dim light."

"Let's get out of here. We'll talk about it later," Jane said.

They retraced their steps but had only gone a short distance when Alex asked, "Is it darker in here than before?"

"It seems like it," Jane replied.

By the time they got to the first landing, there was no light to guide them, so they felt their way up the second flight of stairs towards the hidden door in pitch black, using the wall as a guide. "How can this be?" Alex asked. I know it was a lot lighter when we came here."

"Maybe our eyes have to adjust more after looking at the torches," Diana suggested,

"It can't be that. We came from brightly lit rooms when we first entered this stairway."

When they got to the second landing, Alex inched towards the door with one hand on the wall and the other stuck out to feel for it. His left hand hit the door a few steps later.

He felt around the door briefly before saying, "Can you conjure up some of that magic light, Diana? I can't find the latch."

Diana grunted and slapped her forehead. "I should have thought of that before." She reached down into the pouch at her side, pulled out her fire onyx talisman, and chanted,

*"Dragon's blood and parchment burn*

*Bring the flames for which I yearn."*

A ball of flames appeared in her hand. She waited several seconds to ensure the fire held steady, then moved her hand close to the door to provide light.

Alex reached for the upper left corner of the door, expecting to see the back side of the mechanism that had opened it on their way down, but all he found was the smooth inner face.

"How do we open it?" Diana asked in a nervous tone.

"I'm looking," Alex replied. "Just give me a second."

Cold air crept into the room, and a moment later, a gravelly voice came out of the dark. "Pythia said we should be concerned about you, but it appears she overestimated you. I can't believe you walked right into my arms, helping me complete half of my mission."

Alex was so shocked that Pythia had sent more ghosts after him that he could only gasp.

The spirit didn't notice Alex's reaction and said, "Since you'll be my guests down here for the rest of eternity, I should introduce myself. I'm Friar Tomás de Torquemada."

"What's going on?" Jane asked.

It took Alex a few seconds to recover before he could blurt out, "Some spirit named Torquemada has blocked us in."

"Torquemada! He was a beast, a torturer – an evil man," Diana said as she linked an arm through Alex's.

"We've done nothing to you, so go away and leave us alone," Alex said.

"I intend to. And may you rot in hell down here."

Before Alex could stop the friar, he'd disappeared.

# CHAPTER 19
# DUNGEONS AND SEWERS

"What trouble have you gotten us into now?" Diana asked.

Alex grimaced. "I fear we've stumbled into another one of that Pythia woman's schemes. It sounds like she's enlisted Torquemada to get rid of me, which is why he's trapped us down here and left us to die, while making it sound like he was missing the good old days of torturing people to death."

Diana threw up her hands in disgust. "Oh, great. Now, what do we do?"

"There's no sense in wailing about our situation. We need to focus on finding another way out," Jane said. "Diana, since ye have the light, lead the way."

Diana headed down the stairs to the dungeon floor, hurrying so fast that she left Alex and Jane far behind. She tripped on the last stair and fell onto the cold stone floor. Cursing, she got up and knocked the dust off.

"What's the rush?" Alex asked when he finally caught up with her.

"I wanted to get one of these torches before they go out," Diana replied. "I'm not sure how long I can sustain my magical fire."

Diana shook out her flames, then pulled one of the burning torches out of its wall sconce. She froze when a low rumbling noise caused her to look up in time to see the whole wall shaking. Too stunned to move, she barely noticed Jane grabbing her arm and yanking her away just as a chunk of stone fell off the stairs. A second later, there was a roar as the whole wall collapsed onto where she'd been standing, followed by a thick dust cloud.

Gasping and coughing, Diana waved the dust away until it had settled enough for her to see what remained of the stairway. Trying to sound more confident than she felt, she said, "At least we have torches. Let's see if there's another way out."

While Alex and Jane grabbed nearby torches, Diana started slowly walking the perimeter of the room, looking for a possible exit. After she'd finished exploring three walls, she stopped and said, "This is hopeless. We're going to die down here."

In an encouraging voice, Jane said, "Don't despair. We're a long way from that. Do ye see any ghosts that might help us, Alex?"

Alex turned around in a slow circle, then shook his head. "Nope. It makes sense, though. If this was a torture chamber, then the people who died here probably got a pass to move on in the afterlife."

"What about all the king's slaves in Lamanai?" Diana asked. "They were trapped under that pyramid for a thousand years."

"Yeah, but the king held them there by magic," Alex replied.

"I can't believe it. Ghosts pester you all the time, but where are they when we need them?" Diana instantly regretted raising her voice in the cavernous dungeon as the echoes unnerved her and made their situation seem more dire. She rubbed her arms to get rid of her goosebumps and resumed her search. Just as Diana reached the end of the fourth wall and was ready to admit defeat, her torch fluttered. She gave a tiny yelp and cried out, "I found something. There's a grate at my feet, and I can feel a cool breeze coming out."

Alex and Jane rushed to where Diana stood and looked at where she was pointing.

"Hold this while I lift the grate," Alex said as he handed his torch to Jane before kneeling on the floor. He grabbed the bars and pulled them as hard as he could, but they didn't budge. After several failed efforts, sweat poured down Alex's face. He leaned against the dungeon's wall and rested. The next time he tried, he braced his feet against the wall, grabbed the grate with both hands and pulled with all his might. Despite his best efforts, though, the grate didn't budge. Alex let go and lay back against the wall again.

With a smirk on her face, Diana asked, "Do you need any help?"

"No, I got this. I need some tools." He went to one of the tables he'd seen earlier and rummaged among the items. A minute later, he returned with a long, thick iron bar.

He shoved the bar at an angle into one of the openings until it hit the wall below. Stepping back, he grabbed the upper end of the bar and pushed down. The grate didn't budge, but the pry bar snapped in two, sending Alex sprawling backwards.

Diana chuckled. "Here, hold my torch. There's a much easier way of doing this."

Alex took her torch and watched as Diana took out her talisman.

She nodded to the other two and said, "You better step back." Then she closed her eyes, folded her arms, and started mouthing words. Beads of sweat soon broke out on her face as she concentrated on her task. A couple of minutes went by before she suddenly flung her arms wide and yelled,

*"Asunder!"*

A second later, a small explosion sent debris everywhere. Diana ducked as several chunks of metal and stone whizzed by her head. "Damn. I can never get that spell right," she said.

"Why didn't you tell me earlier you could use magic to open that hole?" Alex asked.

"I was having too much fun watching you trying to open it with brute force. Boys like to think they can be all macho and do things on their own, then get resentful if a girl offers to help. So, I just sat back until you ran out of options. Next time, maybe you'll ask for help first."

Alex grumbled as he stepped towards the hole but pulled back, waving his hand in front of his face. "That smells disgusting."

Diana bent over the opening and gasped, "No, it's worse than that. It looks like our only way out. You first."

"Oh, but that would be so rude of me. Please, ladies before gentlemen."

Diana smiled back at him. "If you were a gentleman, that might be true. But I think you owe us big time for getting us into this situation."

Alex grimaced and pulled the remaining loose pieces away from the hole. He peered into the opening and said, "I can't believe our only way out is through this rat-infested hole."

Diana slumped. "Rats again! Why did it have to be rats?"

As Alex watched the rodents scurry away, he said, "Well, let's hope they're the least of our worries. We don't know where it empties or how deep it is. I'd hate to drown down there. Of course, we could stay in this torture chamber and do nothing. We'd at least freshen up the bone collection in here."

Diana punched him on the arm. "Keep your morbid thoughts to yourself," she said.

"Sorry."

Jane bent over the opening and looked down. "The water is pretty yucky, but it looks shallow enough to wade through. So, unless ye know another way out, I say this is our lead option. And don't worry about the rats, Diana. They shouldn't bother us with our torches."

"I'll go first because I got you guys into this fix," Alex said, handing his torch to Diana. Then he sat down and, after taking a deep breath, slid into the hole. His feet splashed in water that was only a few inches deep. He gasped for breath as the smells of the old sewer system nearly overcame him. He looked up and called out, "It's shallow, so we should be okay. Just to warn you, though, it's breathtaking down here. Hand me your torches when you're ready to come down. But watch your heads. The ceiling is low."

After they'd descended into the ancient sewer tunnel, Alex started heading off into the darkness, but Diana grabbed his arm and said, "I'll go first in case I need to use magic." She wet her finger and slowly turned in a circle to see which direction the breeze was coming from. When she felt the cooling feeling of the draft, she set off down the narrow old sewer system. She'd only taken a few steps when she stumbled on a stone in the dimly lit tunnel and fell. Her torch plopped into the fetid water and fizzled out. She got up, flinging muck off her as she said, "Hand me your torch, Jane. I'll try to be more careful because I don't know how long these will last or how long we'll be down here. Maybe you should put yours out, Alex, to ensure they last. One should give off enough light for all of us."

The smell was so overpowering that Diana thought she would throw up, but she overcame her gag reflex and pushed on. Her torch soon started sputtering, but Jane pushed past Alex and touched her torch to Diana's to relight it. Jane's torch flared brightly, then dimmed and went out seconds after Diana's, throwing the three into total darkness.

"Are you able to do that fireball thing with your hand?" Alex asked.

"I'm a little tired as magic does take a lot of energy, but I should have enough left to relight the torch," Diana said. After chanting a different fire spell, the torch burst into flame, giving off even more light than before.

"I still wish I could do that," Alex said. "Do you think there's a way I could learn?"

"If a person has the innate ability, then it's just a matter of finding the right talisman to channel their thoughts through the natural forces around them – and a lot of practice. Of course, some people are better at certain things than others, but that's true for everything. But you'll never get any help from our order to learn magic."

"Bummer," Alex grumbled. "But since we're in this together, I'm glad you're terrific at it."

Diana was glad for the dim light as she blushed. "Let's stop talking and get out of here before this torch goes out, and I can't relight it." She pulled her phone out and said, "Here, take my phone and use the flashlight app if you need it."

"I don't know how to use it," Alex said.

"Haven't you learned any technology yet? I know you said you didn't have it when you were growing up, but what's your excuse now?"

"I still don't have one," Alex replied sheepishly.

Diana groaned in mock disgust and handed it to Jane. "Here, you take care of it since Mr. Luddite here isn't familiar with modern technology."

A trembling under her feet caused her to look around. She took off running, not waiting for the others, when she saw a crack developing beside her. Tiny bits of rock started pelting her, followed by a loud rumbling sound an instant later. She glanced back and saw a large section of the wall implode into the tunnel.

A billowing dust cloud blew over her, putting the torch out and making it impossible to see anything. She covered her mouth and nostrils and let the dust settle down. When she could finally see through the haze, she saw Jane standing in front of the pile of rubble, but Alex had disappeared.

# CHAPTER 20
# ARCHIVO GENERAL de INDIAS

The explosion knocked Alex back several feet. Too stunned to move, he sat in the fetid water until he realized Jane was calling for him. He shook his head to clear the cobwebs and saw both girls anxiously looking at him through a hole in the rubble filling the sewer tunnel. "I'm fine," he shouted, his ears still ringing. "Just give me a minute.

"Thank Gaia," Jane replied. "We thought ye'd disappeared on us again."

"You're not that lucky," Alex replied as he slung muck off him. After ridding himself of the biggest chunks, he started scrambling over the rubble pile but stopped when he saw a petite, older female ghost dressed in a floor-length black mantua float through the opening. "Who, who are you?" he asked.

Diana spun around, wondering who Alex was speaking to in formal Spanish. Seeing nobody, she asked, "Who are you talking to now?"

"Some ghost lady. She looks harmless, but after that blast – I don't know."

The Spanish lady curtsied, then said, "I've been expecting you, Señor Scire. I am Doña de Ubilla."

"What do you want?" Alex asked cautiously

"Doesn't my name mean anything to you?"

Memories of the ghost ship came rushing back. "I met a Captain General with the same last name. Are you related?"

"Si. And I'm grateful you took my son's journal so he could move on," Doña de Ubilla replied.

"Why don't you come down here so we can hear what's going on?" Diana asked.

Alex held up a finger. "Hold on." Turning his attention back to the ghost lady, he asked, "Why do you think I have the journal?"

"Because that journal has been the bane of my family's existence for centuries, and my son wouldn't have moved on unless he found someone worthy to protect it. I can't express how relieved I am that we no longer have to care for it. But follow me. I have something to give you."

Alex watched as Doña de Ubilla turned and floated through the hole in the wall, then scrambled down the pile and updated Jane and Diana on what had happened.

A few seconds later, Doña de Ubilla reappeared in the opening. "Forgive me, but you must hurry while the way is clear. I fear I used too much magic to make this hole, for I hear sirens approaching. Please follow me."

As Alex followed her through the opening, Diana grabbed his arm. "Do you trust her? Remember how we got here?"

"Yeah, I do. Now come on." He followed the elderly spirit into a modern, well-lit, air-conditioned tunnel and asked, "Where are we?"

"This is an underground tunnel between the two buildings of the Archivo General de Indias," Doña de Ubilla replied.

Alex turned to the girls and said, "I have no idea what she's talking about, but she says we're in some tunnel between the General Archive Buildings of the Indies."

"Cool," Diana said. "I wanted to go here, but your grandmother didn't want to take the time. This is where they house all the documents about the Spanish Empire in the Americas and the Philippines."

"We can't dally here looking like this," Jane said as she waved at her soiled dress. "We can return when we're clean."

A door opened at the end of the hallway, and a person stepped through carrying an armful of books. The elderly man saw them and called out in Spanish, "Hey, what are you kids doing? You're not supposed to be down here."

Not understanding what the man had said, Alex looked to Jane and Diana for translation. Before he could ask them, he saw Doña de Ubilla fly down the hall, howling at the man. Her yell was so piercing that Alex had to clap his hands over his ears to shut it out. An instant later, she knocked the man's books out of his arms, sending them flying. The man screamed and ducked back into the building he'd come out of.

Doña de Ubilla flew back towards the group, looking as if nothing had happened, and said, "Follow me."

Jane and Diana each stuck an arm through Alex's, then the three followed the spirit through a set of doors at the end of the hallway into a library stuffed with yellowing books, papers, and maps. "Why are we here?" Alex asked.

"Even though it started nearly two hundred years before I died, the Tribunal of the Holy Office of the Inquisition raged on throughout my lifetime," Doña de

Ubilla said. "I was never at risk of the Inquisition targeting me since I'd descended from a long line of Spanish nobility. But my husband, being of distant Moorish descent, worried that the Inquisition's tribunal would eventually accuse him of heresy, strip us of everything we owned, and execute him. He wasn't concerned about losing his wealth or life so much as he wanted to ensure the safety of documents his family had been guarding for centuries. They were of such great importance that my husband and his brothers left for the New World to protect them. Alas, I never saw my husband again.

"When our son grew up, he, too, left for the New World. He stayed there for most of his life, continuing to protect his father's family secret. He became quite successful and eventually became the commander of the ill-fated treasure fleet of 1715. He must have stayed with his ship, guarding that secret until you came along."

"Hold on a minute," Alex said. "Should I tell her what we're doing? My gut's telling me it's the right thing to do."

"Do what ye think is right," Jane said. "Maybe we'll get lucky, and she'll help us figure out how to use the journal."

Doña de Ubilla led them to an old desk and said, "Underneath this is a secret compartment with the other document my husband's family protected for centuries. You may have it. All I ask is that you finish what they were unable to accomplish."

"And what is that?" Alex asked warily.

"I'm not sure," she replied. "As I said, I don't know what was in the journal. But there's a map in the desk that goes with the book." She motioned to the desk and said, "It's yours."

"I can't take it from here," Alex said. "I'll get in trouble."

"I don't know what she's told you," Diana said, "but when have you worried about something that might get us in trouble? Whatever she's talking about seems like too good of an opportunity to pass by. Go for it."

Alex frowned and turned back to Doña de Ubilla. "Won't the security cameras see me doing this?"

The elderly spirit smiled. "Apparently, I have the effect of disrupting their systems. No one will bother you. Find a little bump at the far back right-hand corner and press it."

Alex felt around until a faint click told him he'd found it. "Now what do I do?"

"Look under the drawer. You'll see a small drop-down slot. Reach your hand in and pull out the paper you'll find there. It must have dropped out of my husband's journal because I didn't find it until long after he'd sailed for the Americas. I hid it in the desk, then donated it, thinking it would be safe here."

Diana and Jane joined Alex in kneeling on the floor to look at the bottom of the desk. He reached into the opening and felt a single sheet of parchment. He pulled it out, pushed the hidden slot back, and stood.

As Diana leaned on his arm to get a good look at the paper, Alex said, "Do you think it might show us where the…."

Doña de Ubilla cut him off. "Please, don't say anything else. I don't want to know what this is about, because whatever it is, it destroyed my family." She sat in a nearby chair, closed her eyes briefly, and sighed. When she opened her eyes again, she had a serene smile. "You know, I had no idea I could feel so good just by showing you that scrap of paper."

Alex watched in fascination as a soft rainbow-colored light suddenly shone through the museum's ceiling onto the elderly spirit. She covered her heart with her hands as her eyes grew wide with wonder. In a low voice, she said, "Something strange and wonderful is happening. My whole body is tingling in delight." She glanced at Alex and mouthed, "Thank you."

As Alex watched, she slowly turned into tiny sparkles of light. A few seconds later, she was gone, leaving him too stunned to move.

Worried that something terrible had happened, Diana shook Alex and asked, "Is everything okay?"

"Yeah," he replied. Then, in a daze, Alex turned and searched for the nearest exit. When they found their way out, a cacophony of sirens rushing to the area to deal with the collapsed tunnel greeted them.

"Come on, let's go back to where I'm staying," Diana said. "I'm filthy and can barely stand the smell of myself."

Alex stopped. "I can't go with you," he said.

"Why not?" Diana asked.

"If I go, my grandmother will send me home, or even worse, to Scotland. Finding this map is a signal that I must push on, if for no other reason, then it's the last best chance to help my sister. I mean, it's the Holy

Grail. It's got to be an object that can help her move on. Right?"

"You know, your grandmother's not the monster you make her out to be," Diana said. "Trust her for once. Come with me. I bet when she sees this map, she'll change her mind and ask you to help her find the Grail."

"I doubt it. Besides, can you imagine the trouble I'll be in if we show up looking like we do? Everyone will assume I've done some new horrible thing to you."

"Well, in a way, they'd be right. You did get us into this mess," Diana replied.

"I think it's the right next step," Jane said. "Get over yer worries, and let's go with Diana."

"But Alex does have a point in one aspect," Diana said. "We should get somewhat clean before heading back. And I know the perfect place to wash off most of this grime."

"I don't like the grin on yer face. What have ye done with the quiet, unassuming girl I used to know?" Jane asked.

"If you're willing to risk it, we can get cleaned off in the fountain back at the Plaza de España."

"I'm up for it," Alex said.

Jane rolled her eyes and motioned for Diana to lead the way.

It was nearly a half-hour walk to the plaza. Quite a few people stared at them, and a few waved their hands in front of their noses to get rid of the stench, but Alex was able to ignore them as the sights and sounds of Seville were so fascinating. As soon as they entered the park side entrance, all three started running for the inner plaza where the fountain was shooting water high into the sky.

Diana sat on the fountain's edge and surreptitiously splashed water on her face.

"Come on, is that all you're going to do?" Alex said. He looked around and, not seeing any police, slipped his pack off and jumped into the fountain. He came up a second later, sputtering with a big grin.

"I didn't mean for you to swim in it," Diana said. "You've got to get out of there, or we'll get in trouble."

"Not until ye get in, too," Jane said as she followed Alex in.

A little gust of wind reminded Diana of the sewer slime covering her. She rolled her eyes and jumped in.

Jane splashed Alex, quickly turning their outdoor bath into a full-fledged water fight until a loud whistle caught their attention. Alex looked up and saw a policeman running at them. He jumped out, picked up his backpack, and shouted, "Run."

They ran out of the main entrance to the plaza and dove into the park just outside. Weaving through the trees, Alex kept running until Jane caught his arm and gasped, "I need a breather."

Alex slowed to a walk, looked around for the police, and was grateful when he didn't see any. But he only had a moment of peace because the ankh suddenly started vibrating against his chest. Alex looked around at the people passing by but saw nothing unusual. He tried ignoring the sensation but couldn't shake the idea that his little looped cross was telling him something was wrong.

Seeing his anxious glances, Jane said, "I swear, you make me more nervous than anybody I've ever known. Now what's wrong?"

Alex absent-mindedly replied, "I don't know exactly. But I have this feeling that someone's following us."

"Maybe it's all the extra commotion for whatever's going on over by the cathedral," Diana said.

"Maybe," he replied. But they had only gone a hundred yards when Alex spun around to look behind him. He scanned the park but still didn't see anything unusual. After a minute, he gave up and turned back to Jane and Diana. "Come on. I've got an idea how to see who's following us."

They worked their way out of the park and soon found themselves near the banks of the Guadalquivir River. Then they turned and walked towards the city center until Alex found a small café. Pretending to read the menu in the window, he motioned for Jane and Diana to his side.

Alex watched in the window for several minutes but didn't see anything. He was about to give up when he noticed two rough-looking men across the street creep into the reflection. Both quickly looked away when they saw Alex staring back at them. "We've got to get out of here," he said.

"Follow me," Diana replied. "We'll lose them in the tourist crowds."

## CHAPTER 21
# TO FIGHT ANOTHER DAY

Diana led them back towards the cathedral, hoping to hide in the tourist crowds. But, instead of the hordes of people she'd hoped to find, the police had cordoned off the entire plaza. Fire trucks, police cars, and heavy equipment dotted the plaza they had walked across several hours earlier.

As she steered them through a narrow alley on the backside of the cathedral, Alex asked, "Where are we headed?"

"Because of the nature of your problems, I don't think going to the police is the best idea," Diana replied. "So, I thought we'd go to the grove's headquarters and ask your grandmother for protection."

Alex stopped. "You guys go, but I'm not. I'll figure something else out."

"It's too dangerous for ye out here," Jane said. "In the last couple of hours, one ghost locked us up, and now two thugs are chasing us. Plus, ye're so close to achieving a breakthrough for yer sister. That map could be the key."

They became so caught up in arguing their course of action that none of them saw the two men creeping up on them until they jumped out of the shadows brandishing guns. The taller man said, "If you come with us quietly, we'll go easy on you. But if you make it difficult, well...." Instead of finishing the sentence, he made a threatening gesture.

Diana shrank back, pretending to cower before the bandits while surreptitiously slipping her hand down to her pouch. Then she pulled out her talisman and quietly chanted,

*"Clouds of black, clouds of white.*
*I summon thee to show thy might.*
*Bring thy winds and bring thy might,*
*Hurl these cans and drive their flight."*

Several garbage cans flew across the alley, slamming into their attackers. Alex dropped his head and charged the nearest thug, ramming his shoulder into the man's belly. The first bandit staggered backwards and slammed into the second one, sending both to the ground. Unable to stop his momentum, Alex fell on top of them.

Jane ran over to Alex, grabbed a hand, and jerked him up. Diana grabbed his other arm and took off running, leading them back towards the Alcazar. She didn't slow down until they were in the middle of the crowd, ogling the collapsed plaza.

Hoping they'd ditched their attackers, Diana looked back and saw their assailants fighting to get to them through the crowd.

Diana motioned to Alex and Jane, ducked under the police tape, dodged between two police officers, and headed for a large yellow excavator crawling up to the damaged area. Cutting alongside the tracked equipment, she jumped over the partially collapsed pavement.

After making it across the plaza, she paused to ensure the other two were keeping up with her, then turned into one of the narrow streets surrounding the historical buildings. She went through a short tunnel, barely noticing the bronze Carmen plaque in the ground, across a small courtyard, and into the next narrow road. Diana didn't hear anything but saw two puffs of dust and some chips flying.

Diana turned right at the next intersection and started zig-zagging through a bunch of narrow streets until she came upon a major artery leading into downtown. The light turned from green to yellow, but not wanting to wait for their attackers to catch up, she darted across the road with Jane and Alex on her heels.

She glanced back and was relieved to see that the two men were caught at the light. Diana turned off the main boulevard and ducked into a narrow alleyway. Over her shoulder, she shouted, "This is crazy. How could they know about the map? We just got it."

"I don't think they're after it," Jane shouted back. "They're going after Alex, and we jest happen to be in the way."

"Do you have any ideas on how to ditch these guys? I thought about the police, but I don't think that would stop them," Diana shouted.

After several more turns, they popped out on a broad avenue with a large modern building and dozens of cars in front of it. Pointing at it, Alex said, "Over there."

"But that's the train station," Diana said, gasping for air.

"Good. There'll be lots of people inside, which means we should be able to ditch them."

They dashed across the road but were so exhausted that they slowed to a walk to climb the bridge towards the train station. Pouring sweat from the long run under the hot Castilian sun, Diana was glad to get inside the air-conditioned building and sat on a nearby bench to catch her breath.

"We can't wait out here in the open," Jane said, breathing raggedly. "Let's get in a line and mingle so it'll be harder to spot us.

Diana was too tired to argue, so she stood and shuffled towards the nearest ticket line. She was so intent on watching for their pursuers that she didn't notice bumping into a cold metal ledge.

Alex nudged her and whispered, "The man behind the counter is asking us something in Spanish. What's he saying?"

Diana pulled out her phone, turned to the cashier, and asked in fluent Spanish when the next train was leaving. After getting the information, she glanced at the giant board and saw they barely had time to make it. "Come on."

Diana rushed to their assigned gate and led them out of the air-conditioned terminal building and onto the escalator heading down to the trains. When they neared the tracks, she called over her shoulder, "We've got to hurry. We've only got a couple of minutes before our train leaves."

They ran down the remaining steps, jumped onto the train, and were still looking for their seats when the train pulled away from the station.

"Do you think they followed us?" Alex asked.

"I didn't see them get on, but who knows," Jane replied. "So, where are we going?"

"Cordoba," Diana answered. "It was the first train leaving, and it's only a half-hour train ride. There should be plenty of trains coming back to Seville, so all we have to do is get off this one and book a passage back. But first, I've got to call my mom, tell her what's going on, and ask her to call the police."

"I'm sorry about all of this," Alex said. "I never meant to get you into more danger."

Diana studied Alex for a moment. "You're not arguing? I thought you wanted to avoid your grandmother."

"I do, but as you said, I don't have a plan, so I might as well give up and go home."

When Diana finally hung up, Alex asked, "What did she say?"

"Quite a bit. The bottom line is that you and I are in big trouble. When we get back, she's sending you to Scotland, and I'm never supposed to have anything to do with you again. Of course, Jane gets a pass since she's supposed to keep an eye on you."

Alex stared out the window at the countryside, zipping by without responding.

"Did you hear what I said?" Diana asked.

"Yeah. Hates me. Dead meat. Got that."

Diana was about to argue but decided against it. The hair-raising events of the day had taken their toll on her. She closed her eyes and laid back, thinking she would rest for a few minutes and sort things out.

The next thing she noticed was the train lurching as it slowed down coming into Cordoba. It took her a moment to clear the sleepers from her eyes and realize all three had fallen asleep. She felt a pang of jealousy seeing Jane's head resting on Alex's shoulder. Then, as if she could read Diana's mind, Jane woke with a start and blushed when she noticed where she'd been sleeping.

Diana got up, exited the train, and pulled out her phone to check the train schedule to Seville. Another passenger bumped into Diana, causing her to drop her phone. It skittered across the platform and onto the tracks where a train was pulling in. She couldn't hear the crunching sound, but she could imagine it. Diana threw her hands up and screamed, "I can't believe it." She turned to Alex and shook her empty phone hand at him. "This is the third time I've ruined my phone chasing after you. I can't believe you jinxed it by calling it Kenny. I swear, if my mom forgives me and buys me another phone, I'll make her happy by keeping as far away from you as possible."

"I'm sorry," Alex said. "But now what do we do?"

"We do it the old-fashioned way," Diana said. "We'll have to go to the terminal and use your credit card to buy tickets."

"But we didn't have to pay for tickets on the way here," Alex said.

"Yeah, we did," Diana replied. "Remember when I took your credit card and put the info in my phone? Well, that's how I bought the tickets, which is why I said I was sorry earlier."

Alex grinned. "You know what that means? This incident proves that my old-fashioned methods are more reliable than your newfangled ones."

"You're hopeless," Diana retorted.

"Ye're both hopeless," Jane said. "Ye two bicker like ye're siblings. Now, let's go upstairs and get some lunch before we head back. Then we can get some return tickets."

They walked up to the main terminal, bought some sandwiches and drinks, and were just finishing their lunch when the two thugs from Seville came through the doors.

## CHAPTER 22
# CORDOBA

"Let's get out of here," Diana said as she jumped up and ran away.

Alex and Jane hurried after her but didn't catch Diana until she was outside. "What do we do?" she asked, looking around in panic.

"First of all, calm down," Jane said. "They won't attack us out in the open with all these people around. Let's find a policeman and have those men arrested."

"I don't think that'll work," Alex said. "They'll deny everything and come after us later. We need to ditch them. Diana, do you have a spell to get us out of here?"

Diana thought for a moment before saying, "No, but I've got an idea. Get close, and don't move or speak." She reached into her pouch, pulled out her talisman, and chanted under her breath,

*"Oh, sacred land of Avalon,*
*I call now on your might.*
*Help us hide from the light,*
*And keep us safe and shrouded."*

Diana hoped the spell would work but had only practiced it a couple of times in a classroom with her teachers. She saw the men come out of the station and repeated the spell more fervently. To her amazement, the station disappeared as a dark mist descended over them. She whispered, "Let's just hope nobody bumps into us."

The three stayed huddled together for several minutes until Diana saw the two men split up and run in different directions. When no one was looking, she waved her hand to dismiss the haze surrounding them. "Thank Gaia," she said. "I can't believe that spell actually worked."

"That was weird. What did you do?" Alex asked.

"It's an obscuring spell, but almost nobody uses it."

"Why not?"

"Because it creates a lot of consternation if there are people nearby. My teachers taught us this spell but recommended we never use it. So, what do we do now?" Diana asked. "We missed the train I had booked us on."

"When's the next train back to Seville?" Alex asked.

"A couple of hours from now," Diana replied. "But what do we do in the meantime? We can't wait here at the train station. It's too open, and there aren't enough people to hide amongst.

"I think it's too risky to return today, so I suggest we find a couple of rooms for the night and hole up," Jane said. "Then we go back tomorrow when they'll probably have quit looking for us."

"I'm okay with that plan," Alex said. "As long as we get something else to eat."

Diana rolled her eyes. "We just ate. You can't possibly be hungry already."

"Since I've arrived, all I've had are those bocadillos. They're just pieces of bread and thin slices of meat. I want some real food."

"We'll have to feed the beast eventually," Jane said, "but right now, we need to get out of here."

Since the two thugs had gone in opposite directions, Diana split the difference and led them into the narrow confines of the old part of the city."

Wanting to stay out of sight as much as possible, they found a small café and went in. While Jane ordered takeout, Diana borrowed Jane's phone and looked for an Airbnb room. She found a two-bedroom apartment a half-hour away and led them to it as soon as the food was ready to go.

After they'd eaten, Diana said, "I've been thinking and believe we should call my mom and have her get the police to escort us back to Seville."

"I've got a different thought," Jane said. "Of course, we need to let your mom know we're safe, but I don't think we should tell her where we are just yet."

"Why not?" Diana asked.

"I think we have a leak in the order, and am unsure who we can trust. By now, dozens know about Elizabeth's quest to find the Grail. Unfortunately, it also appears that one too many people know Alex found the journal. Otherwise, why would those thugs chase us only after he shows up? And there's no way they could know about the map because they were pursuing us within minutes of us finding it."

"There's a flaw with your theory," Diana said. "How could they know he was coming? He didn't know until he ditched you in Edinburgh yesterday." She snapped her fingers and said, "Unless they've been tracking him from the States."

"You know I'm right here," Alex said. "You're talking about me as if I'm some inanimate object."

"So, what do you suggest?" Diana asked.

"Well, I agree with Jane and think we should hole up here in Cordoba for another day, then return to Seville." Seeing both girls staring at him, Alex hastily added, "You look at me like I'm crazy, but I'm guessing that they think we're scared out of our minds and will do something rash – like run."

"We are scared," Diana said.

"We all are, but I bet they'll be watching the train and bus stations like hawks because I also think you're right, and they've been following me since I left home. They probably have people spying on where Grandma and the others are staying. Knowing we've been running from them half the day, what are the odds of them thinking we'll stop running and hang around here?" Seeing Diana wavering, he said, "Besides, you say you've wanted to see this city. Well, let's do it. They'll never expect we're sightseeing in a million years."

Diana looked at Alex in amazement. "I can't believe you're suggesting we do something I want to do. In some ways, this sounds too good to be true. From what I've read, this city has an interesting blend of Islamic and Christian cultures, especially the cathedral. We could catch a bus and go to the Medinat al-Zahra ruins outside of town tomorrow morning, then come back to see the Mezquita Cathedral, the old town walls, the Roman ruins, the gate tower overlooking one of the bridges, and all sorts of other cool things. There's an added bonus for me if we go sightseeing here – I get to add two more UNESCO sites to my list." She grinned and added, "Besides, Cordoba also has an Inquisition Museum."

Alex sat up with a grin. "Now you're talking. When do we go?"

"As for that last place," Jane said, "I'd rather not go there. We barely escaped from a real one in Seville, so I have no desire to see more torture devices."

"Good point," Diana replied. "We'll skip that."

"I'm curious. What do you think your mom will say about all this, Diana?" Alex asked.

"I'm sure she won't be happy," Jane said, "but I'll talk with Lady Yvaine and tell her about our situation. I'm sure she'll support our choices and smooth things over with Sophie and Elizabeth."

As they stepped onto a tour bus the next morning, Alex asked, "Why are you so excited to see this Medinat-whatever, Diana? It sounded like there are all sorts of cool things right here."

"It's the history. Muslim forces conquered the Iberian Peninsula a few centuries after the fall of the Western Roman Empire. After the Gauls stopped them from expanding into the rest of Europe, they settled in Spain. For the next several centuries, Christians, Jews, and Muslims got along fairly well. As a result, art, philosophy, the sciences, and architecture flourished. The Moors were so successful here that they became a challenger to the Caliphate in Baghdad and built an entire royal complex on the hills outside the city over a thousand years ago. Then, less than a hundred years later, they left and moved their capital to Granada."

An hour later, they reached an overlook of the ancient Muslim city. "It's a bunch of ruins," Alex said. "I thought it was going to be a real city."

"You're hopeless," Diana said before heading down the steps.

As they stood on the far side of the ruins sometime later, looking out over the hazy plains below, Alex said, "Okay, I'll admit it. This place was way cooler than I thought it would be."

A man standing nearby pointed to the southwest. "Kids, you might be interested to know that you can see Almodóvar Castle on a clear day."

"I saw a big castle on the hillside when we came in on the train yesterday," Jane said. "Is that the one they filmed some of *Game of Thrones* at?"

"Si," replied the man.

"I wish we had time to see it," Jane said. "It looked so interesting."

"You're starting to sound like Diana," Alex said. "And anyway, I hate to burst your bubble, but we're running out of time. We should be heading back if we're going to catch our bus back to town."

Diana sighed and turned to Alex. "At least you're good for one thing. You get into trouble in the coolest places."

After lunch in the city, they headed down to the Guadalquivir River, crossed over a massive stone bridge, and climbed the steps in the gate tower to get a view of downtown Cordoba. A light breeze and heavy clouds made it so pleasant on the battlements that Diana said, "I wish we could spend more time here. It's so beautiful."

"Beautiful? It's a desert here," Jane said.

"I understand what Diana's saying. I grew up at the edge of the plains and loved gazing out at the landscape with nothing to see for miles and miles," Alex said. "It's ...."

"It gives you a sense of peace and freedom," Diana interjected.

"Well, give me trees and water," Jane said. "But right now, let's go see the Cathedral."

They toured the Mezquita-Cathedral in silence as the inside was a fascinating blend of Moorish architecture and Gothic Catholic Church trappings, including almost a thousand red and white arches. Unfortunately, the clouds had thickened by the time they'd exited, turning dark grey. It soon started raining and thundering, sending them scurrying for the giant glass and metal train station.

Sopping wet and having almost an hour before their train left for Seville, they got food at one of the station's restaurants and were sitting down to eat when Diana spotted the two men chasing them the day before, standing near the doors leading to the trains below. She nudged Alex and hissed, "They're here."

"I can't believe this," he said. How'd they find us?"

"I don't think they found us. I think they've been waiting all this time," Jane said. "The bigger question is, what do we do?"

Alex groaned. "You guys probably aren't going to like this, but I have an idea. The next train leaves in ten minutes. Diana, if you can get us tickets for the next train, we'll take it. They won't dare attack us in a security line, not with armed guards patrolling the terminal. And I'm sure they don't have tickets, so they can't get to the train platforms fast enough. Then, when we get to the next city, we hop a train back to Seville. There's no way they can keep up with us."

"I think we'll have to come up with a new plan," Jane said. "They have to be working for someone with lots of resources because these guys are relentless."

"Okay, but now's our chance to escape," Alex said. "We can figure out the next steps on the train."

"Brilliant," Diana said. "That sounds like one of your typical plans."

"Do you have a better idea?" Alex asked. "If so, you better hurry because the clock is ticking."

Diana hesitated for only a few seconds before thrusting her hand out to Jane and asking for her phone. She was just finishing the reservations when they reached the security checkpoint. Seeing the two men looking around in confusion, she pulled out her talisman and pointed it towards the two men. The mischievous side she'd suppressed for so long in the order popped out, and she chanted,

*"I call upon the ancient spirits,*

*To manifest my will times three.*

*Listen to me and abide,*

*Shove that can in their side."*

She paused before getting on the escalator and watched as the large trash can she was focusing on flew across the floor, knocking both men to the ground. With a smile, she turned and ran down the escalator steps, stepping onto the train a moment before the doors closed.

## CHAPTER 23
# TOLEDO

As the train pulled out of the station, Alex looked for the two men but didn't see them. Turning back to Diana, he said, "I'm sorry for having gotten you guys into yet another mess. I've been in a lot of hairy situations over the last year, but those guys are scaring the wits out of me."

Diana smiled and patted his knee. "That's sweet, but you and I both know you don't have any wits to scare."

"Good one," Alex replied, grinning. "But seriously, I don't know what I'd have done without your help these last two days."

"It's our order's mission to find things like the Grail," Diana said. "And, since you keep finding things like that Grail map, I'd be breaking my vows if I just let you go off on your own. I have to help try to recover the objects."

Jane stuck a finger in her mouth and pretended to throw up. "Be honest, Diana. It's not about duty. Ye're loving these adventures. I've never seen ye smile this much in all the years I've known ye."

"Enough about the mushy stuff," Alex said. "Where are we going?"

"Madrid," Diana replied.

"Madrid! That's in the middle of the country?"

"I'm surprised you know where it is."

Alex blushed. "I happened to see a map in the train station. Otherwise, you're right. I'd have no clue where it is."

Watching the countryside flashing by, Diana looked up at a digital readout at the front of the car and exclaimed, "Wow! We're going 300 km/hr."

"What's that in miles per hour?" Alex asked.

"200 mph. At this rate, it'll take less than three hours to get there, but it means we can't get back until tomorrow morning. I just hope you have enough money to pay for all these trips, Alex. This one cost almost fifty euros for each ticket."

Alex waved the concern aside. "Don't worry, we'll be fine. What I'm wondering, though, is how we're getting back to Seville without those guys tailing us. They seem to have tracking devices on us because there's no way they could've found us when we don't even know where we're going."

"They don't," a new voice said. "They just have incredible amounts of resources."

Alex jumped when he saw his sister floating in the aisle. "Deb!" he shouted.

"Yer sister's here?" Jane asked, jumping out of her seat. "Where?"

Remembering they were in public, Alex ignored Jane's question and, in a lowered voice, asked, "Where have you been?"

"Well, hi to you too," Deborah replied.

"I'm sorry. I'm a little frazzled because of what's been happening, but I'm glad you're here, Sis."

Deborah smiled and sat across from Alex, who was squeezed between Jane and Diana when both girls switched seats so they could hear her. "I don't know how you do it, but you've really gotten yourself into a mess this time."

"What's going on?" Diana asked.

"Hold on a minute. I want to find out why my sister is here." Turning to Deborah, Alex asked, "Where have you been all this time? I've been hoping you'd moved on."

"I wish, but it looks like it's still not in the cards for me. Anyway, when I said earlier that you'd gotten into a mess, I didn't mean just now. I'm talking about back on Blackbeard's Island when the pirates attacked you the second time. I was able to use my magic to get away, but something stopped me when I tried to find you. By the time I figured you'd gone to Salem, you'd already left for your home. Then, when I tried to see you at Grandpa's, the spirit Indians on the reservation wouldn't let me near you. So, I left for a while. When I returned, you'd already left for Scotland. And silly me, I thought you'd be at Stormhold. I finally tracked you down in Seville but decided I should follow those men chasing you rather than going with you. I don't know who those guys are, but they have some serious money. They've been able to keep catching up to you because they have a helicopter at their disposal."

"A helicopter! At least that explains their speed. What else have you learned?" Diana asked.

"Well, this is just speculation, but I don't think they're after the Grail. I haven't seen any signs of them trailing my Grandma or hanging around the grove's headquarters. All they seem to care about is my brother. Which is why, after you ditched them in Cordoba, I came to warn you."

"That would indicate they're part of some bigger organization with lots of resources. Which begs the question – why are they following you? Despite what your sister said, I can see only one answer – the Grail," Diana said. "But I don't get why now. We've had the journal since last summer but only got the map yesterday."

"And don't forget about Torquemada and those other two ghosts we saw in Seville's cathedral," Jane said. "It can't be coincidence. It's got to be the Grail."

Alex shook his head. "I don't know. I think this is all a continuation of what I first experienced going to Lamanai and has to do with the Maqlû and that Pythia woman."

"I know ye've said ye've heard her name bandied about, but that was a role title for a series of women a couple of thousand years ago. I did a quick search when ye first mentioned that name and learned that the average number of people born each year with that name worldwide is essentially zero. Which means it's useless information to us."

"Well, we can't do anything about it now," Alex said as he turned back to look out the window.

He didn't join in the rest of the conversation until Diana roused him as the train slowed. "Jane and I thought it'd be better to get off in Toledo. Those guys probably know this train is heading to Madrid, so I doubt they'd guess we'd get off here. Madrid is a much more likely spot for us to hide in."

A few minutes later, as he stepped into the Toledo train station, Alex was surprised at how different it was from the stations in Seville and Cordoba. It was much smaller but more ornate and decorated in the Moorish style. He and Jane stepped outside and took a minute to adjust to the bright Spanish sunlight.

When Diana joined them a few moments later, she said, "Hey, I know I sound like a broken record, but since there are so many trains going between Madrid, here, and Seville, would you be okay wandering around the old section of Toledo for a bit? It's another UNESCO site, and we're so close. Besides, I don't see those two men, so we should be safe."

Alex didn't hear what she said as his sister called him.

"I'll scout the area," Deborah said. "After seeing how those guys move around, I don't feel comfortable with you out in the open." Before Alex could respond, she'd flown off.

"So, what do you think?" Diana asked.

Seeing both Jane and Diana looking questioningly at him, Alex said, "What?"

"Weren't you listening?" Diana asked.

Alex shook his head. "I'm sorry. Deb was letting me know she's going to scout the area for those two men. What were you saying?"

"I was just wondering if you'd be okay if we look around Toledo for a bit. There are plenty of trains back to Seville."

"Sure," Alex replied. "We'll be less obvious blending in with all the tourists walking around in the city, then waiting here at the station."

Fifteen minutes later, they were at the entrance to an old Roman bridge. A castle overlooked one end of it, while a large stone tower stood on the far end, guarding the entrance to the city of Toledo rising above it.

Diana launched into the bridge's history, but Alex didn't hear what she said. He was so enamored with the stunning beauty of the river gorge that he didn't pay any attention to a helicopter landing on the main street they'd just come from. Nor did he notice it take off just seconds later. Diana and Jane headed towards the city while Alex leaned onto the stone railing and gazed at the rocky gorge cut through the millennia by the Tagus River far below.

He was so relaxed that he didn't react immediately when the ankh suddenly started thumping against his chest. Before he knew what was happening, a hand covered his mouth, and an arm wrapped around him with an iron grip. His eyes flared open in horror as his attacker lifted him and tossed him over the stone railing. As he fell towards the rushing river far below, he briefly saw his sister hovering in mid-air at the end of the bridge, seemingly talking to herself while looking directly at him.

## CHAPTER 24
# A QUICK DROP AND A SODDEN STOP

Alex felt like he fell forever towards the roiling green waters. Halfway down, though, a large gust of wind pushed him up, and for a moment, he thought his sister's incantation would save him. But an instant later, he resumed his descent. As the wind whistled around him, he struggled to straighten up, barely managing to close his legs and clap his hands to his sides before hitting the water. His neck snapped back so hard that he felt like his head had hit a wall.

It had happened so fast that he didn't worry about the river being too shallow until after his feet touched the river bottom. Luckily, his knees only partially buckled. Alex pushed up hard, and moments later, his head shot briefly above the surface before the river tugged at him, trying to pull him down.

Waves kept rolling over his head, reminding him of his experience of being adrift in the ocean a year earlier. He tried calling for help, but no sooner did he open his mouth than he hit a small tree floating in the river, knocking the air out of him, and causing him to swallow a mouthful of water. He choked and nearly vomited but overcame his gag reflexes and started swimming for the shore. But with the wind cord on his Tilley tugging at his throat, and his soggy clothes and pack weighing him down, he made no progress.

Alex heard a roaring sound and knew it wasn't a good sign. He redoubled his efforts, kicking and pulling harder, but for every stroke he took to the side, the river swept him downstream double the length. Seconds later, he smashed into a rock that sent him whirling back into the center of the river. His right leg hit something hard, causing him to spin around then shoot down a gently sloped concrete spillway.

He tumbled into the swirling pool at the base of the dam and struggled to get to the surface as the thundering river falls kept pushing him under. When he finally broke free, he was so tired that it was all he could do to stay above water.

The river pushed him swiftly along, but it wasn't as turbulent as above the dam. He managed to keep his head above water long enough to see a relatively flat spot in the gorge just beyond a bridge. Alex struck out for it and felt immense relief when the river washed him onto a stone walkway, where he ground to a halt. The waters kept wanting to push him downstream, but the stones were rough enough that they provided resistance against the river. With one last surge of energy, he got up on his hands and knees and crawled a short distance to where the river was only a few inches deep before plopping down again to rest.

Despite the hot Toledo sun, Alex shivered as shock set in. He struggled to stand up but was so exhausted that he managed only a few steps before collapsing onto a nearby stone path. His head started spinning, and his vision blurred. A moment later, he blacked out.

When he woke, he thought he'd dreamed about falling off the bridge and pulled the cool, clean sheets up to his chin, wiggling his fingers and toes to ensure he wasn't dreaming.

A balding man with a fringe of white hair around his head, wearing glasses and a black cassock with black buttons down the middle, walked to Alex's bedside and took his pulse. The man looked him over carefully, lifting each eyelid before gently pulling up a bandage on his head.

Alex pushed the man's hand away and tried sitting but groaned and collapsed back onto his pillow before he got halfway up.

"That was a nasty concussion you got," the unknown man said. "How are you feeling, my son?"

"Who are you?" Alex asked.

"Relax, you're safe. My name is Father Torri."

"How did I get here?" Before the priest could answer, Alex blurted out, "Where are my friends? Are they okay?"

"Relax, they're fine. They're in the next room, sleeping. You know you've got true friends there. They've taken turns staying up with you half the night, especially the red-headed one. I finally convinced her to get some sleep only half an hour ago."

"How long have I been out?"

"It's been about twelve hours. I happened to be nearby and saw you fall in. I was just starting to tend to you when your friends came running up."

"Why am I here and not in a hospital?"

"The only thing they could have done that your friend hasn't, is run a CT scan," the priest said. "Besides, the Bandruí have not been discrete enough. We learned of your discovery in the Americas last year and know your grandmother has launched a search for the Grail."

"Why are you telling me this? If you're like everyone else, you only want it for yourself."

The priest smiled and asked, "Would you like some food? I imagine you're famished."

Alex's stomach took the opportunity to remind him that he hadn't eaten in almost a day. "Yes, please."

Father Torri brought his cleaned clothes in and left the room, saying, "When you're dressed, come out to the main room, but be quiet. I have something I wish to talk to you privately about."

It took Alex longer to dress than he expected, as every muscle seemed to scream in pain as he climbed back into his clothes. Walking was even more painful as he felt as if his entire body had gone through a wringer then pounded dry.

Father Torri saw Alex's discomfort sitting down at the dining table and said, "You took quite a beating in the river, so you need to take it easy for a few days."

"I can't," Alex replied. "We need to get back to my grandma's and let her know Diana and Jane are all right."

"Don't worry. Your friends have already contacted your grandmother. She knows you're safe and that I'll send you back as soon as your head has healed."

The priest placed a bowl of hot cinnamon oatmeal with fruit and a glass of goat's milk in front of Alex. "It isn't fancy, but it'll be good for you. When I see you moving around more easily, I'll give you more substantial food."

"Regretfully, I've heard that line too many times in the last year," Alex growled.

Father Torri sat silently as Alex ate. When he'd finished, Alex pushed his chair back from the table. "I don't know how to thank you for your hospitality, but we've got to get going when Jane and Diana wake up."

With an intensity that surprised Alex, the priest leaned over the table and said, "We only have a little time before your friends wake up, so I'll get to the point. I know you have a map because I saw it while washing your clothes."

Seeing Alex start, he hastily added, "It's all right. I only glanced at it and didn't copy it. But I doubt whether that, or the journal, will help you find what you're looking for. So, trust your instincts but no one else – even your friends. There's much more at stake than you know."

"How do you know what I'm trying to find? And why should I trust you?"

Father Torri didn't answer at once. He sat for some time, staring at the floor. When he did speak, it was in a voice barely above a whisper. "I'm part of a brotherhood of men and women who have devoted our lives to seeking out and safeguarding Christ's sacred relics – things like the real Shroud of Turin, the Crown of Thorns, the Spear of Destiny, and so on. We have sought the Holy Grail for two millennia but have come up empty-handed. You've probably heard stories about some of our members – King Arthur and the Knights Templar. Their stories were based on our members searching for those holy artifacts."

"They're just tales," Alex said.

Father Torri shook his head. "I'm afraid not."

"But didn't someone like Galahad already find the Grail?"

"So, the tale goes, but he never returned from his quest. We're not sure what happened, but interestingly, sightings of the Grail suddenly stopped and remained that way until you came along."

"Why are you telling me this?" Alex asked.

"It wasn't chance that I was at the river yesterday. You came to our attention last summer when you found a journal we didn't know existed. Some people in our order think you're the one who will find it. Others, well, let's just say they're uncertain. I'm assigned to tail you and am trying to figure out what you're up to.

"You mean they fear me?"

Father Torri dipped his head. "Just so, but I'm not one of them. I've done some research on you and am hopeful that you might help us. It's why I've come to ask you to bring the Grail, if you should find it, to us in Avalon so that we may protect it for eternity." Seeing Alex look at him skeptically, Father Torri said, "You're right not to trust me blindly, but at least think about it. If you are who I hope you are, I'm confident you'll do the right thing."

The priest heard one of the girls stirring in the next room and stopped talking. A minute later, Jane appeared with her hair completely disheveled. She smiled sleepily at Alex, then stretched. "I'm so glad ye're awake," she said. "I was worried sick about ye."

Alex shifted his chair to give Jane more room at the table and said, "Father Torri told me what you guys did for me. I can't thank you enough – again."

Diana entered, looked at his empty bowl, and said, "Breakfast. I'm starved."

He noticed she had an ugly purple bruise on her forehead and was walking with a limp. "You look terrible," Alex said. "What happened to you?"

"I thought I told you never to say things like that to a girl," Diana replied as she winked at Jane.

Alex didn't realize she was kidding and turned beet red.

Diana took pity on him. "Relax. I'm joking. Besides, have you looked at yourself in a mirror yet?"

"No, do I look that bad?"

She waved the question off and limped over to the table. Alex watched as she slowly lowered herself into her chair. "Are you all right?" he asked.

Diana winced as she sat down. "I've felt better. I was running down the hillside to reach you when I fell. I must have banged into every rock and boulder on the way down before I fell into the river. I barely made it out and don't see how you survived a fall from the bridge. How in the world did you fall in?"

"I had help," Alex replied.

"What! Did those thugs do this to you?" Diana asked.

"I'm not sure who did it because they came up behind me. But I'm guessing you're right."

"Which, again, raises the question of why they're going after you," Diana said.

Jane gave her a quelling look, but Alex said, "Father Torri already knows about your order's search for the Grail. He said there's a leak in your order. But it can't be for the map. Otherwise, they'd have searched me first, then tossed me."

"Good point. So, what do we do now?" Diana asked.

"This could be a blessing in disguise," Jane said. Seeing the questioning looks on Alex and Diana's faces, she added, "It means they're probably not going to be chasing us since they think you're dead. I say we ask your grandmother for a ride back since it wouldn't be wise to take public transportation."

"I still suggest you rest here, at least for today," Father Torri said. "Alex is in no shape to be traveling around the country right now, and I can take you into Ávila first thing tomorrow morning, where you can catch a ride home."

Diana smiled. "You know, every once in a while, good things come from hanging around you, Alex."

"What good things are you talking about? I don't see any," Alex said.

"Are you kidding? Here I am in Spain, surrounded by all this history and natural wonders, and all my mom, your grandmother, and Señora de Leon want to do is talk about that book you found. If you hadn't pulled me into your latest escapade, I'd never have seen Cordoba or Toledo. And now, we get to see Ávila."

"I'm sorry. What's in Ávila?" Alex asked.

"It's only one of the most fairytale-like cities in the world," Diana replied. "There is a gigantic stone wall surrounding the city that's almost a mile and a half long with nearly a hundred huge turrets. Heck, even the church is part of the wall system. It's so amazing that I thought it was fake the first time I saw a picture of it."

"Is it another one of your UNESCO World Heritage Sites?" When she nodded, Alex said, "I have to admit that they've all been really cool places so far." Alex saw that Diana was looking at him expectantly. It took him a moment before he realized what she was driving at and said, "I'm up for touring Ávila before we go back to Seville. But one of you will have to tell my grandma."

He furtively touched the ankh and felt its reassuring pulse. Alex tried to get out of his chair but was too stiff to stand up. He sat down and said, "But I definitely need a day to rest before touring it."

# CHAPTER 25
# WHEN WE DIFFER

Elizabeth and Señora de Leon had debated the meaning of every page in the Grail journal for weeks. They'd often had to do deep dives – searching for information on long-forgotten events and places that no longer existed on maps. Occasionally, they'd even called in outside resources to help with some of the journal's more cryptic notes. It had been difficult work at times as they had to sort out two thousand years of history from distorted legends. Then, a single phone call made all the work seem like a wasted effort.

With a stunned look, Elizabeth put her phone on the coffee table, sat back, and stared at the bubbling fountain in the courtyard. Señora de Leon sat up. "Is everything all right?" she asked. "You seem to have gone through a roller coaster of emotions the last few days. First, you were worried about the girls. Then, you were jubilant. But now, you're back to looking like you've seen a ghost. What's wrong?"

"That was Jane again. There's been an accident that has forced them to delay their return another day. She also suggested I invite my grandson to help us because he's found a new lead."

Señora de Leon shook her head. "There is no way I'm letting that boy in my house."

"You don't understand," Elizabeth said. "Jane believes my grandson has found a map of the Grail's hiding place in Romania. Think about how many Eastern European clues we've rejected in our research

– because they don't fit our paradigm that the Grail is somewhere in Western Europe. This map might make our work much easier."

"Surely you're not going to listen to that girl. Why, she's not even truly one of us."

"I know, but Lady Yvaine trusts her implicitly. She's a level-headed girl with a keen mind who's dedicated to our cause. Diana is also supportive of the idea."

"I respect you, Señora Adler, but I will never trust anything your grandson says or does. And I will not condone any action that involves him in our affairs."

"I understand your position, but I must check out this lead. I can't ignore the possibility that he might have found something crucial. If it's not promising, then I've only lost a day. But you should know I'm beginning to fear this journal won't help us as much as we'd hoped. I feel like we're no closer to finding the Grail than King Arthur's knights. If my suspicions are right, then you may want to reconsider your position about him helping us."

"I don't understand why you think your grandson can find it when no one else has been able to. I'm starting to revert to my original thoughts and doubt the Grail exists."

Elizabeth looked at Señora de Leon and said, "There's something I haven't told you yet because I have no proof." She took a deep breath and exhaled. "The reason I think we should consider asking my grandson for help is because I believe he might have found one of the Maqlû."

Señora de Leon's mouth gaped open. "I knew you had stopped all operations in Lamanai, but I thought it was because you believed it was a false clue. Why haven't you said anything before?"

"Because I'm not sure what the truth is," Elizabeth replied. "He keeps hiding things from me and has never admitted to anything. The only information I have is what Diana and Jane have told me, and they're not sure either."

Seeing Señora de Leon glaring at her, Elizabeth said, "Fine. I'll tell Sophie she's to go to Ávila to pick up her daughter and ensure she sends my grandson and Jane back to Stormhold. But, when Sophie returns, I plan to take that map Jane has told me about and leave immediately for Romania in the hope that it will build on our work here."

Lucrecia sighed. "You're a stubborn woman, Elizabeth Adler, but I suppose there's no harm in you attempting this. People have searched for the Grail for millennia with less to go on than you have. May Gaia bless your work."

# CHAPTER 26
# ÁVILA

As soon as she awoke the next day, Diana went to Alex's room and prodded him awake. "Come on. If we're going to see any of the city before your grandma picks us up, we've got to get going."

Alex blinked his eyes open and said, "Fine, but you have to promise me that you'll take it easy as I still ache all over."

She smiled brightly and said, "Breakfast is ready, so hurry up."

After breakfast, they all crammed into the priest's Biscúter. The beat-up old car was so small that Alex and Diana had to crawl into a tiny seat in the back while Jane squeezed into the passenger seat for the trip into town. Father Torri stopped at one of the main gates on Ávila's historic medieval wall to let them out. "I'll find a parking space and meet you at the Puerta de San Vincente gate as soon as I can." Seeing a questioning look on Diana's face, he said, "It's easy to find. You can either go through this gate and wind your way to the right through the city or walk around the outside and turn left when you get to the end of this wall. You can't miss the entrance. It's also the closest place to get tickets to climb up on the battlements."

When they reached the main gate a few minutes later, Diana looked across the city plaza and said, "Hey, before we go in, let's tour that church. The window at the top looks interesting, plus the church is so simple versus all the cathedrals we've seen that I'm interested in checking it out."

"Why don't you two see it?" Alex said. "I'm going to limit my walking around, so I'll head up to the battlements."

"Okay, but we'll need some money to get our tickets to join ye," Jane said. "And don't go too far. We need to be able to find ye because it's a big place, and we don't have much time to spend here."

Alex gave them twenty euros, then walked through the enormous front gate of Avila as Jane and Diana headed across the plaza. After buying his ticket, he headed up a set of steep, narrow steps to the parapet. He went to the outer wall, looked for Diana and Jane on the city's plaza far below, and quickly spotted Jane's ginger-colored hair. He was about to call out to them, but a gust of wind nearly blew his hat off, forcing him to turn away and pull the wind cord down over his chin.

Unsure which way to go, he saw a large, boxy-looking cathedral supported by flying buttresses tied into the crenellated wall off to his left. To his right, he saw a range of mountains in the distance that reminded him of the front range of the Rockies and followed the wall around to get a better view. He considered climbing into each turret along the way but decided to wait until Jane and Diana rejoined him.

The three-meter-wide walkway led him past a large circular fountain in the courtyard below, through a curved tunnel, and turned to go along the south wall. Alex was surprised when the wall ended a short distance further on, but he shrugged and climbed up into the last accessible turret on that side. He was about to lean out one of the merlons when he felt the ankh beating wildly against his chest.

Alex whirled around and saw Torquemada plus the two well-dressed ghosts he'd seen in the Seville Cathedral's dungeon.

"I see now that I should have listened more closely to that demon witch," Torquemada said. "She was right. You're quite a resourceful heretic. I don't know how you escaped from the dungeons, but you're a danger to our plans and must die."

Trying to buy time, and with a lot more bravado than he felt, Alex said, "You know you should watch more movies as the bad guy always talks too much right before they die."

"You can't hurt me, for I'm already dead, but I can end your worthless life," Torquemada replied as he reached into his tunic and pulled out a sickly-looking whitish-grey hand.

Alex laughed. "What are you going to do? Beat me with that putrid thing?"

Torquemada's eyes narrowed. "In my day, my presence alone would send heretics like you fleeing for their worthless lives. Soon, you'll see why." Raising the grisly-looking object, he said, "This is my hand of glory. All I have to do is touch you with it, and it will cause you so much pain you'll be begging me to kill you quickly."

Alex couldn't help but laugh. "You're just like all the other holier-than-thou people my dad used to rant about. Preaching against the very thing they do. You're just a big hypocrite."

It took Torquemada a moment to recover from Alex's unexpected verbal attack. His face turned red as he clenched his magical hand. "How dare you. I did not rise from a family of conversos to earn the trust of the most holy Catholic Monarchs, Isabella and Ferdinand, only to have you mock me."

"I've heard what you three did – torturing and killing innocent Spaniards in the name of purifying your country. It's almost assuredly why you're stuck here in the afterlife."

"How dare you insult Their Majesties," Torquemada screamed.

"Oh, that's who those two are. Well, they're losers just like you," Alex said as he backed away.

Torquemada raised his hand of glory and shouted, "Die, infidel!" The ankh flared and threw a crackling force field around Alex just as the spirit lunged with his magical hand.

The ghost hit the force field and bounced off, flying across the turret and onto the walkway beyond. Torquemada shook his head and warily advanced toward Alex. "I see I keep underestimating you, but no matter, I will still send you to hell."

With no weapons, Alex slipped off his pack and held it in one hand. As Torquemada rushed towards him, he swung it like a bat to clobber the spirit priest. He missed the priest but knocked the hand of glory free.

Both dove for the magical hand, skittering across the stone floor – reaching it at the same time. A wave of cold passed over Alex, but a second later, the now familiar feeling of an energy surge built up inside Alex, causing the hand of glory to start sizzling. An energy bolt shot out of his hand and blasted Torquemada across the turret and over the walls of the old medieval fortress.

Alex lay on the stone, watching Torquemada sailing into the distance for only a second. Some movement to his side brought his attention to the two remaining ghosts. He raised himself on one elbow, but both vanished before he could stand up. Relieved at having survived, he lay back down and stared at the clouds scudding by.

He felt something jump on his chest, immediately followed by a rough tongue licking his chin. Alex looked down and saw Sadie sitting on his chest, a concerned look in her eyes. Images began flashing through Alex's mind, but they were too confusing to make sense of.

A familiar voice called out, "Unbelievable. We leave you alone for a few minutes, tell you to stay put, and what do we find? You playing around on the ground with another stray cat," Diana said. "Although I have to say, except for the coloring, it looks a lot like the one I saw you with in Seville."

Jane pushed Diana aside and rushed to Alex's side. "That's not important right now. I think he's hurt."

Sadie jumped off and ran away as Alex struggled to sit up. He gave up when Jane pushed him down. "Take it easy for a minute. It looks like you've had some sort of shock. Your hair is sticking out, there's dust all over you, and your eyes are dilated. What's happened?"

He grinned weakly. "Just taking care of some business from Seville. I'll tell you more about it on our tour of these walls. It's been a real blast up here so far."

# CHAPTER 27
# TO BE LOCKED OUT

Diana looked down at her watch for the hundredth time that morning and sighed. "We should get going, as Elizabeth will be at the front gate soon."

Alex began fidgeting as they waited.

"Do ye have to go to the bathroom?" Jane asked.

Alex blushed. "No. I'm having second thoughts about giving the map away. Like, what if the Grail causes as many problems as the Maqlû? How can we be sure that your order will safeguard it correctly? And what if someone else is supposed to protect it," he said, remembering Father Torri's comments.

"Like who?" Diana asked.

He was glad he didn't have to answer when he heard an unwelcome voice calling Diana across the plaza.

A few seconds later, Sophie rushed up, grabbed her daughter's hand, and started pulling her back the way she'd come. "Come on. We're heading back to Seville."

"But what about Alex and Jane, Mom?"

"They're not coming with us. Elizabeth tried getting the others to accept him but failed because nobody wanted to work with her if her grandson was involved. So, they're going back to Stormhold," Sophie said while glaring at Alex. "Lady Yvaine is taking care of them."

"But, Mom, that makes no sense. Alex is the one who found the journal you're using, and now he's found this," Diana said, waving the Grail map.

Sophie hesitated, then grabbed the old document from her daughter's hand. "You three run off, get into all sorts of trouble, then say it's because men were chasing you for this thing. Do you know how implausible that sounds? This map is probably about as useful as that *Sibylline Book* he found."

"Yes, but as I told Elizabeth, we shouldn't rule out the chance that it's the real deal," Jane said.

Sophie glared at Alex standing a short distance away, before unfolding the map and glancing down at it. "Tell me again, how did you get this?"

Seeing the pleading look on Diana's face, Jane said, "It's like I told Lady Yvaine and Elizabeth. It was pure luck. We were looking around the General Archives of the Indies when Alex started messing with this old desk. He thought something was off, so I knelt and found a secret drawer. I know we should've returned it to the museum, but when I saw what it was, I figured it was too important to leave behind. To prove my point, two men started following us as soon as we left the building. We weren't able to ditch them until yesterday. Look, I know ye don't want Alex around, but I believe he can help us find the Grail. Jest look at the map. If I remember right, the name on it is the same as the one in the journal. And those men who chased us for the last two days must think it's the real deal. Otherwise, they wouldn't have kept chasing us like they did."

Sophie seemed to relent a little. "I have no idea if this map is legitimate, but it sounds like someone thinks it might be. But if it's just the map they're after, why didn't they steal it rather than toss him off a bridge?"

"I'll be the first to admit that it doesn't all add up," Jane replied. "But something's going on."

Sophie went quiet and seemed to be in deep thought until she shook her head to rouse herself. "You're right. It can't be a coincidence that someone attacked you right after you found this map. If we're to find the Grail before anyone else does, we'll have to assume they're watching all our movements and become more unpredictable."

Sophie grabbed Diana's hand and started walking away. "Hurry. We've got a plane to catch."

"Are you just going to leave Jane and Alex here?" Diana asked.

"I forgot." Sophie stopped, reached into her purse, and pulled out a wad of Euros, which she thrust at Alex. "This should take care of your immediate needs. Lady Yvaine will take care of the rest. I hope you take this, go home, and never bother anyone in our order again. You invite trouble, and this mission is too important to let you screw it up."

She started walking away again, then paused and looked back at Jane. "You can come with us if you want."

Jane shook her head. "My responsibility is to look after Alex. Lady Yvaine will understand."

"Just as well," Sophie said, "because you make everyone in the order uncomfortable."

Jane didn't say anything until Sophie and Diana were out of sight when she turned to Alex and, with a straight face, said, "That went well, I thought."

Alex burst out laughing. "You know, I'm actually relieved at not having to be around a bunch of people who don't trust me. So, now, what do we do?"

"Isn't it obvious?" Jane replied. "We go after the Grail."

"But they have the map."

"Why should that stop ye? Besides, we have an advantage over them." She tapped him on his chest and said, "We have ye, and I'll take ye over that map any day."

Alex didn't know what to say.

Jane continued, "I believe it's more important than ever to search for the Grail – not for Deborah's sake, but for whatever else is going on. Whether ye like it or not, people keep coming after ye. So, if yer to survive, I believe ye must take the initiative."

"But we only have the clothes we're wearing and nothing else."

"We have yer credit cards and that wad of cash. We can get whatever else we need on the way. Besides, ye need to look at this on the bright side. Would ye rather be here with me and free, or with Sophie and yer grandmother?"

"Good point. But where should we go?"

"Romania, at least Diana said that's where the journal leads them to believe it is. Plus, the map ye found also indicated Romania as a good starting point."

Both were so deep in thought that neither one noticed Father Torri had come up and was standing to one side. He cleared his throat and said, "I agree with Jane."

"What all did ye hear?" Jane asked.

"Relax. I'm not going to tell anyone what you've been discussing. But, if I'm not mistaken, I'm stopping you from getting on with your work." He bowed to

Jane, then grasped Alex's hand and said, "It was a privilege to meet you."

Alex was walking away when the priest added, "Don't forget about my request."

When the priest was out of sight, Jane asked, "What was that last comment about?"

"It's not important. Right now, I'm more worried about figuring out what we do next."

# CHAPTER 28
# FEAR IS THE MIND KILLER

"Damn, damn, damn," Stafford yelled into the Italian night sky.

The door opened, and Sidney Carton came running onto the patio. "What's wrong, brother?"

Stafford tucked his cell phone back into the folds of his robe and shook his head. He started pacing back and forth along the railing, looking out over the slopes of Mount Subasio. It was some time before he said, "I don't want to hear your criticisms."

"I haven't said anything," Carton replied.

"I know, but you will. I went against your advice and have been trying to get rid of the boy. But I've failed yet again."

"Who made you judge, jury, and executioner?"

"I had to try," Stafford said. "We've spent most of our lives trying to fix the mess we helped create. And now, that boy is undoing everything."

"You don't know that," Carton replied. "So, what if you gave him the Palantir book? Nothing has happened because of that incident."

"We don't know that to be a true statement. Although I still wonder how he compelled me to give it to him, that's not what I'm most concerned about," Stafford replied. "It's everything else since then that bothers me. Somehow, he has managed to win over the Guardians while simultaneously antagonizing the witches, Pythia, and us. He's destroyed one of Pythia's magical objects, disappeared in broad daylight, and has defeated all our attempts to stop him. I'm telling you, something's not right."

"I bet that if we left him alone, all of this would be a moot point," Carton said.

"You don't understand. Now he's gotten the witches to start actively searching for the Grail. I never thought it existed, but the boy has provided them with enough information for them to act. Someone who can do all that is dangerous."

"Why are you so upset about the witches chasing after a fable? That's of no concern to us."

"I disagree. I can feel it in my bones that something's drastically off," Stafford replied.

"Maybe so, but you can't go around killing people just because you think they might be dangerous."

"But I haven't told you about his latest escapade. After my first attempts at eliminating him failed, I had Brothers Arkan and Ratko tail the boy. They flew to his home but found he'd already left for Europe. So, they hacked his credit card accounts and followed him to Spain. I told them to take whatever steps were necessary to eliminate the boy, but he continued eluding them despite all the resources I'd allocated to stopping him. They eventually caught up with him and tossed him off the bridge in Toledo."

"Oh my god!"

"They're safe," Stafford said. "They did it so fast that no one called the police, so both got away with no problem."

"I'm not talking about them. What happened to the boy?"

"Him? He survived a nearly twenty-story fall, of course. That boy has more lives than a cat. That alone should tell you that he's using dark magic."

"No, it doesn't tell me that at all," Carton retorted. "It tells me that you're out of your mind. If you're so worried about him, try talking with Lady Yvaine again. Get her to control him."

"I've told you. She won't do anything to him and has made it clear that she's just going to observe him for now. Besides, she can't control him either. She sent one of her aides to escort him to Stormhold, but he somehow eluded her, which is how he ended up in Spain. I also know that she's told all the groves to keep their hands off him. And she's never done that for a warlock. I don't know what she's up to, but we can't trust her. For all I know, he's put a spell on all of them."

"I highly doubt it," Carton said. "Why don't you invite him to join our order? Helping boys like him is one of our key missions. That way, we can keep an eye on him and make sure he doesn't do anything to hinder us."

"I will never let him join us," Stafford said, pounding the railing. "He messes with people's minds. I will not stop hunting him until that boy joins his family in the afterworld."

"I will never understand why you're so afraid of him," Carton said. "If you don't watch out, this obsession of yours will kill you one of these days."

When his brother didn't reply, Carton said, "So, what are you going to do now? If the witches are after the Grail, will you follow them, the boy, or both?"

"Who cares about the Grail when that boy is on the loose. Besides, I can always decide what to do if the witches should be so lucky as to actually find it."

## CHAPTER 29
# SOME OTHER BEGINNINGS END

"I think we should head for Romania," Jane said. "Unless something is telling ye we shouldn't go there."

"That would suggest I had a plan, but the only one I had just blew up when Sophie took the map," Alex said.

"Well, knowing ye, I'd say ye're about to get hungry, so let's go find a café and talk it over."

Alex stayed silent while eating, but as soon as he finished, he said, "I think you're right – we should go to Romania and look for the Grail, or Sangreal, or whatever you call it. But what about those men who've been after us? Father Torri believes they've hacked my credit cards and are watching my transactions to find out what we're doing."

"I've been thinking about that," Jane said. "Ye probably don't want to hear it, but ye'll have to thank Sophie next time ye see her because she gave me the idea on how we get to Romania."

Alex looked questioningly at Jane.

"We'll pay for everything in cash. I'll contact Lady Yvaine, tell her what's happening, and ask her to wire transfer me some money. All ye need to do is go to a local bank and max out yer ATM withdrawals. We stay in town tonight, then repeat your withdrawals tomorrow. We should have enough to last us some time between what Sophie handed ye, yer bank funds, and Lady Yvaine."

"But if they can hack my cards, what's to stop them from figuring out our airline reservations? They'll know where we're flying to and be waiting for us."

"Who said anything about flying?" Jane asked.

"We can't drive there," Alex protested. "Neither of us is old enough to rent a car."

"I know, but we can take trains. I doubt they'll look for us to take the slow way there. Plus, I'd imagine we'll have to change trains several times."

After thinking it over for a minute, Alex nodded and said, "I like the plan. Let's do it."

Executing Jane's plan was more difficult than expected. It took an extra day to get the wire transfer from Lady Yvaine and pull out enough cash for the trip. Then, it took them much longer than she expected to make it from Ávila to Romania. They had to switch trains in Madrid, Barcelona, Zurich, and Budapest, missing two connections. When they finally stepped off the train in Bucharest almost a week later, all Alex wanted was to get a hotel room, shower, and sleep. But Jane caught his arm and steered him to another platform.

"Why can't we take a break here?" Alex asked. "You've got to be as tired as I am."

"That might be, but we're close now. So, the more we keep moving, the better our chances of avoiding whoever might be chasing us."

Alex sighed. "Where's our next stop?"

"Curtea de Argeş," Jane replied. "Ye said ye wanted to get to Dracula's old stomping grounds. Well, Curtea is at the entrance to Transylvania. Plus, ye can rub it in next time ye see Diana that we went there. She'd probably go gaga over the place because it's a cute little town with an interesting-looking monastery. Once we get there, we'll rest and figure out our next steps."

"I'm too tired to think straight, so lead the way." He followed Jane to an older-looking train with faded, peeling brick red paint. He was about to step on when he saw a young, clean-shaven man in a brown robe staring at him. The man reminded Alex of a young Brother Stafford. Grabbing Jane's arm, he said, "Look at that guy over there."

By the time Jane had turned to look, he was gone. "Who?" she asked.

Alex continued staring at the spot where the man had been standing a few seconds earlier, then rubbed his eyes. "He's gone now. Maybe I'm just tired, but he spooked me."

"I've learned not to take yer worries lightly. Let me know if ye see him again because we might have to run. At the very least, we need to keep our eyes open now that we're in Romania. I'm guessing that some of the men who chased us in Spain have been waiting here for ye."

The rail car was much older than anything else they'd ridden and was hot, smelly, and stuffy, with no air conditioning and windows that didn't open. Unlike other trains they'd taken, this one had no assigned seating, and since families that had gone to the city to do their shopping packed the train, it made finding seats difficult.

The train had barely pulled out of the station when the occupants seemed to come to life. One boy started riding his tricycle up and down the aisle while a little girl approached Alex and stared intently at him before rubbing her stomach with one hand.

"I think she's asking you for some food," Jane said.

"What should I do?" Alex asked. "Her parents are right over there but don't seem to be watching her very closely." Before he had to decide, a conductor came by and shooed the girl away.

His resolve to be alert for potential threats didn't last long, as he was so tired from their travels that he fell asleep within minutes. He woke sometime later with an aching shoulder, opened one eye, and noticed that Jane had fallen asleep using him as a pillow. His movement caused her to nestle her head further into his side before she settled back down. Alex was surprised that the ache suddenly disappeared. Not wanting to disturb her, he laid his head back against the window and went to sleep.

A short time later, Jane stirred, waking him again. He found it hard to look away as she sat up and stretched, her tousled hair hiding most of the sleepy smile she gave him. She looked out the window and said, "Don't worry. We'll be arriving soon and can eat there. I didn't think the trip would take this long, but I didn't know it would make that many stops."

Alex felt the ankh suddenly start thumping against his chest in warning. He abruptly stood and looked around the train car. "Something's wrong," he said. "Come on."

"Ye're probably jest tired," Jane said. "We've been traveling for days and haven't had any problems."

"Trust me. Something feels off." Alex grabbed his pack and slid past Jane. He stopped in the aisle and looked around the crowded rail car. Feeling the ankh tug him towards the rear of the train, he motioned for Jane to follow.

As he was about to open the door to step into the gangway, he saw the man he'd seen in the train station in Bucharest stand up and move towards them. The ankh changed the direction it was tugging him, pulling him towards the door leading outside. Alex looked from the approaching man, to the grassy hillside rolling past, to Jane.

"Oh no. Ye can't be thinking of jumping off a moving train, are ye," she said, her blue-grey eyes dilating, making the freckles on her face stand out.

He looked down to where the ankh lay hidden beneath his shirt. "It's telling me we need to go now. Besides, it doesn't look too far to jump. Just remember to bend your knees when you hit. Don't try to stick the landing. Let your momentum carry you down the hill." Before he could talk himself out of it, he pulled the door inward, took one step down, and jumped. He hit on soft grass, stumbled, and fell. A second later, Jane tumbled past him.

Alex pushed himself up and looked to see if anybody had followed them off the train. His heart sank when he saw the man he'd been watching jump from the train just before it disappeared around a corner. But an instant later, he heard a cry of pain from the direction where the man had jumped.

He looked at Jane and asked, "Are you okay?"

"No thanks to ye." Shaking her head in disbelief, she added, "I can't believe we jest did that."

He looked to where he thought their pursuer was but didn't see any movement. Another groan of pain drove him to help Jane up. "Come on. Let's get out of here while that guy can't follow us."

Alex had only taken a step when Jane grabbed his arm and pulled him back. "Jest, where do ye think ye're going?"

"I'm getting the heck out of here. This is our opportunity to escape, and I'm taking it."

"Ye can't run away when a fellow creature is hurt."

"If he's trying to kill me, I can," Alex replied.

A moan in the distance caused Jane to run towards where the man was lying. Alex watched for a moment, then threw his hands up and followed her. By the time he reached the man, Jane was already checking his injuries.

Without looking up, she held a hand out. "Quick, give me the t-shirt in yer pack."

"What! It's the only one I've got. What do you have against my shirts?"

"Hurry up," Jane said. "He hit a rock when he landed and is bleeding badly."

Alex grumbled as he dug his shirt out and handed it to Jane. He watched as she cut off one of the man's pant legs, pulled out some medical supplies from her daypack, then cleaned and wrapped the wound with his shirt.

"I need ye to flag someone down on the road and get them to call an ambulance," she said. "I don't have the right supplies because I never planned on this trip. Now hurry."

Alex followed her instructions and was glad it wasn't too long before someone stopped. The language barrier made it difficult for Alex to get his request understood, but he eventually managed it and stayed by the road until an ambulance came. Then, he led the medic to the stricken man to assess the situation.

When the driver headed back to the ambulance to help get the gurney down the hill, Alex headed back down to their pursuer. "Who are you?" he asked. "And why are you following us?"

Despite the man's pain, his eyes narrowed as he said, "We cannot let you live. You're a threat to both the witches and us." He grimaced in pain, then went silent.

Alex wanted to ask more questions, but the ambulance crew came with their gurney just then and proceeded to evacuate their unknown assailant.

With Jane in tow, Alex clambered up to the road and began walking in the same direction the train had taken. Neither one said anything until Alex asked, "How could you help someone trying to kill us?"

"I'm a healer first," Jane replied. "I cannae look away when someone's hurt, no matter what they've tried to do to me."

"Well, you're a better person than me," Alex said. "I think we should have left him there and let him figure out how to get out of his situation."

"Ye don't really believe that, do ye? What about all the ghosts ye've helped or the fortunes ye've given away. I don't see much of a difference."

"Well, I do," Alex replied grumpily.

They lapsed into silence until Jane said, "So now what? I was planning to stop and rest in Curtea, but I think that idea's nixed now. I'm sure they'll have someone else waiting for us there."

Alex wasn't paying attention as he was looking up at the snow-capped Carpathian Mountains in the distance. "We're close," he whispered to himself.

"Close to what?" Jane asked.

"Nothing," Alex replied. "I was just thinking out loud." He shook his head to clear his thoughts and said, "We still have a way to go. Let's see if we can hitchhike because I don't think I'm up to a long hike."

"But that's dangerous."

"And what we're doing isn't? Come on. It'll be all right."

It wasn't long before an old orange and white Volkswagen van pulled over. The sliding door opened, and a college-aged girl leaned out. In a British accent, she asked, "Need a lift?"

Jane looked to Alex, who clapped a hand over his chest. When he didn't feel the ankh warning him, Alex nodded.

As they clambered in, the girl said, "You're packing pretty light for this far out."

"We tend to do things on the spur of the moment, so we always pack light," Jane said as she nudged Alex in the ribs. "Isn't that right?"

"Yep. We've had less on some of our trips," Alex said. He looked around for a seat, but the only chairs were the two up front – both filled. A shag rug covered the rest of the van.

The girl asked, "Where are you headed?"

"We're playing it by ear," Alex replied as the door closed, and the van continued north.

Jane elbowed him again. "Oh, come on. It's nothing to be ashamed of." She turned to the girl and said,

"We're following Dracula's trail, so we plan on visiting Poenari, Bran Castle, and Sighisoara."

"We just finished doing that ourselves," the girl replied. "I should warn you that it's probably going to be pretty cold in Poenari the next couple of days, what with the winds, the overcast sky, and the temperatures. You don't look like you're going to be warm enough."

"We'll be fine," Jane said. "Where are ye headed?"

"We can take you as far as Albesti. We've got friends there, so you'll have to find another means of transportation if you're going to keep going. It might be easier if we drop you in Curtea, though."

Alex threw out his hands. "No. Albesti is perfect."

The conversation drifted to other topics, making the time fly by. All too soon, they were standing on the side of the road in a small city. Looking around at the peaceful town, Alex said, "All in all, I'd say we did all right. Nobody killed us, no broken bones, and we're in a city where we can get food and shelter for the night."

It didn't take long before they found a small lakeside bed and breakfast. After dinner, they cleaned up and headed to bed. Exhausted from all their traveling, they slept in the next morning. When they finally woke, they went on a shopping excursion for warmer clothes, supplies, and food, preventing them from getting back on the road until after noon. As they walked up the road, Jane said, "Ye know, one of the things I've been wondering about is how we get away with so much on our travels."

"What do you mean?"

"I'm sixteen, and ye're only fourteen, yet we've traveled across Europe on planes, trains, and automobiles. And no one's questioned it."

"It's my charm," Alex replied flippantly.

"No, I'm serious. I can't help but wonder if it's yer ankh putting a spell on people."

Alex stopped, looked around, and put a finger to his lips. "Not so loud. I don't want anyone to know I have it. Besides, how could it do what you're suggesting? Maybe it's because you're older than me and taller."

"I don't think so. But whatever has caused it, it's strange."

They had walked only a short distance before a farmer let them hop in the back of his truck. As they bumped along, Jane stared at the mountains towering over them. At last, she said, "Are ye sure we're going the right way? There's not much ahead of us except wilderness."

"Of course not, but the ankh isn't fighting the direction, and it's done me right before. So, I'll keep trusting it."

A short time later, they passed a funeral procession going in the opposite direction, consisting of two horse-drawn wagons and a crowd of people. The first wagon carried the casket with flowers strewn around its bed, while the second held a cross and was followed by the mourners.

Jane stared at it until it passed out of sight. Then she sighed and said, "That's how I'd like to go. Simple, elegant, and sincere."

"I agree," Alex said.

Half an hour later, the farmer stopped and let them off in front of a newer-looking stained wooden building with a bright red metal roof and a sign saying Poenari Fortress off to the side.

"Are ye sure this is where ye wanted to go?" Jane asked. "There's nothing around here except wilderness and some tourist stuff."

Alex craned his neck to look up the steep forested hill to where a crumbling old castle stood. "Yep, but I have no idea why the ankh told me to get off here."

"But, I read there are 1480 steps to the top. And we have to wait for a guide to take us up because they've had bear problems around here."

"Well, let's get our tickets and find a spot to get out of this wind."

They had to wait two hours for the next tour, with the group consisting of a few twenty-year-olds and a middle-aged couple. Their guide called them together for a quick briefing, patted the holster on his hip, and said, "This isn't to keep you in line – it's to chase away any brown bears that might come nosing around while we're climbing to the top. So, everyone has to stick together for safety purposes."

"Wouldn't it be cool to see one?" Alex said as he looked into the forest above them.

Jane rolled her eyes. "Ye needn't look so excited. Remember, even though this is probably a wild goose chase, we're here for another purpose. I jest hope your hunch makes this climb worthwhile. I don't know if I could muster enough enthusiasm to keep looking around the rest of the country for the Grail if we have to keep doing this type of searching."

As the guide moved off with the rest of the group, Jane looked at the castle far above, stepped up on the first concrete step, and grumbled, "1479 to go."

Alex ignored her complaints as he was more interested in a pair of dogs that had joined the group. The heavily forested mountainside kept the winds out, making the walk up pleasant. It also wasn't that hard of a climb, as their guide walked slowly and had the group make frequent stops. The two dogs, one a black lab mix the other a shaggy black and auburn dog, stayed with them the entire way. As soon as they cleared the tree line for the final climb, the winds made themselves known, turning a pleasant climb into a chilly summer day.

When their guide finally stepped out of the way, Alex raced to the top of the steps onto the old castle ramparts. He reached the side that overlooked the Arges River Gorge and stood mesmerized by the beauty of the wilderness surrounding him. Alex could barely hear the water boiling over the rocks far below because of the moaning wind, but he felt at peace on the isolated hilltop, as it reminded him of home.

A strong blast of wind whipped around him, causing him to shiver. He stumbled and hit the metal railing on the ramparts a second before hearing a strange woman's voice cutting across the wind. "I'm so glad you've come."

# CHAPTER 30
# **BUCHAREST**

Upset at how the order had left Alex and Jane to fend for themselves, Diana gave Elizabeth the cold shoulder treatment the entire trip to Romania. It wasn't until they'd cleared customs at the airport and gotten into the waiting minivan that she finally relented and asked the questions that had been bugging her ever since Ávila. "Why did you want me to come on this scouting trip? You've spent months studying that old journal but haven't told me anything about your plans."

Elizabeth waited until they were heading into town before she answered, "I don't want to make the same mistake we did at Lamanai and assume we know exactly where to search for the Grail. So, I wanted to make this reconnaissance trip while your mother organizes the rest of the women and equipment.

"Okay, that makes sense. But you still haven't answered my question. Why me?"

"I hate to admit it, but I've often thought we'd stand a better chance at finding the Sangreal if my grandson came along with us. But, as you know, it would have caused too great of a rift in our members. Since we can't use his talents, you're the next best thing. You know my grandson as well as anyone. Since he's the one who found the Grail documents, I figure I could use someone who can think like him."

Diana snorted. "Nobody thinks like him. Besides, this is already more of a plan than he ever has."

"Then it makes it even more important that we get to know the countryside, get a feel for places that the journal and this map highlight. I want to get to know the area where Vlad Tepes III lived and died. Then, unless some new information comes to light, we could start by scanning the ruins in Targoviste. But tonight, we'll go into Bucharest and take it easy because the next few weeks will likely be long and tiring."

"I still don't understand why anyone would think the Grail is in Romania," Diana said.

"I agree that it doesn't make sense, but that's what both the journal and map indicate," Elizabeth replied. "I've spent the last year authenticating the journal and following up on leads. All the data leads me here. Besides, if you think about it from a historical perspective, it's not that far-fetched of an idea. Most Grail lore is based on Western European legends, but the northernmost Crusade route went through Vienna and Belgrade. Since Romania is much closer to Jerusalem and the Middle East than most European countries, it's possible one of the Crusaders found it, brought it back here, and hid it. It might explain why the rulers of this area fought so hard against the Ottoman Empire and why no one has ever found it. Most people link the Grail to France or England, but nobody has ever found a trace of the Grail there.

"The map you three found indicates the northern part of Wallachia, just south of Transylvania. So, tomorrow, I was thinking we'd go see Targoviste, the capital of Wallachia when Vlad was alive. Then we'll keep heading north and visit Poenari, a castle he used in the Carpathian Mountains. After that, we'll stop for the night in Sibiu, then head further north to Sighisoara, where he was born. After that, we'll take stock of what we've learned and figure out where to go."

They encountered heavy traffic in Bucharest, turning the trip into a crawl. Diana, who had her face stuck to the window looking at the sights, said, "This is such an odd mixture of ugly blocky-looking communist-era buildings and beautiful French-style mansions, but I can see why they used to call it the Paris of the East."

She stopped talking when their driver suddenly cursed and turned off the engine. Diana looked outside and saw they were at a red light at the biggest traffic circle she'd ever seen. She was still staring at the mass of vehicles circling when the driver popped the hood, picked up a wrench from the door pocket, and got out of the van. She couldn't hear the driver cursing or the banging, but she could feel the vibrations running through the vehicle. The hood dropped a minute later, and the driver got back in, acting as if nothing had happened.

After checking into their hotel, the two Druids went out for dinner. The weather was pleasant enough that they decided on an outdoor café. Unable to read the menu and unwilling to look dumb in front of Elizabeth, Diana sat staring at the menu. When the waiter asked what she'd like, Diana heard a sizzling sound at the table next to them. She pointed to the fellow customer and said, "I'll have what he's having." She noticed Elizabeth looking skeptically at her and defensively asked, "What? It sounds delicious. Plus, I'm starving."

When the waiter put a plate with a huge hunk of bone and meat in front of her sometime later, Diana looked up and asked, "What's this?"

Elizabeth quickly covered her mouth with a napkin to muffle the sound of her laughter and said, "It's a pig knuckle, a typical dish in this region."

"But it's enormous," Diana said. She looked up and saw tears streaming down Elizabeth's face – the first time she'd ever seen the high priestess laugh. Embarrassed at having ordered so much, Diana tried eating all of it but didn't come close to finishing. As a result, she got an upset stomach that kept her up half the night.

Trying to take her mind off her discomfort, she reviewed Elizabeth's plan, but something felt off. She hadn't figured out what when she finally fell asleep. It wasn't until breakfast the next morning that she figured out what was bothering her. She studied Elizabeth, looking for signs of irritation. When she didn't see any, she took a deep breath and said, "I think you're going about this search wrong."

Elizabeth was surprised but calmly replied, "What are you talking about?"

"I'm not sure if this will make sense, but you asked me to think of this search from Alex's perspective. I know Alex gave you a map and journal that indicate the Grail might be somewhere in Romania, and it may have something to do with Vlad Tepes. But just like Lamanai, I think you're leaping to a logical conclusion on how to proceed." Diana hesitated, unsure how the high priestess was taking her challenge, and was pleased when Elizabeth urged her to go on.

Reassured by Elizabeth's willingness to listen, Diana said, "One of my biggest frustrations with your grandson has been that he seems to go into things without having any plan whatsoever. It drives me crazy, but it seems to work. Think about Lamanai. You and my mom studied the *Palantir Sibylline Book* for months and devised a very logical plan. Yet, he went off and did his own thing. Jane and I tried arguing with him to get with the program, but he kept saying he was following his hunches. And, if our suspicions are right, he found the Palantir, but in a very different place than where you were looking."

"I'm confused. It sounds like you think my plan is sound but wrong."

"Exactly. You say you want to get an overall feel for the area, but it feels more like you're biding your time until the equipment and everyone else arrives, whereupon you'll go straight to the most logical place to search for it."

"So, what would you suggest I do?" Elizabeth asked.

"I don't know. Maybe reverse your plans for this week. I know you said you wanted to start with Targoviste. Make that the last stop of our exploration instead."

"What would that accomplish?"

Diana shook her head. "I have no idea, but I do know Alex wouldn't look at things the way we are. Besides, what harm is there in shaking things up?"

"Where would you suggest we go first?"

"I've been looking at the maps and suggest we make a big loop around Transylvania. We can go to Brasov today, maybe even see Bran Castle, which some call Dracula's castle."

"But it has nothing to do with Vlad Tepes. It was all a tourist push by the Romanian government to take advantage of Dracula's link with Transylvania."

"I know, but there's a link with the Dracula legend. Besides, don't you want to go see it? And if we go there, I was also hoping I could talk you into seeing Prejmer, one of the UNESCO fortified churches sites."

"Are you trying to find the Grail, or is this just a vacation for you?" Elizabeth asked.

"I admit I love visiting new places, so yes, in a way, it's a vacation. But Alex was always willing to make side trips to see these places, and half the time, it seemed to help our search. Don't ask me how it works. It just does."

Elizabeth sat, lost in thought for some time, before finally saying, "There might be some method to the madness. So, rather than waiting around here and talking, let's get moving."

Half an hour later, they were on their way. The crowded streets of Bucharest soon gave way to flat farmlands, which Diana found to be an interesting mix of old and new technologies. She saw tractors in some fields, horse-drawn plows in others, and men with scythes in still others. They gathered hay in small and large square bales, round bales, and sometimes even dried it using teepee-like structures.

As they headed north, the landscape gradually changed to rolling hills. Even the houses started changing, with Bavarian-style housing slowly becoming more predominant as they headed up in elevation. The biggest surprise was when they passed a covered wooden wagon pulled by two horses hauling a load of scrap metal. "Did you see that…?" Diana's words trailed off as they passed the cart, and she saw it was pulling the trunk of a white car. Before she could close her mouth, they passed another wagon carrying more scrap metal, including a washer and dryer.

As they climbed higher into the Carpathians, Diana began seeing miniature house structures by the road. Embarrassed by her lack of knowledge about them, she finally worked up the courage to ask what they were.

"Those are wayside shrines," Elizabeth replied. "They're built for all sorts of purposes. Some are memorials to the dead. Some are meant to keep demons away. They use the rest as small chapels."

Farming gradually gave way to sheep herding as houses became fewer and farther between. After what seemed like forever, their driver pulled off onto a gravel shoulder in front of a convenience store and said, "Bathroom stop."

Diana jumped out and ran inside but was back so fast that Elizabeth hadn't gotten out of the van. "Do you have some coins I can use? It costs two lei to use the bathroom here," she said. As soon as the coins dropped into her hand, she darted back inside.

The next few days became a dream vacation for Diana as they visited castles, fortified churches, medieval cities, and the most incredible graveyards and churches she'd ever seen. A couple of times a day, Elizabeth would ask her if she'd had any insights about the location of the Grail, but each time she shook her head.

After seeing the Greek Orthodox Church in Sighisoara, Diana couldn't help but fill Elizabeth's ears with excited chatter. "Have you ever seen anything like it?" she asked. Without waiting for an answer, she kept on talking. "There's a simple beauty to these churches that speaks to me more than the Spanish churches with all their gold and silver stuff. I love how the pictures on the walls tell so many stories from the bible. It was quite beautiful in an altogether different way."

Her excitement quickly faded, though, when news that Alex and Jane had disappeared finally reached them. She was even more disheartened to learn that neither Lady Yvaine nor Alex's grandfather had called the police to search for them. Diana became so consumed by worry that she barely noticed the Eyes of Sibiu and climbed the observation tower beneath the shiny outstretched arms of the statue of Prometheus overlooking the Vidaru Reservoir without thinking about her fear of heights.

She was so deep in thought as they headed down the mountain from the reservoir that she didn't notice Elizabeth telling the driver to pull over and turn off their vehicle.

"Are you listening to anything I'm saying?" Elizabeth asked.

Diana sat up. "I'm sorry. What were you saying?"

"You know this isn't the first time my grandson has disappeared. Just wait and see, though. He'll show up – just like a bad penny. But while you were daydreaming, I was saying that I got an update from your mother. She expects to be in-country with everyone by the end of the week, which means we don't have much more time. So, what about Targoviste? We'll be coming up on it in another hour or so, and I was wondering if we should go anyplace else first."

"Well, I can think of three other places we haven't seen yet. There's Snagov, but I think that's just a lot of tourist hype, like Bran Castle. It's cool looking but not to the point. There's also Poenari just ahead of us."

Elizabeth cut her off. "I'm not going to climb all those steps just to see a ruined castle. If you want to, be my guest. I'll wait in the restaurant down the street."

"As much as I'd like to see Poenari," Diana said, "I doubt it'll help us any more than the other places. So, we might as well start searching Targoviste because Vlad lived there both as a youth and as ruler of Wallachia. And if your theory about the Grail's location is right, then all the battles in this area could have been to protect it."

A short time later, they passed Poenari. Diana ducked down to catch a glimpse of the castle high on the hill and thought she saw a glimpse of ginger-colored hair on the hillside, but it was gone in a flash. Shaking her head, she told herself it was just her imagination.

An hour later, though, as she and Elizabeth ate lunch at the restaurant a short distance from Poenari's entrance, she thought she caught another glimpse of Jane's signature locks. But this time, they were in the back of a horse-drawn cart going down the Arges River valley.

Diana sat for a minute, thinking she'd seen a ghost. Then she threw down her napkin, said, "I'll be right back," and ran out.

# CHAPTER 31
# **POENARI**

Alex whirled around and was surprised to see a young woman wearing a medieval-styled red and white woolen dress with her brown hair pulled into a tight bun at the back of her head. He wiped away the tears from the cold that blurred his vision and only then realized he was staring at a ghost.

"Who, who are you?" Alex asked.

"My name is Elisabetta. I was the first wife of Vlad Tepes III of the family Dracul."

Alex was too stunned to do anything but gape at the spirit hovering a few feet away.

"I apologize if I scared you, but I was so anxious to meet you that I didn't think about how shocked you'd be seeing a ghost."

"I'm used to seeing ghosts. I was just surprised hearing you were married to Vlad the Impaler."

Elisabetta's eyes grew as cold as the wind flowing over the battlements. "I'll have you know that he did more for our country than anyone before or since. Did you know that one of the first things he did when he ascended to the throne was to stop the abuses of the Boyars, who'd run roughshod over this land for centuries? Then he helped the peasants of this country by building better houses for them and improving their farming methods so our people wouldn't constantly be starving. I'm not proud of his penchant for impaling his enemies, but the scare tactic was necessary, as all his so-called allies found it convenient to desert him every time the Ottomans invaded. He was always the first line of defense against the Ottomans taking over all of Europe. Even though they vastly outnumbered our armies, my husband won battle after battle against them. So, before you complain again about his tactics, think about how many innocent women and children the Ottomans and Boyars would have killed if they had their way. Sometimes, the end justifies the means."

Elisabetta paused, took a deep breath, and smoothed her dress. In a much calmer voice, she said, "I'm sorry I exploded like that, but it's been so hard hearing him vilified for centuries and not being able to defend his honor." She waved her hands impatiently as if to dismiss her comments. "That's not what I came here for, though. I came to ask you to free my husband. He's a good man at heart."

"How am I supposed to help someone who's been dead for centuries?"

As Elisabetta gazed down at the river far below, she said, "I've always believed that God would hear my prayers and send me someone to save him. And today, praise be to God, I felt a disturbance in the life force. It was like nothing I'd ever felt before. I rushed here and saw you standing on the exact spot where I threw myself to the rocks below. I knew then that you were the one to free my husband from his unnatural bonds."

"I have no idea what you're talking about."

"My husband isn't dead. He's trapped somewhere nearby," Elisabetta said.

"How can that be? He died hundreds of years ago."

"But I'm telling you, he's not dead."

"You'll have to explain what you're talking about because I'm not following anything you're saying."

She took a deep breath and said, "My husband was away battling the invading Ottoman army led by his brother Radu Right before my death. The enemy had so many soldiers that it seemed like a hopeless cause. Fearing what would happen to us if the Ottomans defeated my husband's army, we fled from Targoviste and holed up here.

"News from the battlefront seemed to get worse by the day, and it seemed like only a matter of time before the end came. Then, one of my husband's supporters raced here to give us news. Only he was so afraid of the Ottomans that he shot an arrow up here with a warning attached. The coward disappeared down the road, leading us to believe his warning was accurate."

Elisabetta grew quiet and stayed that way for so long that Alex was about to say something when she said, "It landed near where you stand."

Alex leaned forward. "What did it say?"

"That we'd lost. Thinking my husband was dead and unwilling to be an object of the Turk's victory celebrations, I decided to join my husband in death. I leapt over the side here onto the rocks below. Only later did I learn that my husband had turned certain defeat into victory. He even managed to capture twenty thousand enemy soldiers. But it was too late for me. When he learned of my suicide, he went mad with grief and impaled all the prisoners. I've been wandering around this citadel ever since."

"I don't get it. If he was so in love with you, why didn't he join you here in the afterworld when he died?"

"That's what I want to know. I saw him sink into the depravity and madness everyone remembers him by. Then, one day, he just disappeared I don't think he moved on. His rivals told stories that his enemies killed him and hacked him to pieces, but no one ever found his body. I waited for him to appear here in the afterworld, but he never has. I don't know what happened, but I can still sense his presence."

"Do you know where he might be? We're here looking for him because we think he's hiding a magical object, and we want to ensure it's safe."

Elisabetta nodded. "It's beginning to make sense. I thought he was hiding some secret the entire time I knew him. I just didn't know what."

"If he's alive, where do you think he might be?"

"I didn't say he was alive. I said he wasn't dead. There's a difference. As for where he is, I'm not sure. My intuition says he's not far away. He often told me that this area was the only place he felt safe in, which is why I can't see him leaving here." Elisabetta drifted a little ways off as she thought about her long-lost lover. After a few moments of silence, she roused herself and returned to the present. "Will you help me find him?"

"Let me get this straight. You say he's not dead, but you also say he's not alive. You don't know where he is, but you think he's nearby. And you want me to find him. Did I get that right?"

She nodded excitedly.

"How am I supposed to find someone you haven't been able to find in centuries?" Alex asked. "I mean, you can go anywhere you want. I have to hitch rides."

"I don't know, but your aura gives me hope," Elisabetta replied.

Alex heard footsteps approaching. He turned towards the sound and saw Jane's head appear above the battlement floor.

"I've been looking all over for ye," Jane said. "It's getting late. I'm cold, and I want to find a hotel before it gets dark."

Alex heard Elisabetta's voice die away in the wind, "Please help him."

Ignoring Jane, he said, "Where am I supposed to look?" But Elisabetta was already gone. He stared at the spot where she'd stood until Jane called again.

"I'm coming," he replied. Another blast of cold wind hit him, driving him to stick his hands in his pockets and follow Jane down.

It wasn't until they'd entered the shelter of the woods that Jane slowed down and asked, "Who were ye talking to? Or do I want to know?"

"Well, there's good news and bad news. Vlad's first wife showed up and asked me to help him. She says he's somewhere nearby."

"That sounds like great news. Surely ye'll be able to find him. I mean, how hard will it be to find such a notorious spirit?" Jane stopped and turned on Alex. "Wait. What aren't ye saying?"

"Well, the bad news is that he's not dead, but he's also not alive."

"Huh?"

"I don't know what she meant."

"So, what now? Is yer spidey-sense tingling and telling ye anything?" Jane asked.

"My skin is tingling, but it's from the cold. It was freezing up there, and it's June. Can you imagine how cold we'd be if we hadn't picked up gloves and scarves?"

When they reached the entrance, Jane asked, "Which way?"

Alex looked off to his left. "Definitely not that way. I don't want to climb a mountain to nowhere with night coming on."

"Ye know, that's probably the most logical decision I've ever heard ye make," Jane said. "So, that means we go right."

They'd gone only a short distance when a farmer with a horse-drawn wagon pulled up alongside and motioned for them to get in. Alex didn't need any urging as he thanked the man, helped Jane into the back, then followed her up.

Jane tried to converse with the man, but since neither could speak the other's language, they soon lapsed into silence broken only by the clip-clop sounds of the horse's hoofs on the pavement, the sound of the river's rapids off to their left, and the moaning of the winds.

Alex started thinking about food as they passed a nearby restaurant and jumped when he heard a familiar voice calling out. "Wait. Where are you guys going?"

Jane had the presence of mind to tap the man on the back and motion for him to stop. But all Alex could do was stare at Diana running down the road towards him.

# CHAPTER 32
# CROSSING OVER

After thanking the farmer for the short ride, Alex hopped out of the wagon and helped Jane down before turning to watch Diana arrive. "What are you doing here?" he asked.

"What am I doing here? The better question is, what are you doing here?" Diana said. "I heard you disappeared after my mom dragged me away from Ávila."

"We're here to find the Grail, jest like ye are," Jane said.

"Are you trying to beat us to it?" Diana asked.

Jane shook her head. "Relax. We're not competing with ye."

"Well, knowing the kind of trips you normally take, you must be exhausted. Why don't you come back to the restaurant with me? You can tell Elizabeth what you found and volunteer your help."

"No, thank you," Alex replied. "Your mom made it abundantly clear I'm not wanted."

"I'll admit my mom doesn't want you around, but your grandmother is a different story. I even heard her say she wished you could come with us. She's under a lot of pressure to exclude you, but I bet she'd welcome your help until the other women arrive."

Jane looked at Alex expectantly. "That sounds like it could be a win-win. What do ye say?"

When Alex didn't reply, Jane turned to Diana and said, "We had quite an adventure getting here, which

I'll tell ye about later. But the big news is that when we finally get to Poenari, he runs into…."

"Who? Who did you meet?" Diana asked.

Jane leaned in and lowered her voice. "Vlad's first wife."

Diana grabbed his arm. "What! What did you learn?"

Alex looked at the restaurant Diana had run out of and was about to say something but shook his head. "

"Oh, don't act that way," Jane said, nudging him. "I saw ye acting all weird in Poenari but chose to let ye process whatever ye learned. So, out with it. What happened?"

"Shouldn't you be getting back to my grandma, Diana? If she knew we were talking, she'd probably think I'm corrupting you."

Diana stepped back, a shocked lock on her face. "Are you trying to get rid of me? What have I done to you?"

"Nothing. It's just that I don't want you to get in any more trouble. Your mom made it very clear that everyone would quit and desert my grandma if I got involved in your search."

"Nobody else is coming until the end of the week. Then, if you find something important, either you can disappear again, or maybe she can talk the others into accepting you," Diana said.

"I'm tempted," Alex replied, "but I don't know."

"I'm sure I can talk your grandma into letting you stay. In fact, she'll probably take it as a good omen that you showed up at the same time and place as we did."

The three had been so focused on their discussion that they didn't see Elizabeth walk up until she stopped a few feet in front of Alex and exclaimed, "You!" She turned to Diana with her eyes storming, "Has this been your plan all along – making me look like a fool by sending me on a merry chase around the Romanian countryside?"

"No, ma'am," Diana replied. "I had no idea they were here until I caught a glimpse of Jane's hair. That's why I ran out of the restaurant so fast."

Elizabeth turned on Jane. "Did Lady Yvaine send you to spy on me?"

"Hardly. She doesn't even know where I am. All I told her was that yer grandson and I were going to pursue the Grail. We have been incommunicado ever since because we were worried those men chasing us in Spain would track us down. We jest arrived in Romania yesterday because we took the slow way here."

Alex leaned toward Diana and said, "I told you she'd get mad just seeing me."

Elizabeth didn't hear what Alex said as she was still working through what Jane had said. Finally, she scratched her head and asked, "Then how did you wind up in the same place at the same time as we did?"

"That is the question, isn't it?" Diana replied. "Remember what we talked about when we arrived in Romania? You said you wanted me to think like your grandson. All I knew was that he doesn't go in a straight line, which is why we went a roundabout way to get here. And voilà, here he is. But believe me, finding him here is as big a surprise to me as it is to you."

Elizabeth turned to Alex and, in a calmer voice, asked, "So, what will you do next?"

Alex looked at the hillside across the river and scratched his head. "I don't know. I feel like I'm in the right area, but I have no idea what to do next. Before Diana came out, all I could think about was getting a meal and finding a place to stay tonight."

Elizabeth turned back to Diana. "You're not going to tell your mother about what's happened, are you?"

"Are you crazy? I'm not telling her anything. She'd ground me for a year if she knew I was with your grandson."

Elizabeth smiled. "I think you're exaggerating, although maybe not that much. But I asked because as much as I dislike hiding the truth from your mother, I'd like to get my grandson's thoughts on next steps before she arrives. Why don't we see if we can get rooms here at La Cetate for the night? Then, tomorrow, we could talk about how to approach the search."

Alex looked to Jane, who motioned for him to accept the offer. He took a deep breath and said, "Fine, at least for your offer of hospitality."

"Are you saying you won't tell me what you know?" Elizabeth asked. "Are you working against me?"

"It's not about keeping secrets," Alex said. "It's about your safety. I believe someone's trying to kill me. I don't know who they are or what they want, but I don't want anyone getting hurt. And the less you know, the safer you'll be. Besides, I'm not here to find the Grail so much as I'm using the search to smoke out whoever's pursuing me."

Elizabeth stuck out her hand. "I won't pretend to understand everything you just said, but it'll have to do for now. I'll put you up and feed you tonight, and we'll talk more about what you know tomorrow. Do we have a deal?"

Alex shook her hand and said, "You'll probably be disappointed with how little I know, but I'll tell you one thing. As I told Jane earlier, I think we're in the right area. But mind you, it's just a guess."

Later that night, Alex heard a knock on his door. When he opened it, Diana and Jane barged in and closed the door. Before he could protest, Jane said, "Out with it. What haven't ye told us about what happened at Poenari?"

Alex hesitated before saying, "I've already told you the key parts. The only part I left out was Elisabetta telling me about her history with Vlad. But what's bugging me is a comment she made about him not being dead, but he's not alive, either. She did say she thought he was hiding something but had no idea what."

"That actually sounds promising," Diana said. "But I don't see your grandmother listening to you unless you tell her you can see ghosts."

"Well, that ain't going to happen," Alex said.

"So, what are ye going to tell yer grandmother?" Jane asked.

"I have no idea," Alex replied. "That's why I said I needed to think about it tonight. Well, that plus I was tired, dirty, and hungry."

After the girls left, Alex paced around his tiny room, wondering what he would tell his grandmother the next morning. When he finally lay down, he was surprised that Sadie had somehow entered his room without his noticing. He curled up with the little dragon and instantly fell asleep. But it wasn't restful, as dreams soon invaded his sleep. Elisabetta was the first to invade his thoughts, reminding him of her request. Then,

Captain General de Ubilla and his mother followed, begging for his help to fulfill their family's duty.

No sooner had the ghosts left his dreams than the strangest one began. He found himself climbing a coastal mountain. A large lake lay before him with a bridge cutting across the middle. He heard the jingle of bells and saw a procession descending the hill, heading toward him, led by a regal-looking woman. The spectacle was so unexpected that he didn't notice the rest of the procession. When the dream finally faded away, he was able to fall into a deep sleep.

He woke with a start when the first rays of daylight peeked into his room. Alex sat on the edge of his bed for several minutes, wondering if the dreams were actual visitations by spirits or the wild imaginings of his mind. Anxious to clear his head, he dressed, slipped on his pack and Tilley, and headed outside. He stopped when he saw Diana and Jane waiting near the front door.

"What are you two doing here?" he asked.

"The more pertinent question is, what are ye doing here at this hour?" Jane said.

"I thought I'd walk around a bit and clear my head. I had some really bizarre dreams last night."

"Uh, huh. If that's all you were going to do, then you won't mind a little company, will you?" Diana asked.

Alex shook his head.

"Hold on a minute," Jane said. "I'll leave a note with the desk clerk to tell Elizabeth what we're doing."

A couple of minutes later, the three were standing outside the hotel.

"Okay, you know the drill," Diana said. "Which way do we go, George?"

"Why do you think I'm going somewhere? I told you I just wanted to get some fresh air."

"I don't know if ye're trying to convince us or yerself, but ye've got that far-away look in your eyes as if ye're here, but ye're not," Jane said while handing over a breakfast sandwich. "Maybe this will help ye think."

Alex absent-mindedly took the sandwich and started eating. When he'd finished it, he tilted his head and sniffed the air. Then he licked his finger and raised it while turning in a circle. "Can you feel it?"

"Feel what?" Jane asked, looking around. "There's not much here. It's a river valley with a two-lane road and forested mountains on either side."

"You guys don't feel it?" he asked again. He pointed down the river valley and said, "There."

"There's not even a gentle breeze blowing. What is it?" Jane asked.

Alex could feel the ankh tugging at him, along with another sensation he couldn't figure out. After a minute, he said, "It's like a giant vacuum is sucking at my gut."

"What are you talking about?" Diana asked.

"I don't know, but whatever it is, it's coming from that direction." Without warning, Alex headed down the valley at a trot.

Diana was the first to catch up to him. "Where are you going in such a hurry?"

Alex slowed to a fast walk. "I don't know, but I can't seem to stop myself."

Less than a hundred yards further on, Alex abruptly turned and scrambled down the riverbank. He raced across the flat ground, stopping just short of the raging water just as thousands of ghosts emerged from the woods. Most were men in battle dress, but there was also a sprinkling of women and children. All were staring directly at him – their faces showed a mixture of pain, anger, and hope. Unsure what to do, he stared at the mass of spirits until he felt something bump his leg.

Looking down, he saw Sadie winding through his legs. The ghosts disappeared, and an image of a whirling dark tunnel with a multitude of pin-pricks of light filled his mind. He didn't emerge from his trance until Jane grabbed his arm and shook him just as Diana ran up.

"Are ye all right? The look on yer face is scaring me," Jane said.

Alex pointed to a shimmering spot in the forest across the river. "Can you see where the forest looks like it's rippling like water?" Both Diana and Jane leaned forward and peered at where Alex was pointing.

"I cannae see anything except trees," Jane said at last.

"Me neither," Diana added.

"I've never seen anything like it. A minute ago, there were thousands of ghosts over there staring at me. Some looked like they wanted to kill me, while the rest looked incredibly sad."

"Maybe they're Vlad's victims," Diana said.

"That makes sense, but …."

When Alex didn't finish his sentence, Diana asked, "But what? That stare of yours is unnerving me."

"As scary as all those ghosts were, what's bothering me the most is that sucking feeling I was telling you about earlier. It's like it's calling me, and I'm having difficulty resisting it. I feel like I've got to check out that ripple over there."

It was Diana's turn to grab his arm. "You can't go. I don't know what you're seeing or feeling, but it can't be good. You have no idea what's there."

"I know, but I've got to check it out. Besides, I promise I'll only go a couple hundred yards in, then head straight back. Do you want to come with me?"

"You know what curiosity did to the cat," Diana said. "I have a horrible feeling about this. I've already lost you twice when you've followed your hunches. I don't want to lose you a third time. Please don't go into those woods. I won't ever talk to you again if something happens to you."

"I don't get a sense that there's danger ahead. And I don't think the ghosts will harm me because I feel like they're waiting for something to happen. The problem is that I don't know what."

When neither Jane nor Diana replied, he started making his way over the Arges, jumping from rock to rock to keep from getting wet. Halfway across, he turned to see where Jane and Diana were and noticed neither were following. "Are you coming?" he called out.

He saw Jane hesitate, then jump to a rock, followed by Diana. Feeling better about them coming with him, he continued across. Alex temporarily forgot about the horde of ghosts waiting for him when he saw an opalescent-colored flash in the forest. Relieved that

Chrys was nearby, he quickly crossed the rest of the river.

After climbing up the bank on the far side, he cautiously approached the area where the air was rippling. He noticed Sadie standing alongside him, an instant before the image of the star-lit tunnel flashed into his mind.

Alex heard a new voice calling out to him. He whirled around to see his sister waving frantically at him. Surprised by her sudden appearance, he tripped on a rock and fell into emptiness.

He never heard Diana's and Deborah's frightened screams. Nor did he see who followed him in right before the opening closed.

# CHAPTER 33
# A CHANGE OF WORLDS

Diana saw a flash of color follow Alex into the opening an instant before it closed. Not caring whether she got wet or not, she plunged into the river, heading towards the spot where she'd last seen him. Diana screamed his name over and over, hoping he would reappear as magically as he'd disappeared. But the shock of his disappearance caused her to stop short of the far bank in knee-deep water.

Jane came splashing up. "What happened?" she asked.

Before Diana could answer, a man in a brown robe ran up and shoved the girls aside. He reached the spot where Alex had disappeared and looked around for signs of him. After a minute of futile searching, he turned on the girls. "Where is he?" the man shouted.

"You!" Diana said, staggering backwards as she recognized one of the men who chased them in Spain. "We need to get out of here. Now!"

"I can see him," Jane replied. "But don't ye think there's a better way of handling him – one that ye're uniquely qualified in?"

Diana looked over at Jane. "Huh?" Realization of what she meant dawned on her. "Oh yeah." She slowly reached into her pouch for her talisman, saying, "We're just as confused as you. What do you want with him?"

"It's none of your business," the man growled, not noticing Diana was silently moving her lips. He pulled out a pistol and waved it in the air. "I don't want to use this, but I will if I need to. Now tell me. Where is he?"

"Move away from me and be prepared to duck," Diana whispered. When she thought Jane was far enough away, Diana threw her arms forward, sending hundreds of rocks from the river flying at the man. Most missed their mark, but over a dozen large stones hit him. Screaming, he dropped his gun, flung his hands over his head, and ran towards the river, blood streaming from multiple wounds.

Diana watched as the man frantically waded across the river. Wanting to make sure he left them alone, Diana conjured a fireball and flung it at him. The flames hit him squarely in the back, catching his clothes on fire. The man screamed again and plunged into the river, rolling around in the water until the flames were out. Then he scrambled to his feet, took one last look at Diana, and fled. She watched him until he'd disappeared, then sighed and turned back to where she'd last seen Alex.

"It's at times like this that I wish I had yer magic powers," Jane said. "Are ye all right?"

"Yeah, but I'm trying to figure out what we saw." She picked up a rock and threw it into the forest. It landed far beyond the spot where she'd last seen Alex. Unsure what to think, she picked up a handful of pebbles and threw them scattershot at the point. They, too, sailed into the forest beyond. Still not believing there wasn't some invisible wall, she climbed out of the river and tentatively poked at the spot where she'd last seen him. "Nothing's happening. Now, will you believe he's a warlock? Because nothing else can explain what we saw."

"We've discussed this before, and ye know I don't think he has any innate magical abilities. Besides, why would he come all this way only to use magic to disappear here? No, I think there's some other explanation, like maybe he stumbled into some opening to the afterworld."

"Well, whatever it is, it's like nothing I've ever seen or heard of before," Diana said.

Jane didn't reply as she continued staring at where Alex had disappeared. Tapping a finger on her chin, she said, "I think this is something very different than an entrance to the afterworld. I saw the air shimmering briefly right before that tunnel appeared – jest as he mentioned. Besides, he didn't disappear on purpose. He accidentally fell in."

Diana shook her head and waded back to the west side of the river. After climbing out, she said, "Come on. We need to hurry and get back to the hotel so we can request a search and rescue team."

"They'll never find him," Jane replied.

"But what if he's simply lost? The longer we wait to act, the harder it will be to find him. We need to tell Elizabeth what's happened and get her to call local law enforcement to help search."

"Before ye do that, try a search spell. I know ye've said ye never quite mastered it at school, but it can't hurt."

Diana grabbed her talisman and started singing,
*"From rushing river to deep dark forest*
*From rolling plains to snow-capped mountain*

*Please, dear Gaia,*
*Help me find what I seek*
*So mote it be."*

But instead of seeing a vision of Alex, she felt a sucking sensation – something so powerful that it took her breath away. She blacked out and woke to find her head on Jane's lap.

"Are ye okay?" Jane asked, a look of concern clouding her face. "You've been out for half an hour."

Diana had to blink a few times to focus her eyes before she struggled to a sitting position. "I'll be fine. Just give me a minute. My head is still spinning."

"What happened?" Jane asked.

"I'm not sure," Diana replied. "It felt like something was sucking all the air out of me. I wonder if that was what Alex was talking about earlier."

"Are ye sure it wasn't yer imagination?" Jane asked.

Diana shook her head and instantly regretted it. She clapped her hands to her head to stop the dizziness that threatened to overwhelm her. When the sensation passed, she said, "No. It was unlike anything I've ever experienced."

Jane helped Diana walk back to the hotel, where they told Elizabeth what had happened. After hearing their bizarre tale twice, the High Priestess repeated what they'd said before lapsing into silence. At last, she roused herself. "I'm not sure how I'll explain this to the authorities because I can't tell them we believe magic was involved."

"I agree," Diana said. "If it makes you feel any better, I don't think yer grandson was planning for anything like this to happen to him. I'm convinced that some outside force snatched him away."

"I understand," Elizabeth replied. "I think we should tell the police and treat this like a lost person situation."

"I can't help but wonder if he was getting close to finding the Grail, and this was the Grail's protective measure," Jane said.

Elizabeth shook her head and said, "I'm not looking forward to telling his grandfather that we've lost him again. But, I'm curious as to how he'll react."

"What do you mean?" Diana asked.

"Well, I've gotten the impression that he was half-expecting something strange to happen when I've made this type of call before. I'm also curious how Lady Yvaine will respond because I have no idea what to expect from her. I could see her being either curious or furious."

The police arrived within half an hour and immediately started a search of the area.

After the first searchers had disappeared into the woods, Diana asked, "What should we do next? We can't just wait around here forever."

"I've already given the police my contact information," Elizabeth said. "I suggest we return to Bucharest and wait for your mother and the others to arrive. The police will let me know if they get any leads."

"Ye're not going to stay here and see if they can find him?" Jane asked. "How can ye be so cold-hearted?"

"You know what our order's rules say about boys like him. And even if I was to try to find him, the police have more resources and will do a better job. Come on now, girls, our ride is waiting for us."

## CHAPTER 34
# WHEREVER HE MAY GO

Alex felt like something was tugging at his insides, trying to turn him inside out while simultaneously hurling him through a long curving tube. He couldn't see anything except a few pinpricks of light that appeared and disappeared in the blink of an eye.

He had no idea how long he'd fallen when a light suddenly appeared at the end of the tunnel. An instant later, he tumbled onto a thick carpet of moss in the middle of a forest. It took him several minutes before he regained his senses and looked around. The first thing he noticed was the total silence. There wasn't even the sound of wind rustling through the leaves to break the unnatural stillness. The second thing he noticed was that the tree leaves had gone from the emerald green of early summer to the golds and reds of fall.

He looked around but didn't see Diana, Jane, Deborah, or the river he'd crossed moments earlier. All he could see was a forest stretching in all directions.

Alex struggled to his feet and walked towards where he thought he'd crossed the river. But he'd only gone a few yards when he found a thick wall of brambles blocking his way. He circled the area, looking for some way out, but he kept encountering a living fence of bushes and trees hemming him in.

Panic welled up inside him, driving him to sit down and think through his options. He blindly stared at the plants walling him in, wondering what he was going to do, when he felt a bump. An image of a path suddenly flashed into his mind, causing him to look down and see Sadie sitting at his feet, looking at him expectantly.

"Did you get me into this, or are you trying to help me out of this mess?" Alex asked the little dragon. He was surprised to have the image of the trail flash in his mind again. Alex sat up and studied his winged companion for a bit. She'd changed colors and was now a mixture of earthen tones perfectly matching the fall colors of the forest surrounding her.

Sadie continued staring at him, sending him images of the trail, until he said, "Fine. Lead the way." He stood and was surprised when she flew up to his shoulder, craned her head around, and nipped him lightly on the ear.

Alex yelped, "Ow! What was that for?"

The little dragon dipped her head and nuzzled his cheek. Caught off guard by the unexpected affection, Alex reflexively rubbed her furry neck, drawing a low rumbling noise from her. "All right. You seem to be a lot more comfortable with this situation than I am, so lead the way."

Sadie flew a short distance to a large branch on a spruce tree, then turned and sent the same image of the trail. Alex followed her from tree to tree until they finally came on a small path that led off to his left. For the first time since he'd entered the tunnel, Alex felt a sense of hope. He followed the little dragon for almost a mile before seeing an opening in the distance. As quickly as his hopes rose, though, they crashed as he realized he'd been so focused on finding a way back that he hadn't thought about any possible danger ahead of him. He quickly pulled the ankh out, hoping it would give him guidance, and was surprised when it lay inert in his hand.

He looked from Sadie to the opening, hoping she'd provide some insight on what lay ahead – but got nothing. Figuring he couldn't fight whatever had lured him into the forest, he took a deep breath and plunged on. After half an hour, though, the clearing seemed as far away as before. Unsure what lay ahead, he pulled a power bar out of his pack and sat down.

But when he looked around, he saw the forest had closed behind him, covering up the trail he'd been on, and realized there was no turning back. When he'd finished eating, he took a swig from one of the water bottles he kept in his pack and pushed on. Instead of getting lighter, though, the forest grew darker. He knew it had been mid-morning when he'd crossed the river and wondered if he'd lost track of time, as it seemed much later in the day than he thought.

Not wanting to wander in the dark in the strange forest, he decided to camp for the night and looked around for materials he could make a fire with. It took him some time to find enough dry tinder, but he eventually got a fire started and sat down with his back against a nearby tree.

He was glad he'd stopped when he did because the fire quickly became his only light source, as the sky was as dark as a cave. After the unnatural silence of the day, the forest seemed to come alive at night. The strange noises spooked him, causing him to put more wood on the fire and scoot closer.

Exhausted from the worry and effort of the day, he soon drifted asleep with Sadie curled up beside him. He awoke to a howl off in the distance. Several cries immediately answered. Alex sat up and fed more wood onto the fire, listening as the howls came closer. He glanced at the pile of wood he'd collected and mentally kicked himself for not getting more, as it didn't look like it would last the night.

The howls kept growing closer until he saw a wolf, its yellow-black eyes peering at him out of the forest's depths. Alex yelled at the wolf, hoping it would scare the beast away, but all it did was blink its eyes in response.

Another pair of eyes popped out of the forest off to the left of the first animal. More than half a dozen pairs of eyes soon joined the first two sets. Alex looked from one to the other before focusing on the first set, figuring it was the alpha member of the pack. Neither blinked for what seemed like an eternity as the two combatants sized each other up. Before Alex could figure out what to do, the first wolf growled and jumped straight at him.

The animal never reached him as Sadie jumped in front of it. Alex wasn't sure what the little dragon did, but the fire suddenly turned into a roaring inferno. Flames jumped towards the wolf, lighting the beast's hair on fire and sending it howling and careening around. It bumped into a second one, which also caught on fire. Soon all the wolves were howling in panic. Seconds later, they ran away, leaving Alex and Sadie alone by the fire.

The flames died down as quickly as they had roared to life, leaving the rest of the forest in silence. Alex looked down at his companion, ran a hand over Sadie's fur, and said, "I'm glad you came with me. Thank you."

Sadie nudged Alex, forcing him to come out of his crouch. She kept at it until he finally leaned back against the tree. Then she curled up in his lap and went to sleep. But Alex's nerves were still on high alert, so it was some time before sleep overtook him.

# CHAPTER 35
# THE ENCHANTED CASTLE

The whispering of the wind through the leaves woke Alex, making him briefly think he was back home on a camping trip. He sat up and rubbed his eyes, hoping to see the tent his dad always used. But all he saw was the dense forest surrounding him.

Smoke from the still smoldering fire reminded him of the previous night's events and drove him to listen for signs of predators. But the forest had returned to near-total silence. A grumble from his stomach and the dryness of his throat reminded him that he still had to eat and drink. Worried that he might run out of food before finding more, he took only a few sips from one of his water bottles and grabbed a single power bar from his pack.

Something else bothered him, but he couldn't quite put a finger on it until he realized Sadie had disappeared. Figuring she'd gone hunting for her breakfast, he mashed his Tilley on his head, shouldered his pack, and stepped onto the trail.

He finally reached the opening he'd seen the day before and saw a meadow of waist-high grass surrounded by a dense line of hardwood trees. But what caught his attention was the castle on the far side.

Relief at finally finding some civilization warred with his frustration at having spent the previous night in the woods when he was so close to shelter. He heard a rustling sound and turned just in time to see the trail completely disappearing behind him. Alex looked back at the castle and wondered who was putting so much effort into luring him in.

Knowing he had no choice but to forge ahead, he began wading through the grass towards the castle. The rustling sound he'd heard minutes earlier resumed, and when he turned to look behind him, he saw that the forest was slowly swallowing the meadow with each step he took.

He briefly thought about heading back into the woods to find a way out, but he figured it would be in vain, as whoever, or whatever, was controlling the area was forcing him to go towards the castle.

Sometime later, he emerged from the high grass and stepped onto a well-groomed lawn that gently rose to the castle high on a hillside above him. He was staring at the structure, wondering what was facing him, when Sadie appeared and flew at him, chittering loudly.

She landed on his shoulder and instantly sent him a flood of images of darkness and, surprisingly, a sense of excitement. Alex pulled her down and began petting her, trying to calm her. When that didn't work, he tried humming softly to her, but all he continued to see were images of black.

Alex looked behind him and saw that the forest had finally stopped approaching, leaving a narrow grass strip between the hill and the trees. Looking down at his excitable companion, he said, "I guess we don't have much choice. Let's see where this is leading us."

Sadie immediately flew out of his arms and towards the castle. Trusting the little dragon wasn't leading him into danger, he followed her up the hill.

It wasn't until he was almost at the castle's walls that he noticed a drawbridge lay across a moat as if to invite him in. Alex pulled the ankh from inside his shirt and looked down at it, hoping it would give him guidance. But instead of a warning, the little looped cross seemed excited. Shaking his head at its unexpected behavior, he tucked the ankh back into his shirt and headed for the drawbridge.

After passing under a metal portcullis, he saw a large cobblestone courtyard inside the walls. Off to the right stood the horse stables, but there were no signs of horses. To his left were steps leading to the battlements far above and a few small buildings. He thought about going up to get a better view of the area but headed towards a large building across the yard with stone steps leading to two massive oak doors. His foot had barely touched the first step when a deafening roar reverberated overhead. A second later, the ankh's force field flared up around him just in time to deflect a stream of flames.

He jumped backward and looked for where the torrent of flames had come from. His heart skipped a beat when he saw a monstrous black dragon perched on the battlements. Its enormous unfolded wings cast a shadow over the entire courtyard. The dragon's scaly tail wrapped around one of the turrets, its tip nearly touching the ground. It lifted its massive head and roared in anger. Then, uncurling its tail from the turret, it leapt off the battlements landing so hard that it shook the castle grounds like a small earthquake. Alex, who was already running towards the wall the dragon had been standing on, looked back and saw that the giant dragon's smaller front legs, each with five razor-sharp talons, had clamped down on the spot where he'd been standing seconds earlier.

Fear lent him energy he didn't think he had. He scrambled underneath the dragon, trying to cross the courtyard, but only got halfway before it jumped and pirouetted in mid-air in an attempt to catch him. As soon as the dragon left the ground, the ankh jerked him back towards where he'd been standing a moment before. He didn't make it very far, as the beast landed so quickly that Alex accidentally bumped into the beast's scaly belly and fell backward. Lying on the ground, he noticed a jagged scar with golden edges on the dragon's chest, but he didn't take time to study it. Instead, he scrambled to his feet and raced for the drawbridge.

He had barely escaped from beneath the beast when the dragon roared angrily and hurled a torrent of fire towards the open gates. Alex heard a hissing sound and dropped, barely avoiding the fire roaring overhead. As soon as the flames had dissipated, he jumped up and raced towards the stables, where he ducked behind a stone column to avoid the next blast.

For the next few minutes, the dragon chased Alex around the courtyard, trying to stomp him, slice him with its razor-sharp talons, knock him with its tail, and incinerate him. The dragon nicked Alex Several times, but it never made a killing blow. All the while, Sadie was nipping at the head of the giant black dragon, trying to distract it while simultaneously sending out a constant barrage of images. They were so bright, intense, and frequent, though, that they made it hard for Alex to concentrate.

With his breath becoming ragged, his legs feeling like jelly, and every part of his body bruised and battered, Alex knew he didn't have much time before the dragon would end it. He started running towards the gates before abruptly reversing course and heading towards the doors to the main building. As soon as he reached them, he lifted one large iron ring and pushed. The door opened surprisingly easy. Alex jumped in and slammed it behind him an instant before the dragon's flames hit the great oak doors. A heavy wooden beam slid down, locking Alex in as smoke filtered through the cracks.

The room shuddered as the great beast threw its body against the doors and roared angrily. Alex looked for a hiding place in the great hall but didn't see any obvious spots as the only furniture were a few wall sconces, a large oak table, and chairs. A massive fireplace, so big that several people could stand inside it, stood off to the side. The only ornamentation was a greenish-gold rock on the mantelpiece.

Clanking sounds outside drew Alex's attention back to the doors. He found a peephole in one and looked through. To his dismay, he saw the large iron chains on either side of the drawbridge slowly winding around wooden wheels, hauling the gate up. Wondering whether he should be afraid or relieved someone else was inside the castle, he tried seeing if anyone was around the bridge but didn't spot anyone.

He looked for another way out and spotted a door he hadn't noticed before. Hoping it would help him escape the castle, he went through it and was disappointed when he found it only led to the kitchen, where there were several bins of fresh fruits and vegetables. There were no modern appliances, only a few wooden bowls, old-fashioned utensils, and a roasting spit inside a brick fireplace. He thought about eating one of the apples but saw another door on the far side of the room, went over to it, and hesitantly opened the door. Seeing it led outside, he looked around for the dragon. Not seeing or hearing any signs of it, Alex took one step out but stayed inside the doorframe, ready to dart back in if necessary.

The door opened onto a small dirt courtyard with a few buildings that looked like servants' quarters scattered about the perimeter. On the opposite side of the yard was a set of steps leading up to the battlements. Hoping for a way out of his magical prison, he took another step out the door. No sooner did his foot touch the step outside than he felt a rush of air from above. He looked up and saw the black dragon settling on the edge of the main building. Alex had just enough time to jump back in and close the door before a giant fireball coated the courtyard. Growing more worried about being able to escape, he made one more circuit of the floor, hoping to find a way out that he'd missed in his earlier exploration – but found nothing.

Since there were no other rooms on the floor, he headed up the staircase in the great room to search the second floor. Even though every room had beds, armoires, and chamber pots, none looked like anyone had slept in them for ages. Alex felt the bed covers, expecting them to be brittle, but was surprised everything was soft. It was only when he absent-mindedly ran his hand across a side table that he realized everything was immaculately clean, despite the lack of people.

When he'd finished searching the second floor, he returned to the kitchen and sat on a bench near the kitchen door. As soon as he leaned back, the wall gave way, and he fell backwards.

He twisted around and peered into the hidden space, but all he could see were stairs descending into darkness. Wondering if he could escape underground, he pulled out his flashlight and was about to head down when he remembered his experience inside the Moon Temple in Lamanai. Picking up one of the big bowls in the kitchen, he placed it upside down on the floor next to the door jamb before he stepped in. Then he turned on his flashlight and headed down.

The musty air rising from below made it seem like no one had entered for ages. Alex felt the ankh through his shirt and was confused when he discovered it had changed back to excitedly thumping against his chest. The passageway eventually emptied into a large, dank chamber. Alex looked around but couldn't see much as the room was too big for his light to penetrate to the farthest edges. He found the nearest wall and began walking around the perimeter. A short distance after the second turn, Alex spotted a large rectangular object and hurried forward. He gasped when he saw a gigantic marble sarcophagus in front of him, its lid slightly open. An image of Dracula lying inside sent him scurrying upstairs.

As he stepped back into the kitchen, his stomach reminded him how little he'd eaten in the last day. Overcoming his concerns, he grabbed a selection of fruits and carrots, then returned to the main room, where he sat at the dining table.

He was surprised at how fresh and tasty the food was and ate until he was full. Then he filled his pack, unsure when he'd get more food, and leaned back to look up at the ceiling, hoping he'd get some epiphany on how to escape. A yawn escaped him, surprising him since it seemed like it had been only a few hours since he woke. He headed upstairs for a nap, choosing a bedroom that looked out over the drawbridge towards the trail he'd come in on. Alex hesitated, wondering if it was safe, but decided he was too tired to fight it. He lay down and promptly fell asleep.

Alex woke with a start, sensing someone was nearby. The only light in the room came from a flickering candle that obscured the face of the person holding it.

"Who are you?" the unknown person asked.

Alex blinked several times and cautiously lifted himself onto one elbow. He held up his other hand to block the candlelight from shining into his eyes and said, "I'm sorry for intruding, but I'm trapped. My name is Alex Scire. Who are you?"

"I've been known by many names through the years, but my last name before disappearing from the rest of humanity was Prince Vlad Dracul III."

# CHAPTER 36
# VLAD THE IMPALER

Alex sat up with a start and scooted back. He pulled the sheets up to his chin as thoughts of Dracula sucking his blood crowded out everything else.

Vlad lowered his candle. "I didn't mean to frighten you," he said. "But you're the first visitor to Corbenic Castle in centuries, and I had to come see you."

With the candle lower, Alex could see that the man was nothing like the Dracula of the movies. He was short, with a large bushy moustache, sad brown eyes, and a thick head of grey hair that hung over his shoulders. As Alex looked closer, he saw the man was wearing a long white robe with a red cross on his chest. Vlad waved his hand and lit half a dozen candles around the room. He motioned to the end of Alex's bed and asked, "Do you mind if I sit? It's been so long since I've had company that I couldn't wait till morning to talk to you."

Alex moved his pack and waved him to the bed.

"I can see the emotions flitting across your face," Vlad said. "I assure you, no harm will come to you here in my house."

"That sounds like an empty promise," Alex said. "I nearly died because of your guard dog out there."

Vlad smiled. "I can't guarantee your safety outside the walls of this building. My promise is only good if you stay inside."

Alex studied his host briefly before asking, "How could you be who you say you are unless you're a spirit? You should've died hundreds of years ago."

"Has it been that long? I haven't paid attention since time moves at its own pace here. But I must correct you. I am still very much alive."

Alex frowned. "But your wife, Elisabetta, said you were neither alive nor dead."

At the mention of his wife, Vlad leapt to his feet with a vigor that belied his age, strode to the top of the bed, grabbed Alex's arms, and lifted him into the air like he was nothing more than a dishrag. The questions came spilling out. "When did you talk to her? What did she say?"

There was no warmth in Vlad's firm grip, but the absence of cold and the pressure on his arms convinced Alex that Vlad was a living person. "Let me go, and I'll tell you." He waited till Vlad had set him back on the bed before he said, "I talked to her a couple of days ago in Poenari."

"I thought she was dead all this time. How could she be alive and I not know it?" Vlad asked as he began pacing the room.

"She's not alive. I can talk to ghosts, which I thought you were at first. She asked that I free you, although I don't see why you need my help since you're alive."

"How do I know you're telling the truth?"

"Why should I lie to you? I've talked to lots of ghosts who've asked me to help them. Your wife was no different."

Vlad stopped pacing and sat in a chair near the door. He ran his hands through his hair, then asked, "How is she?"

"She looked sad but she was most concerned with your well-being because she worried you'd end up like her – wandering around the Earth forever. She also seemed to think you were hiding some secret, which has kept you from moving on."

Vlad let out a wail that startled Alex. "I wish I'd never found the cursed thing. It's caused me nothing but pain and misery and caused me to be stuck in the afterlife." He started pacing around the room again before sitting down. Vlad remained pensive for some time before abruptly asking, "Have you ever heard of King Arthur and the Knights of the Round Table?"

"Who hasn't?"

"Hmmm. Even in my day, people greatly exaggerated our exploits. Your reaction makes it seem like the tales have grown since I left your world. But in several ways, the tales were right. King Arthur was a great man. Our country was constantly warring until he started uniting the different factions. And yes, just like the stories say, he built a round table for his leading knights. He meant to impress us with the concept that none of us was above the others. Some of the tales about dragons are fictional, but some aren't, as you found out today. Also, Camelot wasn't as fancy as the stories would lead you to believe, but for its day, it was magnificent as we were a poor and uneducated country." He paused to look out the darkened window, then asked, "Do you remember any of the stories about the Holy Grail?"

"I used to think it was just a cool story – until a couple of weeks ago. But now, well, to be honest, it's why I'm here," Alex said. "I met a man who gave me a book that linked you to the Grail. It didn't make any sense, though, because I thought Sir Galahad found it in the King Arthur stories."

Vlad shifted in his chair, looking extremely uncomfortable. "I did, along with Sir Bors and Sir Percival, although we called it the Sangreal."

Alex shook his head. "I'm confused. I thought the legend says Galahad found the Grail because he was the purest of heart and mind. But you earned the nickname the Impaler and a reputation for being one of the cruelest people in the world. How can you be the same person?"

Vlad resumed pacing the room. "You have no idea what a burden the Sangreal has been. My relief at finally being able to tell the whole story to someone is almost as great a joy as when I found it. To answer your question, I have to go back to my youth. I didn't meet my father, Sir Lancelot, until I had bested him in combat. He then knighted me and introduced me to King Arthur. Being young and idealistic, I joined in the quest to find the Sangreal and was successful, along with my brothers-in-arms, Sir Percival, and Sir Bors, in finding the Fisher King. Unlike the tales, though, that's not when we found the Sangreal. Instead, the Fisher King recruited the three of us into an order of men and women dedicated to finding Christ's holy relics and safeguarding them. He took us to Avalon, where we gained immortality by kissing the Crown of Thorns.

From that day on, we searched the world, trying to fulfill our order's mission.

"It wasn't until six hundred years later that Sir Percival, Sir Bors, and I, who were going by different names by then, along with five other members of our order, formed what eventually became the Knights Templar. Our ostensible goal was to protect pilgrims traveling to the Holy Land, but what we were really doing was trying to find and protect the Holy Relics. So, we convinced King Baldwin II, the ruler of Jerusalem at the time, to let us use Temple Mount as our headquarters. Eight poor men entered the building that lay on the ruins of King Solomon's Temple. We came out as the most powerful men in all of Europe. People believed we'd found a fabulous treasure – and we had. Only it wasn't gold or silver. It was the Sangreal. Only later did people start calling it the Holy Grail. We used it to get papal support for our activities and gained thousands of recruits and vast amounts of money, leading us to become the first bankers and pan-national group of knights in Europe. But power corrupts. We forgot our original vows of finding and protecting holy relics and became more involved in politics, trying to reshape Europe to our vision. Only we discovered that power scares those who don't have it.

"So, on Friday the 13th, 1307, the King of France sent troops to imprison or kill all our members – with the Pope's blessing. I barely escaped with the Sangreal. I heard that the Fisher King had returned to Avalon and went searching for him, thinking I would finally fulfill my quest. Unfortunately, I never found Avalon again because I was not pure enough of heart to deserve that state of grace.

"So, I disguised myself, hid the Grail among my belongings, and started wandering across England and Scotland. But after years of failing to find any peace, I crossed the English Channel and continued my wanderings on the continent.

"I'd learned centuries before never to stay in one place long enough for anyone to realize I wasn't aging. Occasionally, I would swap identities with someone I met because they wanted to disappear. I met the original Vlad Dracul in Istanbul shortly after the Ottomans released him from prison. He was bitter about his father sending him as a hostage to the Ottoman Emperor and how well the Turks had treated his brother.

"We swapped identities, and I came here. That's when I met Elisabetta and fell in love. I rebuilt Poenari to protect the Grail and planned to spend the rest of her time on Earth there. I even hoped the magic of the Grail would let her age at my pace.

"Then, that asinine Pope Pius II called for another bloody crusade against the Muslims. He felt that their taking of Constantinople was enough justification for more killing. All it did was stir up the Ottomans, who attacked the Balkans.

"At first, I thought I could ride out the coming war by sitting tight here in Wallachia. But I started hearing rumors that the Ottomans weren't after more land and power – they were searching for the Sangreal. When I came to this out-of-the-way place, I thought no one would ever assume it was here. I realize now that I'd been trusting too much to luck and anonymity to keep it safe.

"How they discovered the Sangreal was here is beyond my understanding. But, as the Ottoman army drew closer, I realized I had to defend it at all costs. Whoever was behind the search was so intent on finding the cup that he was willing to sacrifice the lives of tens of thousands of people. So, I figured I had to be just as ruthless. At first, I tried fighting traditional-style battles and hoped a defeat would force them to retreat. But they kept coming.

"When I discovered Elisabetta had committed suicide, I went crazy and impaled tens of thousands of their soldiers. When I finally regained my reason, I happened to meet a man who looked like me. He was so greedy for the power and wealth I offered him that he readily agreed to swap identities with me and damn the consequences. He became the Prince of Wallachia, and I again became a nobody."

Alex tried to get comfortable, causing Vlad to say, "Patience, my story is nearing the end. I returned to my traveling days and started wandering around this country, but I could never bring myself to go far from the final resting place of my Elisabetta. I'm not sure when I realized something was stalking me, but I could feel its presence long before I saw her. Fearing it was after the Sangreal, I sought a hiding place and found this castle. I hoped it'd pass me by, but it was a trap.

"I'm not sure how it did it, but the dragon you met maneuvered me into this enchanted castle. I was so angry that it had caught me that I turned and fought. Maybe it was my skill as a warrior, or perhaps bad luck, but I slew that dragon and cut out its heart in anger. You might have seen a greenish-gold stone downstairs; well, I found that in the dragon and placed it on the mantlepiece as a kind of trophy. I have no idea how it has continued to live; one of the many things I don't understand about this place.

"But once again, I didn't understand the consequences of my rash actions. Those who used to live here died long ago, but I've kept living. I've tried escaping numerous times, but all my attempts have failed. It's like I'm in some magical prison that cares for all my physical needs. The only good thing about my imprisonment is that I no longer have to worry about protecting the Sangreal – the bane of my existence. I am so relieved that the Lord has finally seen fit to send someone to take on the responsibility of it."

"I hate to burst your bubble," Alex said, "but I'm not staying here. I plan on finding a way out of here when it's light."

"I told you; you can't leave. I've tried, but that dragon won't let you escape." Vlad stood up. "Would you like to see the Sangreal? It's down in the sarcophagus, where I sleep with it in the daytime."

"That's pretty creepy," Alex said.

"It keeps me from having to see the world outside, which is a constant reminder of what I've lost."

Alex thought about Vlad's offer, then shook his head. "I came halfway around the world to find it, thinking I would find answers and solutions. But I've changed my mind. I don't want anything to do with it."

# CHAPTER 37
# THE RESPONSIBILITY OF TOMORROW

"But, you have to take it," Vlad said. "You've earned the right to protect the Grail. I'm too old and unworthy to carry the mantle anymore."

"Aren't you listening? I don't want to have anything to do with it after seeing what's happened to you," Alex said. "It corrupts people just like every other magical object I've encountered. I should've known better than to come looking for it."

"I'm sure you won't succumb to its lure because you have a strength of will I never had. Please, don't throw away this opportunity to ensure the Sangreal's safety." Seeing he wasn't convincing Alex, Vlad said, "It's not forever. All I want you to do is take it to Avalon. They will look after it properly from there."

"But you tried for years and couldn't find it. How am I supposed to find a place that hides from the world? Besides, there's no way I'll give up years of my life to find a home for the blasted thing."

"It won't be like that. I lost my chance of returning because I succumbed to temptation and didn't immediately take the Sangreal to Avalon when I first found it. If I had done what I should have, I wouldn't have endured all this torment. But trust me, as long as you remain pure of heart, the Sangreal will lead you to Avalon."

Seeing Alex looking skeptically at him, Vlad said, "Avalon is real, but it's invisible to those who aren't worthy. Joseph of Arimathea and Mary Magdalene devoted their lives to recovering and protecting sacred relics Christ touched during his last days on Earth. They kept their work secret because they knew what would happen if the unworthy found any of those relics. Thus, their work faded to myth, and they became known as the Fisher King and the Lady of the Lake."

"You're not going to talk me into this. As soon as it gets light, I'll find a way out of here – without the Grail, or Sangreal, or whatever you call it."

"Even if you could avoid the dragon, it wouldn't make a difference. There's nowhere for you to go. As I'm sure you found, the forest will keep you here unless you have the Sangreal."

"I've got friends who are worried sick about me. They probably have search teams looking for me as we speak and will find me any time now."

Vlad shook his head. "You don't understand. The enchantments around this place will prevent anyone from finding you."

Alex got a mulish look on his face and stubbornly said, "My friends will find me."

A sad look came over Vlad. "I wish it were that simple. But think about it. How did you find this place?"

"I literally stumbled. I must've hit my head when I fell, though, because one second, I was near Poenari; the next, I was out in that freaky forest. I eventually found a trail and followed it here, but I couldn't have gone too far."

"Tell me. Did you feel anything strange on your way here?"

"Well, I did feel a strange tugging when I crossed the river. Then there was the falling through a tunnel sensation." Alex suddenly looked up. "Could we be dead, and this is all part of the afterworld?"

"It's possible, but I believe there's another explanation."

"So, you want me to take the Grail to a mythical place, but you don't know where we are nor where I'm supposed to go. And you can't tell me how to avoid the dragon outside that nearly squished and cooked me when I arrived. How am I supposed to do all this?"

"The Sangreal will lead you out."

"You're still not listening to me," Alex said. "I told you I want nothing to do with it."

"You should be excited to take the Grail. It's a great honor. Besides, you'd become immortal."

"And why should I want that? You don't seem happy with your immortality."

"I've made foolish choices. I had the opportunity to do great things or be content, but I threw it all away because I kept wanting more."

"And you don't think I'll succumb to the same temptations? I don't want to test your theory. I think you should destroy it now because I bet it would fix this mess we're in."

Vlad gasped. "That's blasphemy. Please promise me you won't hurt the Sangreal, that you'll take it to Avalon and give it to them for safekeeping."

"Say, I take it to this place, which I'm not agreeing to do. How do I know they won't misuse it?"

"I first met Joseph and Mary when they'd already been guarding Christ's other relics for five centuries.

All the objects have miraculous powers and can do just about anything you wish. Yet, I never saw them use the relics' powers except to hide Avalon."

Despite his misgivings, Alex asked, "Even help my sister move on?"

Vlad backed up. "That's blasphemy. Only God can do that."

Alex huffed. "That's just my luck. I keep finding things that will supposedly help my sister move on, but none work. It doesn't matter, though. When the sun comes up, I'm getting out of here, one way or another. I just have to figure out how to get past that dragon. Any ideas?"

Vlad frowned. "No. Since you got in, I was hoping you'd figure a way out. I told you, I've tried escaping, but even without its heart, it won't let me leave this building. If I stick my head out, it growls and snaps at me. I've tried talking to the beast but accomplished nothing because it doesn't talk."

Alex's hope for escaping was waning. In a resigned voice, he asked, "So, what's it like being the Grail's guardian?"

"Does this mean you'll reconsider?"

"No! I'm just curious."

"I don't understand. God has chosen you for this. Taking the Sangreal to Avalon will be the greatest honor of your life. How could you turn down this once-in-a-lifetime opportunity?"

"You don't want it anymore," Alex said. "Why should I?"

Vlad winced. "I learned my lesson too late, but there's still time for you. And since I'm still hopeful I can change your mind, you need to understand that there are rules you must follow. First, you must not tell anyone you have it. Second, you must keep it hidden at all times. Lastly, you must be willing to risk your life to defend it."

Neither spoke for some time. The first rays of sunshine were streaming through the window when Alex broke the silence. "So, if that's a real dragon out there, how can it still be alive if you cut its heart out?"

"It's just one of the many mysteries of this place, like where does the food come from? Why is the castle always clean? And why does nothing ever decay?"

"Well, do you know where she came from? Because no one sees dragons anymore."

"How do you know it's a she?" Vlad asked. "I've been around it for centuries and had no idea what gender it is."

It took Alex a few seconds before he realized he'd gotten the information in the images Sadie had sent him about the darkness. Not wanting to share his knowledge, he shrugged. "I just know."

"I don't know where dragons came from, nor where they disappeared to, but they were quite common when I was a Knight of the Round Table. Many a knight went on an adventure to slay a dragon. People treated us like heroes whenever we were able to slay one." In a quieter voice, he added, "Although, I must admit that we were a barbaric lot and never tried to understand them. Now that I think of it, they never seemed to do any damage unless we attacked them. It's probably why it doesn't like me. I hope you didn't hurt it."

"Hurt it!" exclaimed Alex. "It nearly killed me a dozen times."

"I'm sure it was only doing its duty as it saw fit. Like you are …."

Alex didn't listen to the last words as the ankh started burning against his skin. He held up a hand to stop Vlad and said, "Something's wrong. Quick, we need to protect the Grail."

"That can't be. This is a magical place protected from the outside world," Vlad said.

"We can argue about that later." Alex jumped out of bed and headed out the door, as he said, "I don't know about your definition of who is worthy to see the Grail, but I think the unworthy are about to invade."

## CHAPTER 38
# THE SANGREAL

Without waiting for Vlad, Alex ran down the stairs, grabbed a torch in the great room, and pushed through the hidden door in the kitchen. He wanted to leap down the steps to the dungeon but forced himself to slow down so he wouldn't fall. When he got to the bottom, he turned and raced for Vlad's sarcophagus.

He stopped short when a roar reverberated through the room, followed an instant later by a heart-rending scream of pain. Alex winced and wondered what was happening above, but he cast aside his questions and tried shoving the lid off. It didn't budge. An explosion, followed by an even louder roar, caused him to redouble his efforts. But they, too, failed.

Knowing he had little time to secure the Grail, Alex searched for something to pry the lid open. He found a pile of iron bars, picked one up, and inserted it into the small open space on the stone coffin. As he pulled down on the bar, Alex closed his eyes and tried shutting out the sounds of agonized screams from above. This time, the ankh sent a surge of power into his arms. He flipped the lid off, causing it to shatter on the floor. Raising his torch for better lighting, he bent over the sarcophagus to look inside. He froze when he saw a jewel-encrusted gold goblet lying deep in the red satin lining. As he reached for the object, a familiar gravelly voice sounded behind him.

"Well, well. We meet again."

Alex whirled around and gasped when he saw Torquemada standing near the base of the stairs, holding the withered Hand of Glory.

An instant later, Ferdinand and Isabella appeared. "You! How did you find this place?" the king screamed.

Torquemada ignored Ferdinand and said, "I see now why Pythia is so impressed by you. Some other time I might have been interested in hearing your story on how you can interact with our world, but alas, I'll never know. Because today you die."

"Wait," Isabella said. "Don't be too hasty to kill him. We need to find the Grail first." She turned to her husband. "Keep your scepter trained on him while I search for it. And don't be afraid to use it this time if he makes a move."

Ferdinand motioned for Alex to move away from the opened sarcophagus, but Alex didn't budge.

"Do you see what I'm holding in my hand?" Ferdinand shouted as he raised his magical scepter. "Did you hear the explosions above? That was me. I blew apart this castle's defenses while Tomás fought the dragon. Now, move so my wife can search. If you don't do as I say, I'll cut off a limb and let you die slowly in agony. But, if you cooperate, I'll be merciful and kill you quickly and painlessly."

Figuring his only hope to survive was to surprise them, Alex charged, hoping the ankh would protect him. He was relieved when he felt the force field popping up around him, but he never made it to the king as a blast of energy struck him so hard that it slammed him back against the wall, where he crumpled to the floor. Alex looked down, expecting to see a hole in his chest. But the only thing out of place was a little smoke rising from his shirt. He staggered to his feet and lurched towards Ferdinand, who launched another energy bolt at him. It skimmed off Alex's force field, missing his ear by less than an inch, before exploding into the wall and sending rocks everywhere.

Remembering Vlad's third expectation of the Grail holder, Alex leaped towards the stone coffin and reached for the cup. Before he could grab it, though, Isabella flew over and yanked it away.

The former queen cackled with glee and cried out, "We found it. Everlasting life is ours. We'll be alive again before the sun has set." Then she backed away, keeping a wary eye on Alex.

Torquemada reached for the golden cup and said, "Give that to me. All my life I've done all your dirty work. I've earned the right to use it to continue our holy mission."

Ferdinand shook his head. "We don't need you anymore, Tomás. We have everything we need to return to the world of the living and continue our reign. It's our divine right." Without warning, he aimed his scepter at the Grand Inquisitor. A bolt of energy shot out and hit the former Dominican friar. Torquemada stood in stunned disbelief before bursting into flames and dropping the Hand of Glory on the floor. An instant later, he was nothing more than a wisp of smoke.

Isabella picked up the ghoulish magical hand and said, "Come, love. I've always disliked seeing violence. We have what we came for, so leave the boy to his fate." She grabbed her husband's hand, turned, and flew up the steps.

They ran into Vlad halfway up. The guardian of the Grail lunged for the object he'd protected for over a millennium but missed and tumbled down the stairs, screaming, "No, you can't take it. You're not worthy."

Ferdinand and Isabella laughed as they flew out of sight.

Alex rushed to Vlad and helped him sit on the bottom step. Blood ran down his face from a gash on his head while his left arm hung limply by his side. "I'm sorry," Alex said. "I couldn't stop them from taking the Grail."

Vlad smiled. "All is well. Quick now. Before they come back, go get the calix from my bed. You'll find a small fountain of water at the back of my sarcophagus. Hurry, and take a drink before they come back for the cup. You'll need the power of the Sangreal to help you survive."

Alex scrunched up his face. "Wait. What are you talking about?"

"The calix is the black clay cup on my bed – the real Sangreal. It's what you came all this way for. Drinking from the cup will protect you from harm, but be wary. Do not partake from it except in the most dire situations, for you'll become addicted to it and wind up like me."

Alex returned to the stone coffin and searched the bedding until he found an unadorned cup that looked like a simple chalice. Its only decorations were a few thin grooves around the top of the cup and a row of beads at its base. Alex bent to pick it up but jerked his hand away when a tingling sensation shot through his body the instant he touched it.

He stared at the cup for several seconds before he hesitantly picked it up and went to a small pipe in the wall where a trickle of water fell into a basin below it. Alex held the cup under the stream of water till the cup was full. Then he raised it to his lips and was about to drink from it when he heard Vlad moaning.

The realization of what he was about to do hit him like a freight train. He lowered the cup, took it over to Vlad, and held it to the old man's lips. Vlad protested, but Alex didn't stop. "It'll at least relieve some of your pain. You've suffered enough."

Vlad nodded, then eagerly drank the contents of the cup. When he'd finished drinking, he said, "Thank you. I'm so old that I find I need the restorative powers of the cup more and more."

A howl of outrage from above caused Alex to lower the cup. He looked up the stairs, wondering what new danger was coming.

He got his answer moments later when Ferdinand and Isabella came rushing back. Despite having no physical presence, their passage sounded like a steam locomotive running full speed through a tunnel. They flew into the dungeon and past Vlad, who lunged at the scepter flying past him. He caught it, jerking Ferdinand backwards, then wrestled the king for the magical staff with a vigor that belied his frail body.

Ferdinand shook Vlad loose and shot an energy bolt at him, tearing a hole the size of a fist in his chest. The ghost king wasted no more time on the dying man. Turning on Alex, he thrust his scepter out and shot another energy blast at him.

Even though the force field popped up around him, Alex reflexively turned his body to protect the Grail. The ankh grew hot against his skin, creating a tingling sensation that permeated his body. He closed his eyes and felt the energy slam into him, knocking him against the wall for a second time, which caused the Grail to pop out of his grasp and fly across the room.

He hit the floor with a thump, causing his eyes to pop open just in time to see the energy bolt ricocheting into Isabella. The ghost queen fell – a hole in her chest where her heart used to be. Ferdinand gasped when he saw what he'd done, dropped the scepter, and rushed to his fallen wife.

Seeing Ferdinand distracted, Alex jumped up and ran toward the two magical objects lying several feet apart from each other. But he'd only taken a few steps when the king grabbed the scepter and pointed it at him.

The ankh yanked Alex to the floor, causing an energy blast to pass over him harmlessly. He scrambled to his knees and jumped for the magical hand. His fingers wrapped around it an instant before Ferdinand's hand wrapped around his arm.

Alex wasn't sure where the energy jolt came from, whether it was the hand, the scepter, the ankh, or all three objects, but it caused his whole body to jerk spasmodically as if everything in his body short-circuited at the same time. The Hand of Glory burst into flames and quickly turned to ashes.

It had a very different impact on Ferdinand. The scepter grew white-hot, causing Ferdinand to scream and try to throw the magical object away. But it was too late – it had fused to his hand. An instant later, Ferdinand's scepter burst into flames that quickly engulfed his arm.

Tiny creatures suddenly appeared and swarmed over the former monarch, tugging the burning spirit into the ground. When only his head was visible, Ferdinand screamed, "I'll meet you in Hell."

And then he was gone.

It became so quiet that it took a moment for Alex to overcome his shock. Finally, he struggled to his feet, stumbled over to where the scepter was still burning, and stomped on it. The crunching sound under his feet caused a weary smile to cross his face.

He shook his head to clear it, then went to where Vlad lay on the floor. The former Sir Galahad turned to Alex with a peaceful look, even as blood gurgled from his mouth. Vlad tried speaking, but Alex couldn't understand what he was saying. Hoping the Grail could save Vlad, he said, "Hold on. I'll put more water in the cup and pour it over your wounds. You'll be better in no time."

With a surprisingly firm grip, Vlad grasped Alex's arm and held him in place. Shaking his head, he managed to say, "No. Let me die in peace. I've been looking forward to this day for ages. You've done more for me than I could ever have hoped." Vlad started convulsing as pain racked his body. When the spasms stopped, he loosened his grip on Alex and said, "Promise me that you'll return the Grail to Avalon."

With tears streaming down his face and a lump in his throat preventing him from speaking, all Alex could manage was a nod.

Vlad grasped Alex's hand, closed his eyes, and breathed his last.

## CHAPTER 39
# WHERE THE STRAIGHT WAY
# WAS LOST

Alex picked Vlad up, carried the frail body to the sarcophagus, and laid him in it. There was still one lid piece that could fit across the stone casket, so he placed it over Vlad's head to cover the dead man's unseeing eyes.

He stood over the legendary man he'd known for only a few hours before starting up the stairs in a daze. Halfway up, he belatedly remembered his promise to Vlad. He rushed back for the Grail and found it in the far corner of the dungeon. After picking it up, he headed upstairs to get his gear. He was about to unceremoniously shove the Grail into his pack when he realized he needed to protect the precious cup. With Jane having taken all his t-shirts, all he had left that was soft was his rain jacket. He wrapped the holy relic in it then placed it in his bag.

Before leaving the bedroom, he looked out the window, trying to spot the dangers awaiting him. Not seeing any signs of the dragon or ghosts, he headed to the kitchen to stuff his pack with food. When he entered the great room, he realized he'd been in such a rush to get his gear that he hadn't noticed the shattered great front doors. The thought of facing the dragon again sent a shudder through him. He was still deciding whether to try escaping through the front or the back when he noticed it was eerily silent outside. Despite his fear of the dragon, he edged towards the front doors.

He peeked into the courtyard to check the dragon's location but didn't spot it. Hoping it had left, he stepped through the front opening and felt something crunch underneath his foot. Alex looked down and saw the mangled remnants of the cup Isabella had taken lying on the stones, its precious gems scattered about. He hesitated, then bent down and picked up the jewels, hoping they'd help him sometime in the future. Then he headed towards the drawbridge.

A whimpering cry of pain off to his right caused Alex to look for the source. He froze when he saw the giant black dragon curled up in a ball in the far corner of the courtyard, her body and wings pock-marked with holes. Her massive head lay on the ground with scorch marks and tiny tendrils of smoke rising from numerous spots on her body.

Staring at the giant beast, Alex couldn't help but feel sorry for it. On an impulse, he rushed back to the dungeon, filled the Grail with water from the spout behind Vlad's sarcophagus, and carefully carried the precious water back outside. He approached the dragon and stopped when the beast raised her head and growled. Hoping she could understand him, Alex said, "I'm not going to hurt you. I'm just going to pour some of this water on your wounds. It should help you heal."

Alex was relieved when a despondent voice inside his head said, "*Do with me as you will. Your kind has pursued us throughout history no matter how much we've tried to help your species. All I ask is that you get it over with quickly.*" The dragon sighed and sank her head even further forward.

He walked to the backside of her wing and poured a tiny bit of the water onto the nearest tear where Torquemada's creepy hand had torn through the dragon. Almost immediately, the bloody skin began bubbling and drawing together.

The dragon jerked, causing Alex to jump back. "I'm sorry. I should have warned you it might sting."

A low rumbling sound, like a giant cat's purr, sounded deep in her belly. Closing her eyes, she flattened her damaged wing, making it easier for Alex to reach some of the damaged spots.

*"Please continue,"* she said.

Alex worked around the edges of the wing, dribbling the healing waters on each wound. Soon, all but the few out of his reach were on their way to closing. Worried about how the giant dragon would react to climbing on her, Alex took a deep breath and said, "I can't reach all of them. I need to climb up on your wing to get to them. Is that okay?"

Surprisingly, the dragon wrapped her tail around Alex and lifted him to the base of her wing. Alex knelt and gently scooted along her side, dropping some of the precious healing water on the last few holes. After mending the injuries on the wing, he slid down and walked around to the front of the wing. The dragon sighed as he neared her head, exposing her fearsome-looking teeth. Alex hesitated, imagining he would be only a bite-sized morsel if the dragon changed her mind. With a shaky voice, he asked, "You've still got some wounds on your head and neck. You won't eat me if I get too close, will you?"

*"No. I'm sorry I attacked you when you first came here. I thought you were like all the rest. I don't know what you're doing, but it feels wonderful, and I promise I won't harm you."*

After finishing one side of the beast's neck, Alex said, "Hold on. I've got to get some more water. I'll be right back." A few minutes later, he started on the other side. Out of habit, he gently stroked the hard, shiny scales on her neck, as he used to do with his dog. He accidentally touched one of the wounds, causing the dragon to lift her head and bellow in pain.

Alex jerked his hand away and said, "I'm sorry. I didn't mean to hurt you. I promise I'll be more careful." He continued sprinkling Grail water on the wounds, gradually working towards her mouth. As he went along, he became more emboldened and started rubbing the water on instead of sprinkling. He heard a low rumbling sound in the great beast's chest and stepped back, thinking he'd done something wrong.

*The dragon opened her eyes and looked at Alex before saying, "That feels delightful. It's not only healing my wounds, but it has been ages since I've had someone care for me."*

Alex continued his work until he thought he'd finished. Then, he looked over the dragon's hide for a moment before saying, "I've got all the ones I can see. Are there any others?"

*"It doesn't matter. You've done all you can, but it's still not enough to help me move on. I fear we're both doomed to stay in this time-space vortex for eternity. I'm sorry you got involved."*

"What are you talking about?" Alex asked. "What vortex?"

*"Compared to you humans, my race lives an extremely long life. But we know when it's our time to move on to the next plane of existence. To do that, though, we need our heart stones. That vile creature inside the castle took mine, which created this netherworld when I tried to return to my home planet. His punishment is fitting, though, as he's trapped here with me."*

"Is it a greenish-gold crystal-looking thing?" Alex asked.

*"Yes, but it would be of no use now. I'm sure my ka is gone forever, and it is nothing but a cold, lifeless crystal now."*

"I wouldn't be so sure about that. Hold on, and I'll be right back." Alex ran back to the castle, filled the Grail with more water, grabbed the crystal off the mantelpiece, and ran back out. When he returned to the dragon, he sprinkled some Grail water on the crystal, then watched in wonder as it grew brighter and started throbbing. "What do I do?"

With a groan, the mighty dragon pushed up on one massive foreleg, exposing part of her chest – enough to expose the gash Alex had seen during their fight. *"Shove my heart stone back into the wound if you can, then pour more of your magical water on it."*

"Won't it have healed shut by now?" Alex asked.

*"There's only one way to find out."*

As Alex bent down to duck underneath the dragon's chest, the ankh happened to slip out of his shirt. Alex jumped back when the dragon suddenly howled in anguish. "What did I do?" he asked.

*"It's not you, little one. It's me. I had no idea you were a member of our weyr. Now my ka will never be at rest."*

"What are you talking about?"

The dragon nudged Alex in the chest with her long snout. *"That ankh. Where did you get it?"* she asked.

"From my dad. It's been in my family for generations. Why do you ask?"

*"A long time ago, a good friend of our species wore a device like yours. She helped us escape the wars on our home world and led us to the planet we now call home. In recognition of her service, we made her a member of our weyr. Forgive me. I didn't realize you were in service with her."*

"I'm not sure who you're talking about," Alex said. "I'm the only one I know who has an object like this, so don't worry about it. I can't imagine the pain and heartache you've endured guarding this place for so long."

Alex stepped forward until he was only a few inches from the gash. He looked up but wished he hadn't because all he could see was the dragon's immense body hovering over him. Knowing she would flatten him if he made a wrong move, Alex took a deep breath and mumbled, "Okay, here goes." He grimaced and shut his eyes while thrusting the stone towards the incision. For a second, he thought it wouldn't work as his hand met resistance. Then, like magic, his hand and the stone slipped through the scales and into the dragon's chest cavity.

The stone softened as if it was coming to life. Images of dragons and more flooded his mind, sending him into a trance that didn't stop until the information flow finally ended. His knees shook as he pulled his hand out. Anxious to escape from under the dragon, he dipped his fingers into the cup and splashed water onto the wound. Seeing the scales fusing, he splashed more water over the length of the incision, then smoothed it with the palm of his hand.

The cut scales started bubbling and sizzling, slowly fusing. Before the gash could close, the dragon lurched to her feet, sending Alex scrambling from under her. She stretched out her wings, blotting out the sunlight. The dragon twisted her head until she could see Alex and thought, *"My weyr will never forget this, Alex Scire."* She dropped her head, nudging Alex towards the drawbridge. *"Hurry now, before you're trapped here forever."*

"Wait, what's your name?" Alex asked.

*"Look inside your mind. You already know it because you are now one of us."*

Alex frowned, trying to understand the dragon's cryptic message. A second later, it hit him. He had no idea where the name came from, but he knew he was right. "Abraxas," he shouted.

The dragon turned towards Alex and roared her approval, forcing Alex to clap his hands over his ears. Abraxas started flapping her great black wings, knocking Alex to the ground with mighty wind gusts as she slowly rose above the castle.

He watched her circle lazily to gain altitude. Another ear-splitting screech drove him to clap his hands over his ears again. When he looked up, he saw Chrysophylax's opalescent-colored scales racing towards her. He smiled as he watched his dragon friend playfully dart around Abraxas, who was several times his size. As he watched mother and son fly out of sight, the meaning of Abraxas' cryptic comment about being one of them suddenly hit him. He realized that handling Abraxas' heart stone had somehow implanted their families' history in his mind.

A loud cracking sound caused him to whirl around. He was just in time to see a turret collapse, sending chunks of stone raining down on the battlements and courtyard. Before he could react, the entire outer wall started breaking apart. Alex ran for the drawbridge, but some unseen vortex-like force started sucking him back to the center of the castle. Chunks of the outer wall broke off and flew past him, causing him to play dodgeball with stone blocks while he fought to get out. Just when he thought he wouldn't make it, Sadie emerged from a black hole in front of him. Alex felt the forces tugging at him lessen, enabling him to reach the little dragon and step into the darkness surrounding her. An instant later, he felt himself falling into the same tunnel that had transported him to the strange world of the Grail.

Spinning and tumbling through the darkness, Alex barely noticed the pinpricks of light flashing past him. Spotting a bright light in the tunnel, he knew his strange trip was about to end and braced for impact. A second later, he slammed into a thick bed of grass.

He was so dizzy that it was some time before he was able to open his eyes. When he did, his first impression was that he hadn't gone anywhere, as the landscape looked like where he'd been minutes before. Except there was no castle – only piles of stone standing on the hillside.

Something else felt different, but he couldn't quite put his finger on it. Alex looked around, but it was some time before he realized that besides the castle lying in ruins, the forest and meadow around him had also changed. Instead of a dense hardwood forest, a thick stand of pines surrounded a field covered in spring flowers.

Alex wandered through the ruins and had just reached the spot where he thought the drawbridge had been when cold air rushed over him. Elisabetta apparated a few feet away and hovered, looking expectantly into the former castle. He was so surprised by her sudden appearance that he stuttered, "I, I wasn't expecting you here." Alex paused and took a deep breath to work up the courage to tell her about Vlad's death. Then he blurted out, "I'm sorry to tell you this, but …." His voice trailed off when he saw she wasn't paying attention to him. Turning to look for the reason, he saw Vlad flying towards them.

Elisabetta flew towards her lover, but an invisible barrier stopped her outside the former walls. She flung her arms out and cried, "Come, my love."

Not wanting to intrude on their reunion, Alex turned his back to the castle and headed across the meadow, hoping to find the forest trail he'd followed when he'd first arrived. He'd only taken a few steps when Elisabetta called out, "Thank you, Alex Scire. We shall never forget you." He turned just in time to see Vlad and Elisabetta disappear.

Alex numbly stared at the spot where they'd vanished. Being alone in front of the now crumbled castle, doubts about what he'd experienced suddenly crept in. Wanting to ensure he wasn't crazy, he yanked his pack off and reached in to see if the Grail was still there. When his hand touched the holy relic, the shock of realizing it had all happened was too much for him. He staggered, tripped over a stone, and fell.

Alex lay on the ground for some time, idly watching the clouds pass by. Finally, he sat up, shoved the cup back into his pack, and began wondering how he'd get to Avalon.

***

### Enjoyed *The Sangreal*?

If you enjoyed this story and have a moment to spare, I'd appreciate a short review on Goodreads or the site where you bought this book. Your help spreading the word is greatly appreciated, as reviews make a huge difference in helping new readers find the series. Thank you!

# ALSO BY THE AUTHOR

After mistakenly taking his dad's magical ankh, Alex Scire suddenly sees ghosts everywhere, including his sister, who's stuck in the afterlife. To help her move on, he joins an expedition headed to the ancient Mayan city of Lamanai to search for a magical object. But to succeed he has to battle a tyrannical ghost king's army and survive assassination attempts by those who killed his family.

After destroying the Palantir, Alex Scire vows to find another magical object that will help his sister move on in the afterlife. He sets out on a ghost ship, along with his Druid friends Jane and Diana, to find the Fountain of Youth. To succeed, though, they'll have to find a place that might not exist, battle pirates, and survive an eerie hurricane in the Bermuda Triangle.

After taking the Holy Grail to Avalon, Alex Scire encounters the ghost of William Wallace. The former Scottish warrior is stuck in the afterlife and asks for help finding his scattered body parts so he can move on. Alex agrees and begins searching throughout Britain to help Wallace. But Alex's sudden reappearance, after everyone assumed he was dead, causes his enemies to redouble their efforts to kill him.

# AUTHOR'S NOTE
## Historical accuracy of *The Sangreal*

As a kid, I loved reading stories about King Arthur and his knights. So, I decided to include one of the central storylines in the Arthurian tales – the Holy Grail, into *The Sangreal.* But I wanted to twist the story, so I gave the Grail a dark side, moved its location from England to Eastern Europe, and took the most 'righteous' of the nights, Sir Galahad, made him immortal, and had him evolve into one of the scariest/most controversial figures in medieval European history.

Despite all those fictional touches, one of the guiding principles I've followed in writing this series is that ***'Truth is stranger than fiction.'*** In *The Sangreal,* I've again drawn inspiration for it from real historical people, places, and events. For instance:

Although I have taken literary license to portray their **characters**, many of the ghosts were inspired by real people.

- Chief among them was the 15th-century triumvirate of terror – Tomás de Torquemada, a Dominican Friar who became the first Grand Inquisitor, and King Ferdinand and Queen Isabella, who presided over the start of the Spanish Inquisition – all in the name of their religion.
- Vlad Tepes (often referred to as Vlad the Impaler and commonly thought of as the inspiration for Bram Stoker's Dracula) was a far more fascinating person than I originally thought. He was ruthless to

his enemies, but he was also a reformer. Many Romanians consider him a national hero, as he defended his country from the invading Ottomans with little to no support from his neighboring countries.

Many of the **locations** in the book are based on places I've visited, including;
- I loved visiting all the Spanish cities in the book (Seville, Cordoba, Toledo, and Avila). The history, the architecture, and the blend of cultures were enchanting.
- The Spanish train system was fascinating in its own right. We rode on modern trains that hit 300 km/hour as well as slow, old-fashioned trains. The stations also varied widely from huge, sleek, modern ones to quaint.
- Bucharest had a fascinating blend of building architecture. You could easily spot the glamorous buildings of the past, the bland communist buildings, and the modern.
- Poenari's 1480 steps weren't as difficult to climb as I thought they'd be, but the views from the castle were well worth it. Except for meeting Elisabetta, our climb to the top was pretty much how I described it in the book (cold, windy, bear threat, and accompanied by a pair of friendly dogs).
- Transylvania was a last-minute add to our trip, but it's my favorite location in all our book travels (so far).
    - If you're ever in southwest Colorado near Memorial Day, I'd highly encourage you to experience the Bear Dance on the Southern Ute

Indian Reservation. I loved the experience. But, hopefully, you'll be more relaxed at it than Alex and I were.
- The weather for our trip was an interesting mixture of storms (in sunny Spain only), heat (also Spain only), and cool/brisk weather (Romania – where it snowed in the Carpathians while we were there in September).

Many of the **backstories** in the book are based on real events and places.
- The locked door I describe in the Seville Cathedral exists. It must go below the cathedral because the passageway it opens onto cannot empty onto the main floor – I checked in all directions.
- Much of what Diana experienced in Romania was a retelling of our trip, including the pig's knuckle dinner (that was me) and the traffic circle/car fix.
- Although the original idea for having Alex and Jane jump off the train came from movies I've seen, my youngest daughter and I got to experience it for ourselves. While visiting Prejmer, Romania, we lined up behind the other people in our train car and had to jump off, down a hill, just seconds before the train pulled away (I have it on video).
- The funeral procession and horse-drawn carts were all drawn from our experiences in Romania.

- I did see several farmers using scythes. But I also saw modern farming equipment in adjacent fields – it was an interesting mix. What was also interesting to me, having bucked hay as a kid, was how many different ways they dry hay.
- The references to the Snickers when Alex was adrift, and Alex and Jane getting picked up by some young people in a Volkswagen minibus while hitchhiking in Romania were based on my hitchhiking adventure the summer after my sophomore year in college, when my older brother and I hitchhiked from Colorado to Seattle (it was in the days before credit cards were ubiquitous and travelers carried American Express Travelers Checks). The Volkswagen experience I describe in the story was based on our trip to Glacier National Park (note, the 'hippies' who picked us up were much nicer than my paradigms led me to believe. The Snickers part of the story was based on the end of the trip when I was getting low on money and ate Snickers ($.25/bar), which were cheap, tasty, and filling.

For more information on the historical places, events, and characters included in this book, go to my web page, where I have posted a glossary about many of the interesting historical facts included in the book.

# ABOUT THE AUTHOR

JC Holmberg is the author of the Young Adult Fantasy Adventure series titled *The Maqlû*. He and his wife Mari live in *The Kentucky Wildlands*, surrounded by nature. John splits his time between working on his forestland most mornings, writing in the afternoon, and continuing his travels to research settings for future books.

The picture below is of the author in Avila, Spain, site of one of Alex's battles in this book.

# FOLLOW THE AUTHOR

Although *The Maqlû* is a fantasy series that includes ghosts and magic, the books are set in the amazing real world with fascinating historical characters. To learn more about the author, the background of each story, and some fascinating fun facts included in the books, go to;

www.jcholmberg.com